Passion for the Game

Passion for the Game

SYLVIA DAY

KENSINGTON PUBLISHING CORP.
www.kensingtonbooks.com

KENSINGTON BOOKS are published by

Kensington Publishing Corp.
119 West 40th Street
New York, NY 10018

All Kensington titles, imprints, and distributed lines are available at special quantity discounts for bulk purchases for sales promotions, premiums, fund-raising, educational, or institutional use.

Special book excerpts or customized printings can also be created to fit specific needs. For details, write or phone the office of the Kensington special sales manager: Kensington Publishing Corp., 119 West 40th Street, New York, NY 10018, attn: Special Sales Department; phone 1-800-221-2647.

KENSINGTON and the k logo are Reg. U.S. Pat. & TM Off.

ISBN-13: 978-0-7582-9043-4
ISBN-10: 0-7582-9043-8

First Kensington Trade Paperback Printing: June 2007

10 9 8 7 6 5 4 3

Printed in the United States of America

To editorial goddess, Kate Duffy.
For everything, but especially for
loving my books as much as I do.
I love writing for you.

Acknowledgments

Thanks to my critique partner, Annette McCleave (*www.AnnetteMcCleave.com*).

Thanks to my dear friends Renee Luke and Jordan Summers for their support on the other end of the IM window.

Thanks to my family, who were orphaned for over a year.

Thanks to my mom, who took over the maintenance of my house while I wrote a bunch of books.

Thanks to my readers, the most loyal, enthusiastic, and fabulous audience a writer could ever ask for.

What a lucky gal I am to have all of you in my life. I'm hugely grateful.

Chapter 1

"If all angels of death were as lovely as you, men would line up to die."

Maria, Lady Winter, shut the lid of her enameled patch box with a decisive snap. Her revulsion for the mirrored reflection of the man who sat behind her made her stomach roil. Taking a deep breath, she kept her gaze trained on the stage below, but her attention was riveted by the incomparably handsome man who sat in the shadows of her theater box.

"Your turn will come," she murmured, maintaining her regal façade for the benefit of the many lorgnettes pointed in her direction. She had worn crimson silk tonight, accented by delicate black lace frothing from elbow-length sleeves. It was her most-worn color. Not because it suited her Spanish heritage coloring so well—dark hair, dark eyes, olive skin—but because it was a silent warning. *Bloodshed. Stay away.*

The Wintry Widow, the voyeurs whispered. *Two husbands dead . . . and counting.*

Angel of death. How true that was. Everyone around her died, except for the man she cursed to Hades.

The low chuckle at her shoulder made her skin crawl. "It will take more than you, my dearest daughter, to see me to my reward."

"Your reward will be my blade in your heart," she hissed.

"Ah, but then you will never be reunited with your sister, and she almost of age."

"Do not think to threaten me, Welton. Once Amelia is wed, I will know her location and will have no further need for your life. Consider that before you think to do to her what you have done to me."

"I could sell her into the slave trade," he drawled.

"You assume, incorrectly, that I did not anticipate your threat." Fluffing the lace at her elbow, she managed a slight curve to her lips to hide her terror. "I will know. And then you will die."

She felt him stiffen and her smile turned genuine. Ten and six was her age when Welton had ended her life. Anticipation for the day when she would pay him in kind was all that moved her when despair for her sister threatened paralysis.

"St. John."

The name hung suspended in the air between them.

Maria's breath caught. "Christopher St. John?"

It was rare that anything surprised her anymore. At the age of six and twenty, she believed she had seen and done nearly everything. "He has coin aplenty, but marriage to him will ruin me, making me less effective for your aims."

"Marriage is not necessary this time. I've not yet depleted Lord Winter's settlement. This is simply a search for information. I believe they are engaging St. John in some business. I want you to discover what it is they want with him, and most importantly, who arranged his release from prison."

Maria smoothed the bloodred material that pooled around her legs. Her two unfortunate husbands had been agents of the Crown whose jobs made them highly useful to her stepfather. They had also been peers of great wealth, much of which they left to her for Welton's disposal upon their untimely demise.

Lifting her head, she looked around the theater, absently noting the curling smoke of candles and gilded scrollwork that shone in firelight. The soprano on the stage struggled for attention, for no one was here to see her. The peerage was here to see each other and be seen, nothing more.

"Interesting," Maria murmured, recalling a sketch of the popular pirate. Uncommon handsome he was, and as deadly as she. His exploits were widely bandied, some tales so outrageous she knew they could not possibly be true. St. John was discussed with intemperate eagerness, and there were wagers aplenty on how long he could escape the noose.

"They must be desperate indeed to spare him. All these years they have searched for the irrefutable proof of his villainy, and now that they have it, they bring him into the fold. I daresay neither side is pleased."

"I do not care how they feel," Welton dismissed curtly. "I simply wish to know who I can extort to keep quiet about it."

"Such faith in my charms," she drawled, hiding how her mouth filled with bile. To think of the deeds she had been forced into to protect and serve a man she detested . . . Her chin lifted. It was not her stepfather she protected and served. She merely needed him alive, for if he were killed, she would never find Amelia.

Welton ignored her jibe. "Have you any notion what that information would be worth?"

She gave a nearly imperceptible nod, aware of the avid scrutiny that followed her every movement. Society knew her husbands had not died natural deaths. But they lacked proof. Despite this morbid certainty of her guilt, she was welcomed into the finest homes eagerly. She was infamous. And nothing livened up a gathering like a touch of infamy.

"How do I find him?"

"You have your ways." He stood, looming over her in the shadows of the rear box, but Maria was not cowed. Aside from concern for Amelia, nothing frightened her any longer.

Welton's fingers lifted one of her curls. "Your sister's hair is so like yours. Even powder cannot truly hide its gloss."

"Go away."

His laughter lingered long after he parted the curtains and exited to the gallery. How many years would she be forced to endure that sound? The investigators who worked for her were unable to turn up anything of value. Brief sightings of her sister and barely warm trails. So many times she had been close . . . But Welton was always one step ahead.

While every day her soul grew blacker at his behest.

"Do not be fooled by her outward appearance. Yes, she is short of stature and tiny, but she is an asp waiting to strike."

Christopher St. John settled more firmly in his seat, disregarding the agent of the Crown who shared the box with him. His eyes were riveted to the crimson-clad woman who sat across the theater expanse. Having spent his entire life living amongst the dregs of society, he knew affinity when he saw it.

Wearing a dress that gave the impression of warmth and bearing the coloring of hot-blooded Spanish sirens, Lady Winter was nevertheless as icy as her title. And his *assignment* was to warm her up, ingratiate himself into her life, and then learn enough about her to see her hanged in his place.

A distasteful business, that. But a fair trade in his estimation. He was a pirate and thief by trade, she a bloodthirsty and greedy vixen.

"She has at least a dozen men working for her," Viscount Sedgewick said. "Some watch the wharves, others roam the countryside. Her interest in the agency is obvious and deadly. With your reputation for mayhem, you two are very much alike. We cannot see how she could resist any offer of assistance on your part."

Christopher sighed; the prospect of sharing his bed with the beautiful Wintry Widow was vastly unappealing. He knew her kind, too concerned over their appearance to enjoy an abandoned tumble. Her livelihood was contingent upon her ability to attract wealthy suitors. She would not wish to become sweaty or tax herself overmuch. It could ruin her hair.

Yawning, he asked, "May I depart now, my lord?"

Sedgewick shook his head. "You must begin immediately, or you will forfeit this opportunity."

It took great effort on Christopher's part to bite back his retort. The agency would learn soon enough that he danced to no one's tune but his own. "Leave the details to me. You wish me to pursue both personal and professional relations with Lady Winter, and I shall."

Christopher stood and casually adjusted his coat. "However, she is a woman who seeks the secure financial prospects of marriage, which makes it impossible for a bachelor such as myself to woo her first and then progress from the bed outward. We will instead have to start with business and seal our association with sex. It is how these things are done."

"You are a frightening individual," Sedgewick said dryly.

Christopher glanced over his shoulder as he pushed the black curtain aside. "It would be wise of you to remember that."

The sensation of being studied with predatory intent caused the hair at Maria's nape to rise. Turning her head, she studied every box across from her but saw nothing untoward. Still, her instincts were what kept her alive, and she trusted them implicitly.

Someone's interest was more than mere curiosity.

The low tone of men's voices in the gallery behind her drew her attention away from the fruitless visual search. Most would hear nothing over the rabble in the pit below and the carrying notes of the singer, but she was a hunter, her senses fine-tuned.

"The Wintry Widow's box."

"Ah . . ." a man murmured knowingly. "Worth the risk for a few hours in that fancy piece. She is incomparable, a goddess among women."

Maria snorted. A curse, that.

The girlish pleasure she had once felt for having uncommon beauty died the day her stepfather leered and said, "You shall fetch me a fortune, my pet."

It was only one of many deaths in her short life.

The first was her beloved father. She remembered him as unrestrained and vital, a dashing man who laughed often and adored her Spanish mother. Then he fell ill and wasted away. Later, Maria would become intimately familiar with the signs of poison. At the time, however, she knew only fear and confusion, which worsened when her mother introduced her to a dark-haired, beautiful man who was to replace her father.

"Maria, child," her mother had said in her softly accented voice. "This is Viscount Welton. He and I plan to wed."

She had heard the name before. Her father's closest friend. Why her mother wished to remarry was beyond her immature comprehension. Had her father meant so little?

"He wishes to send you to the best academies," was the explanation. "You will have the future your father wished for you."

Sent away. That was all she heard.

The wedding took place and Lord Welton took over, whisking them to the moors to a house that resembled a medieval castle. Maria hated it. It was cold, drafty, and scary, so very far removed from the golden-bricked home they had lived in before.

Welton begat a daughter on his new wife and then promptly left them. Maria went to school, and he went to Town where he drank, whored, and gambled her father's money to his heart's content. Her mother grew paler, thinner; her hair began to fall out. The illness was hidden from Maria until the last possible moment.

She was sent for only when the end was near and assured. Returning to her stepfather's home, she found the Viscountess Welton a ghost of the woman she had been only months before, her vibrancy depleting along with their coffers.

"Maria, my darling," her mother whispered on her deathbed,

her dark eyes pleading. "Forgive me. Welton was so kind after your father passed. I-I did not see beyond the façade."

"All will be well, Mama," she had lied. "Your health will improve and we can leave him."

"No. You must—"

"Please do not say any more. You need rest."

Her mother's grip was surprisingly strong for a woman so wan, a physical manifestation of her urgency. "You must protect your sister from him. He cares not at all that she is his own blood. He will use her, as he has used me. As he intends to use you. Amelia is not strong like you. She has none of the strength of your father's blood."

She had stared at her mother in dismay. In the decade of the Welton marriage, Maria had learned many things, but most of all she had learned that beneath Lord Welton's incomparably handsome face, Mephistopheles dwelled.

"I am not old enough," she breathed, the tears falling. She spent most of her time at school, training to become a woman Welton could exploit. But on her occasional visits, she watched the way the viscount belittled her mother with razor-sharp barbs. The servants told her of raucous voices and pained screams. Bruises. Blood. Bed rest for weeks after he left.

Seven-year-old Amelia remained in her rooms when her father was in residence, frightened and alone. No governess would stay long with them.

"Yes, you are," Cecille whispered, her lips white, her eyes red. "When I go, I will give what strength I have to you. You will feel me, my sweet Maria, and your father. We will support you."

Those words were her only anchor in the years that followed.

"Is she dead?" Welton had asked flatly when Maria emerged from the room. His bright green eyes held no emotion at all.

"Yes." She waited with bated breath and shaking hands.

"Make whatever arrangements you desire."

Nodding, she turned away, the swishing of her heavy silk skirts loud in the deathly silence of the house.

"Maria." The soft drawl floated ominously after her.

She paused and faced him again, studying her stepfather with new appreciation of his evil, absently noting the broad shoulders, trim hips, and long legs that so many women found appealing. Despite the coldness within him, his green eyes, dark hair, and rakish smile made him the handsomest man she had ever seen. The devil's gift for his black-as-sin soul.

"Tell Amelia about Cecille's passing, will you? I am running late and do not have the time."

Amelia.

Maria was devastated at the thought of the task ahead. Added to the near-crippling pain of her mother's loss, she almost sank to the floor, crushed beneath her stepfather's heel. But the strength her mother promised her stiffened her spine and lifted her chin.

Welton laughed at her bravado. "I knew you would be perfect. Worth the trouble your mother gave me." She watched him turn on his heel and take the stairs to the main floor, disregarding his wife completely.

What could she say to her sister to ease the blow? Amelia had none of the happy memories that sustained Maria. Now the child was orphaned, for her father might as well have been dead for all the attention he paid to her.

"Hello, poppet," Maria greeted softly as she entered her sibling's room, bracing herself to absorb the impact of the small body hurtling toward her.

"Maria!"

Clutching her sister close, Maria moved them toward the bed draped in dark blue silk that contrasted gently with the pale blue of the damask-covered walls. She rocked the sobbing child in her arms and cried silent tears. They had only each other now.

"What will we do?" Amelia asked in her precious voice.

"Survive," Maria said quietly. "And stay together. I will protect you. Never doubt that."

They fell asleep and when she woke, she found Amelia gone. And her life had changed forever.

Suddenly eager to be productive in some manner, Maria rose to her feet. She pushed the curtain aside and stepped out to the gallery. The two footmen who stood on either side to keep the ambitiously amorous away snapped to attention. "My carriage," she said to one. He hurried away.

Then she was bumped none too gently from behind, and as she stumbled, was caught close to a hard body.

"I beg your pardon," murmured a deliciously raspy voice so near to her ear she felt the vibration of it.

The sound stilled her, caught her breath and held it. She stood unmoving, her senses flaring to awareness far more acute than usual. One after another, impressions bombarded her—a hard chest at her back, a firm arm wrapped beneath her breasts, a hand at her waist, and the rich scent of bergamot mixed with virile male. He did not release her; instead his grip upon her person tightened.

"Unhand me," she said, her voice low and filled with command.

"When I am ready to, I will."

His ungloved hand lifted to cup her throat, his touch heating the rubies that circled her neck until they burned. Callused fingertips touched her pulse, stroking it, making it race. He moved with utter confidence, no hesitation, as if he possessed the right to fondle her whenever and wherever he chose, even in this public venue. Yet he was undeniably gentle. Despite the possession of his hold, she could writhe free if she chose, but a sudden weakness in her limbs prevented her from moving.

Her gaze moved to her remaining footman, ordering him silently to do something to assist her. The servant's wide eyes were trained above her head, his throat working convulsively as he swallowed hard. Then he looked away.

She sighed. Apparently, she would have to save herself.
Again.

Her next action was goaded as much by instinct as by
forethought. She moved her hand, setting it over his wrist, allowing him to feel the sharp point of the blade she hid in a
custom-made ring. The man froze. And then laughed. "I do
so love a good surprise."

"I cannot say the same."

"Frightened?" he queried.

"Of blood on my gown? Yes," she retorted dryly. "It is one
of my favorites."

"Ah, but then it would more aptly match the blood on
your hands"—he paused, his tongue tracing the shell of her
ear, making her shiver even as her skin flushed—"and mine."

"Who are you?"

"I am what you need."

Maria inhaled deeply, pressing her corset-flattened bosom
against an unyielding forearm. Questions sifted through her
mind faster than she could collect them. "I have everything I
require."

As he released her, her captor allowed his fingers to drift
across the bare flesh above her bodice. Her skin tingled, gooseflesh spreading in his wake. "If you find you are mistaken,"
he rasped, "come find me."

He stepped back and she spun in a flurry of skirts to face
him.

She expertly hid the true depth of her surprise. The renderings in the papers did not do him justice. Pale golden hair,
sun-kissed skin, and brilliant blue eyes enriched features so
fine they were almost angelic. His lips, though thin, were
beautifully sculpted by a master hand. The entire sum of his
countenance was so stunning, it was disarming. It made one
want to trust him, something the cold intentness of his gaze
told her would be a mistake.

As she studied him, Maria absently noted the undue attention they were attracting from the other patrons in the gallery,

but she could not spare a quelling glance. Her attention was snared by the man who stood so arrogantly assured before her. "St. John."

Showing a leg in a courtly bow, he smiled, but it did not reach his eyes—glorious eyes that were made more poignant by the shadows that rimmed them. He was not a man who slept often or well. "I am flattered by your recognition."

"What is it that I am supposed to be lacking?"

"Perhaps whatever it is your men search for?"

The surprise elicited by that statement could not be hidden. "What do you know?"

"Too much," he said smoothly, his gaze intensely searching. Sensual lips curved and trapped her attention. "And yet, not enough. Together, perhaps, we could achieve our aims."

"And what is your aim?"

How was it that he would approach her so soon after Welton? Surely it could not be a coincidence.

"Revenge," he said, the word rolling off his tongue so casually she wondered if he was as dead to emotion as she was. He would have to be to live the life of crime he did. No remorse, no regret, no conscience. "The agency has meddled in my life one too many times."

"I've no notion of what you are talking about."

"No? A pity, that." He stepped around her, leaning close as he moved by. "I will be available, should you figure it out."

For a moment, she refused to turn and watch him depart. But it was only a moment, and then she studied him avidly. Starting with his height and breadth of shoulder, down his satin-clad form to his heeled shoes, she missed nothing. Dressed as he was, he could not fade into the crowd that milled in the gallery. His pale yellow coat and breeches stood apart from the darker colors of the other theater patrons. She fancied him as a god of the sun, a shining overpowering presence. His casual stride was unable to hide the danger inherent in him, a fact noted by the peers who quickly moved out of his way.

Now she understood his appeal.

Maria returned her attention to her footman. "Come along."

"My lady," he cried plaintively, stilling her midstep. "Please forgive me." The young man looked as if he might cast up his accounts. His dark hair fell over his brow, framing immature features. Were it not for the livery he wore, he would appear very much the boy he was.

"For what?" Her brows arched.

"I-I did not come to your aid."

Her stance softened. Reaching out, she touched his elbow, a gesture that startled him. "I am not angry with you. You were afraid, an emotion with which I sympathize."

"Truly?"

She sighed and squeezed his elbow gently before releasing him. "Truly."

The grateful smile he gave her made her heart ache. Had she ever been so . . . *open*? She felt so disconnected from the world at times.

Revenge. That goal was all she had. She tasted it every morning for breakfast and rinsed her mouth out with it at night. The need for retribution was the force that pumped blood through her veins and filled her lungs with air.

And Christopher St. John could be the means by which she would acquire it.

A few moments ago, he had been a chore to complete as quickly as possible. Now the possibilities were beyond intriguing; they were seductive. It would take careful planning on her part to utilize them and St. John effectively, but she had no doubt she could manage it.

For the first time, in a very long time, she smiled.

Christopher whistled as he walked away, feeling the weight of Lady Winter's stare following after him. He had not anticipated actually speaking with her. He had merely hoped to see her up close and take note of how well she guarded herself. It was a wonderful turn of events that she had chosen that moment to leave her box. They'd not only met, but he had touched her, held her in his arms and smelled the scent of her skin.

He was no longer dreading boredom in the bedroom, not after feeling the point of that hidden blade. But beyond that, he found that more than his carnal interest was piqued. She was younger than he had assumed, her skin beneath powder and patch unblemished by lines and her lovely dark eyes displaying traces of both wariness and curiosity. Lady Winter was not yet completely jaded. How was that possible, when she was widely considered to have killed at least two men?

He intended to find out. The agency wanted her more than they wanted him. That alone intrigued him no small amount.

As he exited the theater, Christopher noted the black lacquered carriage that bore the Winter crest. He paused beside it. Making a barely discernable gesture, he listened for the answering birdcall that told him his order was seen by at least one of his men stationed around the area. The coach would be followed until he said otherwise. Wherever the fair lady went, he wanted to know about it.

"I shall be at the Harwick house party this weekend," he told the driver, who stared back at him with wide eyes and rigid body. "Make certain her ladyship knows this."

As the man nodded violently, Christopher smiled with deep-rooted satisfaction.

For the first time in a very long time, he had something to look forward to.

Chapter 2

"There is the possibility that she was sold into slavery."
Maria paused her pacing before the fire to stare hard at her investigator and former paramour. Simon Quinn wore only a multicolored silk robe, his tanned throat and chest visible in the parted opening. His eyes, a startling blue, stood out in stark contrast to his dark skin and black hair. Irish coloring. The complete opposite of the golden St. John, and younger by several years, but extremely handsome in his own right.

Aside from his innate sexuality, Simon appeared innocuous enough. Only the intense way he studied his surroundings hinted at a livelihood fraught with danger. In the course of their association, he had broken nearly every law there was.

So had she.

"Odd you would say that tonight," she murmured. "Welton said the same to me earlier."

"That certainly does not bode well, then, does it?" he asked in his smooth-as-satin voice.

"I can do nothing with conjecture, Simon. Find me the proof of it. Then we can kill Welton and give chase."

Behind her, the fire in the grate quickly heated her dressing gown and then the backs of her legs to an uncomfortable degree, but inside she was icy with terror. The thoughts that filled her mind made her ill. How would she ever find Amelia if her sister was in the world at large?

Simon's brows rose. "Taking the search beyond the shores of England would greatly diminish the chances of a successful outcome."

Raising the cordial in her hand to her lips, Maria drained the contents to bolster her spirits and set the small glass on the mantel. Her gaze moved across the room, once again finding comfort in the stained wood paneling and dark green drapes. It was an extremely masculine study, an effect that served two purposes. One, it established a somber mood that discouraged meaningless discourse. Two, it gave her a sense of control she needed desperately. Often she felt like a puppet on Welton's strings, but here she was in command.

She shrugged and resumed her pacing, her black dressing gown swirling around her ankles. "You act as if I have something else to live for."

"Surely there is some goal you wish to accomplish." He rose to his feet, towering over her as most everyone did. "Something more pleasant than death."

"I cannot think of the future beyond finding Amelia."

"You could. It will not make you weak to wish for better things."

The glance she shot him was narrowed and cool enough to discourage most. Simon, however, simply laughed. He had once shared her bed, and with it, the inevitable domestic discord that came with the role of resident lover.

Maria sighed, her gaze moving to the portrait of her first husband that hung on the wall from a length of thick ribbon. The swirls of paint created an image of a portly man with ruddy cheeks and bright green eyes.

"I miss Dayton," she confessed, her restless stride slowing, "and the support he provided."

The Earl of Dayton had saved her from total ruin. Seeing

through Welton's exterior, the kind widower had rescued her, paying a high price to take a girl young enough to be his granddaughter as his second wife. Under his tutelage she learned everything she needed to know to survive. Weaponry and the consummate use of it were only two of the many lessons learned.

"We will see to it that he is avenged," Simon murmured. "I promise you that."

Rolling her shoulders in a vain attempt to alleviate the tension there, Maria moved to the desk and sank wearily into the seat. "What about St. John? Can he be of any use to me?"

"Of course. With what the man knows, he could be of use to anyone. But there must be something to be gained for him. He is not a man known for his charitable tendencies."

She curled her fingers around the carved ends of the chair. "It would not be sex. A man who looks like he does would have women aplenty."

"Very true. He is a man known for living to excess."

Moving to the sideboard, Simon poured his own libation and rested a lean hip against the edge. While he managed the appearance of nonchalance, he never lowered his guard for a moment. She knew this and appreciated it.

"I can only assume it is the death of your husbands and their relation to the agency that has sparked his interest."

She nodded, expecting as much. The only motivation she could find for St. John's approach was his desire to use her as Welton did—for a distasteful task where feminine wiles were required. But surely he had women closer to him who could do the job with similar efficiency? "How was he caught? After all these years, I cannot help but wonder what error he made."

"From what I can discern, he made none. An informant was found who was willing to speak out against him."

"A bona fide informant?" she asked softly, her mind's eye remembering the brief moments she'd spent with the criminal. He was supremely confident as only a man with no fears could be. He was also a man one would be foolish to cross.

"Or simply one who bent to coercion?"

"Most likely the latter. I shall look into it."

"Yes, do." Maria fingered the corner of a piece of parchment on her desk. Her gaze rested on the sparkling amber liquid in Simon's hand and then moved higher, noting his broad shoulders and powerful arms.

"I wish I were of more help to you." The sincerity in his voice could not be mistaken.

"Do you know of a woman we could trust to align herself with Welton?"

He paused with his snifter lifted halfway to his mouth, a slow smile transforming his features. "By God, you are a wonder. Dayton taught you well."

"One can hope, yes? Welton has a preference for blondes."

If only her mother had known that.

"I shall find a suitable female posthaste."

Maria leaned her head back and closed her eyes.

"*Mhuirnín?*"

"Yes?" She heard his glass settle on the surface of the sideboard and then the steady sound of Simon's confident stride. It made her sigh, flooding her with a sense of comfort she struggled to deny herself.

"Time for bed." His large hand covered hers where it curved around the chair arm, and the rich scent of his skin filled her nostrils. Sandalwood. Pure Simon.

"There is too much to be considered," she protested, her eyes opening just enough to look up at him.

"Whatever it is, it can wait until morning." He tugged her up and when she stumbled, he caught her close, embracing her in warmth. "You know I will not be swayed until you do as I say."

Her body attempted to melt against his, and Maria squeezed her eyes shut to fight off the urge.

She could not help but remember the feel of him moving over and inside her, an association she had put an end to over a year ago. When his touch had come to mean more to her than mere physical comfort, Maria had concluded the affair. She could not afford to become complacent or feel contentment. Still, Simon remained in her household. She refused to love him, but she could not send him away either. She adored him and appreciated his friendship and his knowledge of the underbelly of society.

"I know your rules." His hands cradled her spine.

He did not like them, she knew. His carnal interest had not waned. She felt it even now, pressing hard against her stomach. A younger man's appetite.

"If I were a better woman, I would make you go."

Simon sighed into her hair and pulled her closer. "Have you learned nothing about me in the years we have been together? You could not make me leave. I owe you my life."

"You exaggerate," she admonished, recollecting when she first saw him in an alleyway, standing alone against a dozen opponents. He held his own with a ferocity that frightened and aroused her. She almost continued on, her aim that dark night to follow a lead on Amelia that seemed more promising than most. But her conscience would not allow her to ignore the imbalanced battle.

Brandishing sword and pistol, and flanked by several men, she managed to be sufficiently intimidating and the attackers had been frightened away. Left weakened and bloody, Simon had still chastised her roundly. He did not need rescuing, he said.

Then he collapsed at her feet.

Her original intent had been merely to clean him up and ease her conscience. Then he had emerged from a bath, a virile and breathtaking creature. And she had kept him.

Simon stepped back, his mouth curving in a wry smile as if he knew her thoughts. "I would face a dozen men again, hundreds, if it led me back to your bed."

Maria shook her head. "You are incorrigible, and overly randy."

"It is impossible to be too randy," he said with laughter in his voice, leading her toward the door with his hand at the small of her back. "You will not distract me from ushering you into bed. You need rest and sweet dreams."

"Ah, have *you* learned nothing about *me*?" she queried as they stepped out to the hallway and took the stairs. "I prefer not to dream. It makes waking so depressing."

"One day all will be well," he promised in a low, assured tone. "I promise you."

She yawned and then gasped as she was swung up into powerful arms. Within moments she was tucked into bed with a quick good-night kiss pressed to her forehead. As Simon retired, the soft click of the adjoining door made relaxation possible.

But it was a different set of blue eyes that followed her into sleep.

"Good evening, sir."

Christopher nodded at his butler. From his drawing room on the left, raucous laughter spilled out of the open double doors to fill the entryway where he stood.

"Send Philip to me directly," he ordered softly, handing over his hat and gloves.

"Yes, sir."

Crossing to the stairs, he passed the boisterous group of his men and their companions. They called out to him, and he paused a moment on the threshold, his gaze moving over the assembled crowd he considered his family. They were celebrating his release—*the luck of the devil*, they said—but work awaited him. There was much he needed to ascertain and accomplish if he wished to ensure his present state of freedom.

"Enjoy yourselves," he urged before taking the stairs with shouted protests following him to the second floor.

He reached his rooms and, with the help of his valet began to undress. He was shrugging free of his waistcoat when the young man he had requested rapped lightly on the door and then entered at his behest.

"What have you learned?" Christopher asked without preliminaries.

"About as much as one could expect to learn in the space of a day." Philip tugged at his cravat and started pacing, his pale green coat and breeches a stark contrast to the stamped leather that lined the walls.

"How many times must I warn you about your fidgeting?" Christopher admonished. "It betrays a weakness that begs to be exploited."

"My apologies." The youth adjusted his spectacles and coughed.

"No need to apologize. Simply correct it. Stand straight, no slouching, and look me in the eye like an equal."

"But I am not your equal!" Philip protested, pausing mid-stride, looking for a moment very much like the five-year-old child who had appeared on Christopher's doorstep orphaned, beaten, and destitute.

"No, you are not," Christopher agreed, moving as required to facilitate his disrobing, "but you must attempt to face me as one. Respect is earned here and in the world at large. No one will give it to you simply because you are pleasant and thorough. In fact, many an idiot has obtained success merely by acting as if it were his right."

"Yes, sir." Philip squared his shoulders and lifted his chin.

Christopher smiled. The boy would become a man yet. One who could stand firmly on his own two feet and survive the worst life could throw at him. "Excellent. Now speak."

"Lady Winter is six and twenty, twice widowed, with neither husband surviving more than two years in her bed."

Shaking his head, Christopher said, "Can you begin with something I do not know and then continue in that vein?"

Philip flushed.

"Do not become flustered. Simply remember that time is valuable and you want others to consider yours to be of some worth. You should always lead off with the kernel of information most likely to pique interest. Then proceed from there."

Taking a deep breath, Philip blurted, "She has a resident paramour."

"Well . . ." Christopher stilled, awash in visions of a softer Lady Winter, a woman flushed and sated from passionate play. It was his valet's sharp tug to his waistband that pulled him out of his surprise. Freeing the placket of his breeches, he cleared his throat and said, "That's more like it."

"Oh, good! I was unable to gather much aside from his Irish descent, but I can tell you he has been a member of her household since Lord Winter passed on two years ago."

Two years.

"Also, I find something curious about her relations with her stepfather, Lord Welton."

"Curious?" Christopher asked.

"Yes, the servant I spoke with mentioned his frequent visits. I find that odd."

"Perhaps because your relations with your stepfather were less than satisfactory?"

"Perhaps."

Christopher thrust his arms through the robe his valet held out for him. "Thompson, bring Beth and Angelica to me."

The valet bowed slightly before doing as he was bid, and Christopher left the dressing room for the sitting area. "What do we know of her finances?" he tossed over his shoulder.

"Not enough at the moment," Philip answered, following, "but that will be rectified in the morning. She appears flush, so I am curious as to why she feels the need to acquire money in such a gruesome manner."

"And you reached the conclusion of her guilt with sufficient evidence?"

"Ah . . . no."

"I can do nothing with conjecture, Philip. Find proof."

"Yes, sir."

Two years. Which proved she was capable of some feeling. A woman did not share the delights of her body with a man for that length of time without caring at least some small measure. "Tell me about Welton."

"He is a profligate who spends the majority of his waking moments pursing gaming tables and whores."

"Haunts?"

"White's and Bernadette's."

"Preferences?"

"Hazard and blondes."

"Well done." Christopher smiled. "I am pleased with what you accomplished in only a few hours."

"Your life depends upon it," Philip said simply. "Were I you, I would have sent someone with more expertise."

"You were ready."

"That is debatable, but in any case, I'm grateful."

Moving to the row of decanters on the nearby walnut table, Christopher waved off the statement before pouring a glass of water. "What use would I have for you if you remain green?"

"Yes, exploitation was your only aim," Philip said dryly as he leaned against the mantel. "The Lord forbid that my well-being should be the result of a momentary bout of generosity. A recurring bout, I should mention, as all of us under this roof seem to have stumbled upon it at some point."

Christopher snorted and drained his glass. "Please refrain from casting kind aspersions upon my character. It's quite rude to malign me so."

Philip had the temerity to roll his eyes. "Your fearsome reputation has been hard earned and proven many times. Taking in the world's strays will not raise sunken ships from the ocean's depths, replace stolen cargos, or revitalize those foolish enough to have crossed you. You've no cause to worry. My undying gratitude shan't diminish your infamy."

"Cheeky bastard."

The young man smiled and then the moment was broken by a soft knock at the door.

"Come in," Christopher called out, bowing his head slightly in greeting as a statuesque blonde and petite but voluptuous brunette joined them. "Ah, lovely. I have need of both of you."

"We missed you," Beth said with a seductive flip of her loose blond hair. Angelica simply winked. She was the quieter of the two, unless she was fucking. Then she cursed like the crudest of his sailors.

"Pardon me," Philip interjected, frowning. "How did you know Welton would not have a preference for red-haired wenches?"

"How do you know they are not here for me?" Christopher countered.

"Because I am here and you are focused. You never mix business with pleasure."

"Perhaps pleasure is the business, young Philip."

Philip's gray eyes narrowed behind his spectacles, a physical sign of his mental exertions. It was that tendency to reason out everything that had first captured Christopher's attention. A bright mind was not to be wasted.

Setting aside his glass, Christopher then sank into the nearest wingback chair. "Ladies, I have a request of both of you."

"Whatever you need," Angelica purred, "you know we will provide."

"Thank you," he said graciously, having known they would

agree to whatever he required. Loyalty worked both ways in his household. He would fight to the death for any one of the persons under his care, and they offered the same courtesy to him in return.

"The modiste will come by tomorrow and measure you both for new garments." The rapacious gleam in their eyes made him smile. "Beth, you are about to become Lord Welton's most intimate confidante."

The blonde nodded, a movement that caused her large, unfettered breasts to sway within her pale blue gown.

"And me?" Angelica asked, her painted mouth curving with anticipation.

"You, my dark-eyed beauty, will serve as a distraction when required."

He was uncertain whether it was Lady Winter's purse that captivated her lover's attention, her beauty, or both. Taking no chances, Christopher hoped Angelica's exotic features and a carefully crafted façade of wealth would be enough to lure his rival away. She was not nearly as refined as the Wintry Widow, but she was curvy enough and bore the clear hallmarks of Spanish bloodlines. In a darkened room, she could pass.

Rubbing the slight sting left on his wrist by Lady Winter's ring, Christopher found himself desirous of the infamous seductress's company. What a fine piece she was. Fragile in appearance and fierce in temperament. He knew, without question, that his life was about to become far more interesting than it had been of late. It was almost depressing that he had to wait a few days before he could tangle with her again.

In the meantime, his appetites were roused by lack of female companionship. He had been imprisoned for weeks. Surely that was the only reason he was thinking of the Wintry Widow with such fierce carnal interest. She was a task to accomplish, nothing more.

Still, when he lifted his hand and waved his visitors away, he drawled, "Not you, Angelica. I want you to stay."

She licked her lips.

"Lock the door, love. Then turn down the lamps."

Christopher sighed as the lights dimmed. Not Lady Winter. But in a darkened room, she could pass.

Chapter 3

"Can I tell you all the many things I adore about you, *mhuirnín?*"

Maria shook her head, her mouth curving in a faint smile. Arm's distance away, Simon lounged on the opposite bench, his large frame beautifully covered in cream-colored satin embroidered with flowers in fine gold thread. Against the backdrop of a serene lake and green grass, the singular color of his blue eyes stood out with stunning effect.

"No?" he drawled. "Well, then. How about one? I do adore that tilt to your chin you affect when wearing your Wintry Widow façade. And the ice blue silk with white lace is a stroke of genius."

Her smile widened. She was nervous, and Simon had noted the constant twirling of her parasol and sought to alleviate her disquiet. Behind her, the imposing stone edifice that was the home of the Earl and Countess of Harwick provided the roof under which she would pass the next three days. "It is expected, Simon darling. Mustn't disappoint our hostess, you know."

"Of course not. I, too, find it delightful. So what is the infamous widow planning for this weekend's house party?"

"Who can say so early on?" she murmured, her gaze moving over the assembled guests. Some sat on benches like she did, the females reading or working on needlepoint, the gentlemen standing nearby on the lawn. "A bit of mayhem, perhaps? A sprinkle of intrigue?"

"Some sex?"

"Simon," she admonished.

He held up his hands in a defensive gesture, but his eyes gleamed with mischief. "With someone else. Though I do hope you have better sense than to choose St. John."

"Oh? Why is that?"

"Because he is coarse, *mhuirnín*. Tainted, as you are not. I should not have touched you either. You are too fine for the likes of me, but even I am a better man than he is."

She looked down at her lap and the gloved hand that rested there. Why could Simon not see the stains of her transgressions?

He reached over and squeezed her fingers. "The blood you seek is on Welton's hands."

"I wish that were true."

"It is." Simon settled back into his seat.

"Tell me how it is that a known criminal would be invited here."

"Word has it the future Lord Harwick was maimed during a failed abduction attempt. It is said that his father approached St. John to act as the method of his retribution. The miscreants were dealt with, and Harwick's gratitude manifests itself in open invitations to his gatherings, amongst other things."

"A devil's bargain."

"To be sure," Simon drawled smoothly. "So tell me what your plans are, and I will formulate a way to assist you."

"There is too much uncertainty for me to steer a clear course. Why did St. John choose this venue for us to meet? Why not my residence or his?" Maria sighed. "If I were not so desperate, I would not play this game of his."

"You think best on your feet. You always have."

"Thank you," she said earnestly, taking comfort in Simon's esteem. "At present, I wish merely to speak privately with St.

John. Hopefully, he will tell me at least a small measure of how he thinks our association can benefit him. Based on that, I can move forward."

"Ah well, that I can help you with easily. He took that path behind you only a moment ago. I believe Lady Harwick mentioned a pantheon being in that general direction. If you wish to follow, I shall make certain you are not disturbed."

"Simon, you are a blessing."

"How good of you to notice." He smiled. "Are you sufficiently armed?"

She nodded.

"Good. I will see you shortly."

Maria rose to her feet without haste, her movements leisurely as she set the post of her parasol to her shoulder and began to stroll. A carelessly affected glance behind her found Simon intercepting a couple intent on the same gravel pathway she took. Secure in the knowledge that he would handle things beautifully as he always did, she set her mind to the task ahead.

Rounding a large hedge, Maria quickened her pace, her appearance of lazy perusal discarded. She took note of various markers along the way to keep her bearings—a pyramid here, a statue there. A few moments out, she spotted the pantheon up ahead and abandoned the trail, closing her parasol before weaving through the bordering copse. She circled the small building, looking through the pillars to the interior and then through the rear door.

"Looking for me?"

She spun about and found St. John leaning casually against a tree she had passed mere seconds before. Seeing the arrogant curve of his lips, Maria recovered quickly, removing all traces of surprise from her features with a wide smile. "No, actually."

The effect was what she had hoped for. His grin faltered, the smug gleam in his eyes flaring with a spark of awareness. She took that moment to study him in the dappled sunlight, her first clear viewing. His obviously powerful frame was draped in dark blue velvet that matched his irises and set off the golden strands of hair he kept neatly restrained in a queue. His eyes were not the bright blue of Simon's, but a deeper, darker shade. They were startling in contrast to the unsurpassed beauty of his face.

"I do not believe you," he challenged in that delicious rasp that moved like rough silk over her skin.

"I do not care."

He had the countenance of an angel, a man so handsome he seemed almost unreal. It made a woman's brain stumble to see those jaded eyes and hear that husky, earthy voice from an otherwise ethereal masculine creature.

And he was definitely male, regardless of that perfection.

White stockings clung to firmly muscled calves, and she could not help but wonder what activities he engaged in to bear the form of a laborer. A build she admired on Simon, but even more so on St. John, who lacked Simon's softer edge.

"Why, then, are you traipsing through the forest?" he asked.

"Why are you?" she tossed back.

"I am a man, I do not traipse."

"Neither do I."

"I noticed," he murmured. "You, my Lady Winter, were too busy spying."

"What do you call what you are doing?"

"I have an assignation with a lady." He pushed away from the tree in a dangerously graceful movement and she resisted the urge to step back.

"Is she a bit . . . icy, perhaps?"

His gait was slow and blatantly seductive. She admired it even as she marveled at his daring. Her stomach fluttered, but she hid her response.

"Chilly enough to lure men who enjoy a challenge. But I think it's a façade."

She laughed. "Has she given you any reason to doubt?"

St. John came to a halt before her. A warm, gentle breeze blew past her, carrying with it a faint hint of the bergamot and tobacco she remembered from his embrace in the theater. "She is meeting me here. As an intelligent woman, she knows what will happen if she seeks me out."

"You made sure I would come," she said softly, her head tilting back so their gazes stayed locked together. In such close proximity she saw the lines that bracketed his mouth and eyes, signs of a rougher life than his immaculate garments would suggest. "I'm certain you noticed that I did not come alone."

Moving so quickly he took her unawares, St. John caught her waist and nape in his large hands and tugged her into his body. "I noticed you are no longer fucking him."

For a moment his rough possession and the harsh edge to his crude speech startled her into silence. Then she found her voice.

"Are you mad?" she asked breathlessly, panting softly within the unyielding prison of her corset, her parasol dropped to the leafy floor.

The day was warm, but that was not what sent heat racing across her skin. As had happened before, nerve endings flared to painful life at the feel of his arms around her. The mass of her skirts forced her off balance, their chests touching, but yards of material separated his thighs from hers. That did not alter her knowledge that he was aroused. She did not have to feel his cock to know it was erect for her. She could see it in his eyes.

And when he kissed her, she could taste it.

Closing her eyes, Maria told herself to ignore the feel of his lips against hers. Soft, with a brushing touch of the tip of his tongue. But the taste of him—dark and dangerous—was delightful and she indulged, opening to him, and was rewarded with his soft rumble of approval.

He took her mouth as if they had all the time in the world. As if a bed were nearby and he could deliver on the promises made by his deep licks. There was something about the way he handled her, both harsh and tender, that affected her deeply. He stole what he wanted by force, but in a gentle manner so completely at odds with his approach.

For long moments, she allowed him to intoxicate her, her senses reeling behind her closed eyelids. His thumb circled lazily at the back of her neck, an easy rhythmic caress that made her back arch and her toes curl. Her nipples ached, her lips trembled. The quivering in her belly was reflected in her hands, forcing her to cling to his coat to hide the depth of her reaction.

Then she reclaimed her wits and divested him of his illusions.

His posture stiffened the instant the point of her blade pressed against his thigh. Lifting his head, he took a shuddering breath. "Remind me to disarm you the next time I wish to seduce you."

"No seducing, Christopher."

As his embrace slackened, Maria stepped away. "I may call you Christopher, yes? Truly, that was one of the best kisses I have ever had. Perhaps *the* best. That thing you do with your tongue . . . But unfortunately for you, I make it a habit to learn the business end of my liaisons before I even consider the pleasure end of them."

Later, when she was alone, she would reward herself for sounding so strong when her knees were so weak. At the moment, however, she had to face a man who was dangerous in more ways than one. "Tell me what you want from me."

His slow, easy smile kept her heart racing. "Is it not obvious?"

Perhaps it was her inability to breathe properly that prevented clear thought, but no matter how she looked at their situation, she could not comprehend why he affected her the way he did.

"The woman you arrived with can relieve that for you," she reminded.

She had her pick of handsome lovers, like Simon. Dark-haired men were her preference. She disliked scoundrels and rogues and consummately arrogant men. There was absolutely no reason for her to be so aroused by the criminal before her.

"I attempted that substitution the other night." His laugh was a joy to hear. Unlike hers, it sounded as if he gave it freedom often. "I adore Angelica, but sadly, she is not you."

The image that came to mind of the brunette writhing beneath the golden god before her made Maria's teeth clench. A silly, stupid, sentimental response she had no desire to feel. "You have one moment to tell me how I fit into your plans for revenge," she warned.

"I'll tell you in bed."

Her brows lifted. "You think to extort sex from me? When it is *you* who needs help, and not the reverse?"

"You must need me for something," Christopher drawled, "or you would not have come this weekend or sought me out now."

"Perhaps it was curiosity," she argued.

"You have investigators to handle that."

Maria took a deep breath and slipped her blade back into its sheath in a hidden pocket. "We are at an impasse."

"No, *you* are at an impasse. *I* am ready to move on to the sex."

One corner of her mouth tilted in a wry smile. "You do realize that the sex is supposed to come after we settle what we can do for one another. If it comes at all."

Christopher stilled, finding his unwanted fascination for the Wintry Widow sharpening to near painful acuity. Physically, he was staring at the exact opposite of himself. Where he was fair, she was dark. Where he was tall, she was petite. Where he was hard, she was luscious softness. But the brain inside her head was so similar to his, he could scarcely credit it. He had known she would circle the pantheon like a huntress seeking prey, because it was exactly what he would do. And the knife . . .

. . . well, he would have been prepared for that if she had not melted in his arms.

What he had not known was that he would reach for her. Until she had tossed her lover in his face, a man he knew was not warming her bed any longer simply by watching their posture together. Christopher had planned to keep things light. Draw her closer. Not frighten her.

But obviously she was not a woman who was easily frightened. She was presently returning his stare with one finely arched dark brow raised in silent query. "Your time is up."

Then she collected her parasol, moved to the pathway, and headed back toward the manse.

He stared after her, debating whether to stop her or not and then deciding that her egress was so magnificently affected it was too much of a joy to end. So he leaned against a tree and watched her until the flashes of ice blue could no longer be seen. The mere thought of the entertainment ahead made the wait for her almost bearable.

Almost.

Maria took her time in rejoining the rest of the guests. When St. John made no effort to continue their conversation, she knew he would not follow her.

He had approached her in the theater. She had approached him here. The next move was his. She wondered what it would be. Perhaps he meant to wait until curiosity bested her strength of will. If so, he would be waiting a long time.

When she emerged from around the corner, Simon's gaze found her, and he came to her with rapid strides, claiming her elbow before heading toward the lake.

"Well?" he asked.

"He wants sex. That is all I know."

He snorted. "We knew that before you met with him."

"We did not!"

"Very well, then. *I* knew that before you met with him." Simon blew out his breath and came to a halt. "We shall hope the man I sent to join St. John's household succeeds and brings us more to work with."

"That would be excellent," she agreed.

"I'd say the pirate is daft, but that would not be true. He is wily and creative, and damned if he did not take me into consideration."

"What are you talking about?" Tilting her head and parasol back, Maria looked at him, noting his dark scowl and the agitated cant of his torso.

"The female who accompanied him is for my use, not his. She made that quite clear while you were absent."

"Oh." Odd how that bit of news made her grin.

"You like him!" he accused.

"I like the way he thinks, Simon love." Tugging on their linked arms, she drew him along the shore of the lake.

Maria's gaze drifted to the waterfowl that floated serenely beneath the arched walking bridge. "He is also very observant. He knows we no longer share a bed."

"We can change that quite easily," he murmured in a low tone.

Through a lump in her throat, she swallowed hard and said, "Or you can accept the woman's offer and see what more she'll tell you."

He stopped again and glared at her indignantly. "Are you a cock purveyor now?"

"You like her," she argued. "I can tell."

"I like *parts* of her," he corrected. "Damn it all, do you feel nothing for me? How can you suggest such a thing without batting an eyelash?"

"Are you unaware that I would keep you to myself if I

could? If I were a different woman, Simon Quinn, I would lock you away and keep you all to myself. But I am not that woman, and you are not chaste, so do not play the role of wounded lover while making me the villainess. That is a title I earn on my own. It does not need embellishing by you."

Maria stalked away.

"*Mhuirnín* . . ." he called after her.

She ignored him.

"You are creating a spectacle," he said directly behind her.

Spinning about in a wave of wide skirts, Maria forced him to jump back. "That is what I am here for—scandal and entertainment."

"He has you flustered," he breathed with wide blue eyes. "By God, look at you."

"What does this have to do with St. John?"

"I wish I knew. I would have done it long ago, before you pushed me away."

She heaved out her breath. "You do not love me in that way, do you?"

"I do love you, *mhuirnín*." Simon's mouth lifted in a rueful curve. "But no, not in *that* way. I was close once, the closest I have ever been, perhaps will ever be."

The lone tear that hung on her lashes was her reply. She considered the promise that had once hovered between them to be another casualty of Welton's machinations. Another death that he would pay for. "I should not have suggested you bed that woman. I do not know what goaded me to say it."

"I've no notion either," he drawled, capturing her arm again. "You should know me well enough to anticipate the arrangement I made with her for later this evening."

"Later this . . . Oooh!" Maria stepped on his foot and he cursed. "Why did you torment me, then?"

"I am a man, with a man's ego. I wanted to know that it stung, at least in small measure, to think of me with someone else. It pains me to contemplate the same with you."

She might have believed him if he had refrained from laughing.

This time when she pulled away, she did not stop. "I am not in charity with you at the moment."

"You adore me," he called after her. "As I adore you."

If a glance could kill, the one she tossed over her shoulder would have done the deed.

Replete from supper, Christopher stood with his back to the wall next to the parlor window that overlooked the front drive. He could not remove his gaze from the petite but voluptuous form encased in a shimmering fabric that was the exact shade of a ripe peach. The evening candlelight caressed the curve of her bosom, making his cock ache. Lady Winter stared right back at him, bold as you please.

His blood thrummed with the heated awareness that he would have her soon. He had given up trying to reason out why he was suddenly in full rut to have her. He simply was, and he needed to relieve himself of the itch so that he could consider his options properly.

He was well aware that sex with her would not reveal the answers he needed about Welton and her husbands' affiliation with the agency. She was too much like him. A series of orgasms would not suddenly engender in her the desire to share her secrets with him. And he wanted her secrets. Needed them.

The agents who worked under the auspices of His Majesty's Royal Navy were a thorn in his side. They followed him ceaselessly, spied on him regularly, and reclaimed pirated cargo often enough to be annoying. The reason Maria married two of them could be simply that both men had been wealthy peers, but it could also be related to the agency itself, and if it was, he wanted to know why.

The setting of the Harwick country house was perfect in a way few places could be. First of all, he was welcome here. Second, they were forced to share a roof. And lastly, but most importantly, her home was vacant aside from the servants. With careful staging, one of his people would manage to join her household. She would not be able to sneeze without him knowing of it.

Christopher lifted his glass to her in a silent toast and she smiled a woman's smile, one filled with mystery.

To the winner, the spoils.

Chapter 4

"I received word from Templeton," Simon murmured, his hand at the small of Maria's back. "He will be waiting in the pantheon after the clock strikes two. I cannot go to him, *mhuirnín*. I will be occupied."

"I shall go, of course. What do you expect him to say?"

He gave an elegant shrug for appearance's sake, but his gaze was sharp as flint. "I anticipate he has some pressing news about your sibling. He would not risk coming here without just cause."

"You expanded the search of the coastlines?" Beneath lowered lashes, she studied the many occupants of the parlor. St. John was presently charming Lady Harwick, but Maria had no doubt where his attention truly was.

She could feel it—hot and intense.

"Yes. Because of this, the men are spread thin."

"What else can I do?"

He sighed and his fingers stroked over her back. The touch was barely discernable through the layers of her garments, but she knew it was there all the same. "Be on your guard. Templeton is a man for hire. He cares nothing for you or your sister, he cares only for coin."

"I am ever careful, Simon."

She turned slightly and stared up at him. He was a stunning man. Dressed in gray silk with a quilted silk satin waist-coat, there were no distracting colors to compete with his masculine appeal. Unwigged, with his dark hair restrained in a queue, his long-lashed blue eyes riveted her attention. Their half-lidded state gave the appearance of boredom, but as she watched him, his gaze darkened.

"I will turn her away, *mhuirnín*, if you would like to follow through with the promises your scrutiny is making."

"Every woman here is admiring you. Am I to be denied that pleasure?"

His mouth curved dangerously. Simon was rough around the edges, untamed. She had literally plucked him from the gutter, and the sense that he could kill or fuck with equal expertise held a potent allure for most women. "I have never denied you anything." He lifted her hand to his lips. "And I never will."

She shook her head with a soft laugh. "You take care, as well, Simon love."

Bowing, he said, "I am, as always, your servant."

In a few moments, he was gone, and a short time after that St. John's dark-haired companion made her excuses as well, her anticipation palpable. Maria knew firsthand that the woman would not be disappointed.

Turning her head, she saw St. John approaching. Whatever remnant of disquiet she felt over Simon fled in an instant, her senses fully focused on the man whose interest caused butterflies to take flight in her stomach. He towered over her, golden hair and skin burnished by the candlelight. Chain-stitched embroidery accented his cream-colored waistcoat, which in turn accented the lush deep green of his coat. Unlike Simon's, his garments were designed to draw attention, bringing his coloring into stark relief. Once again she felt the weight of female gazes directed to where she stood.

He caught her hand, much as Simon had, and kissed the

back, but her reaction to the gesture was entirely different. She was not touched by sorrow. Not by any means.

"I will make you forget him," he rasped softly, his gaze piercing. He was every bit as rough as Simon, and there could be no doubt that this man had no qualms about anything—killing included.

However, his bearing was not lazily seductive, as Simon's was. It was brazenly sexual. She knew, as only a woman could, that St. John was not a man prone to rolling about a bed with laughter and playfulness. St. John was too raw for that.

She was deeply astonished to realize that she was *attracted* to that primitive quality in the pirate, especially after suffering through Lord Winter's treatment. And not merely attracted, but filled with base cravings.

"Hmm . . ." She tugged her hand free and looked away, feigning a nonchalance she did not feel.

He moved, stirring the scent of his skin in the air. She felt a feather-light touch drift across her throat. "My beautiful deceiver. Your heart races. I can see it here."

Suddenly, in that brief contact, she became fully aroused. Eyes wide, she looked back at him.

His gaze was dark and hungry. Territorial. "A chaste touch, yet it makes you want me. Imagine how much greater the effect will be when I am *inside* you."

She sucked in a breath. "That is all you will be doing—imagining." That her voice remained strong and slightly dismissive amazed her.

He smiled a purely male smile. "Tell me you will not end up in my bed." St. John's voice lowered, his fingertips again brushing across her fluttering pulse. "Say it, Maria. I do so love a challenge."

"I will not end up in your bed." Her lips curved. "I much prefer to have sex in mine."

She could see that she surprised him, then delighted him.

His eyes sparkled and the rumble of laughter that came from him was genuine. "I can live with that arrangement."

"But not tonight," she equivocated. Then she leaned closer and said in a conspiratorial whisper, "Lady Smythe-Gleason has been coveting your form all evening. You might try her. Good evening, Mr. St. John."

The thought of St. John with another woman affected her in a similar manner to such thoughts of Simon. However, it was not as easy to push them aside . . .

St. John caught her arm when she attempted to move away. The heat that flared from where he touched her was undeniable. It was also reflected in the look he gave her. "As part of our inevitable business association, I want the private use of your body. In return, I will offer the same courtesy to you."

Maria blinked. "Beg your pardon?"

Christopher's thumb stroked intimately within the crook of her elbow, hidden from view by the froth of white lace. The caress sent tingles up her arm to her breasts, making her nipples ache. She was grateful for the prison of her corset, which hid her state from him.

"You heard me," he said.

"Why would I agree to such an arrangement? Better yet, why would you?" She arched a brow.

He returned the gesture.

She gave a shaky laugh and attempted to conceal how fascinated she was by the idea of claiming him. He was wild, untamed, a wolf in sheep's clothing. "You amuse me, Christopher."

"That is not what you are feeling." He stepped closer, entering her personal space. "I arouse you and intrigue you and even frighten you. My repertoire of carnal amusements is nearly endless, as you shall soon see. But I am not *amusing*. That requires a level of frivolity I will never achieve."

Her lips parted with softly panting breaths.

"Come to my room when you change your mind," he murmured, stepping back.

Maria managed a mocking smile and then made her excuses so she could retire. She felt him watching her as she left the room, and his words followed her long after they parted.

Leaving the manse without being seen was both simpler and more difficult than Maria expected.

On one hand, it was as easy as tossing her leg over her balcony railing. On the other, it required her to descend using a vine-covered trellis. With custom-made black breeches, it was more of an inconvenience than a true trial. Regardless, the method was not the most desirable means of traversing the distance from her room to the ground level. Especially with a rapier attached to her waist.

She dropped to her feet with enough noise to make her cautious. She looked around, clung to the shadows, and waited the space of several breaths. Once she was certain no one was peering out their windows for trespassers, she pushed away from the bricks and set off toward the pantheon.

The night was still and quiet, the breeze cool but not cold. It was a perfect setting for a moonlit meeting of two lovers. That she was dressed as a man and rushing to meet an unsavory denizen of the streets was simply a fact of her life. There was no room for wasted moments of happiness and comfort. She could not enjoy them in any case, knowing that Amelia was at large, perhaps scared and alone.

As she had earlier in the day, Maria moved from tree to tree, circling the pantheon, her eyes straining to see in the darkness. The canopy above filtered the moonlight enough to make the interior of the structure black as pitch. She paused, her breath held. The hair on her nape stood on end, warning her.

She spun about before a twig snapped to her rear, her blade singing as she yanked it free of its scabbard. A man stood a few feet away, watching her with a cold intensity that put her further on her guard. In the darkness, there wasn't much she could see of him, but he was shorter in stature than Simon or Christopher, and so thin he looked emaciated.

"Where's Quinn?" he asked.

"You will be speaking with me this evening." There was as much steel in her voice as in her blade.

He snorted and turned away.

"Who do you think pays your coin?" she murmured.

Templeton paused midstride. A long moment passed where she could almost hear him considering, then he turned about. He whistled softly, then leaned against a nearby tree and thrust his hands against his pockets.

Maria opened her mouth to speak and then she noted his eyes were shifting, as if he espied something beyond her that she had no view of. His preoccupation alerted her to a rushing movement passing through the periphery of her vision. Suddenly on guard, she leapt back from a lunging foil wielded by a second man.

She recovered instantly and parried the next thrust, the two rapiers meeting in a clash of steel. Her jaw hardened at the sight of the burly man who faced her. She was an expert swordsman, a hard-earned accomplishment made possible by Dayton's largesse. Still, her heart raced.

Sadly, my darling Maria, you are one who will live by the sword, he once said. *Therefore, we must be certain your skill with a blade is unequaled.*

How she missed him!

As always, the memory of his loss sharpened her focus and she began to fight with such fervor her opponent, large as he was, cursed and was pushed back. Her arm lifted, thrust, and moved lightning quick. She kept to a position that allowed her to keep sight of Templeton, who watched avidly, even as she remained engaged by his associate. She was small and fast, but that did not prevent the toe of her boot from catching on a tree root. Maria stumbled with a cry of alarm, the gleam of victory in her opponent's eye undeniable as his foil aimed to take the advantage.

"Easy now, 'arry!" Templeton cried.

She hit the ground and rolled, Harry's downward-plunging blade piercing the dirt, her upward-thrusting blade piercing his thigh. He bellowed in rage, like a wounded bear, then a bright flare of muted white hit the man full bore in the chest and took him to the ground with a brutal thud. The two bodies rolled briefly, a pained groan was heard, and then both men went still.

In the end, it was the figure in the billowing linen shirt who rose, yanking free the dagger that had found its home in the larger man's chest.

Moonlight revealed pale hair and a quick turn of his head in her direction revealed fathomless eyes. Then Christopher St. John moved toward Templeton, who stood frozen nearby.

"Do you know who I am?" he asked in a deceptively quiet voice.

"Aye. St. John." Templeton backed up cautiously. "The leddy's none the worse, you see."

"No thanks to you." Moving as quickly as he had before, with a speed so startling it would be missed if one blinked, St. John had Templeton pinned to the tree with his dagger embedded in a bony shoulder.

What followed was agonizing to watch. St. John spoke in a low, almost soothing tone while twisting the blade into torn flesh, and the frieze-clad man writhed while gasping and sobbing out his replies. Against her will, Maria's gaze moved back and forth between Christopher's broad shoulders and the dead man a few feet away. She fought nausea, repeating a familiar litany in her head, one that absolved her of guilt because the end had been necessary to preserve herself. And Amelia.

His life or mine. His life or mine. His life or mine.

It never quite succeeded, but what more could she do? If she took too long considering how far in the mire she had fallen, she would sink into a melancholia that took weeks to run its course. She knew this from experience.

"Restore the area to its previous appearance," St. John said, pulling away and watching as the man fell to his knees before him. "When the sun rises, this spot should be pristine and undisturbed, do you understand?"

"When I works, I'm careful," Templeton said, his voice strained.

Christopher turned his full attention to her then, striding to her side and catching her elbow before dragging her away.

"I must speak with him," she protested.

"A governess was hired and sent to Dover."

Maria tensed, and perceptive as he was, he did not fail to notice.

"He said no more than that," he assured. Despite the controlled quality of his voice, there was a dangerous undercurrent beneath the façade. "Trust that your need for such information is a secret saved. Wise of you to keep the reason for your inquiries a mystery. He has nothing with which to leverage extortion."

"I am not a fool." She shot him a sidelong glance, and the tiny hairs on her nape stood on end. He was leashed for the moment, but barely. "I also had the situation firmly in hand."

"I will debate the use of the word 'firmly,' but I agree, you were doing well enough without my intervention. Blame my intrusion on a heretofore unknown speck of chivalry."

Although she said nothing aloud, Maria had felt relief at his appearance and a softening she had not expected. At first, her examination of this new regard for him yielded no answers. Then she realized, with great surprise, that it was the first time since Dayton that someone had saved her.

"Why were you there?" she asked, noting as they left the cover of trees that he was nearly undressed, wearing only shirtsleeves, breeches, stockings, and heels. There was blood on his shirt and hands, an outward sign of his proclivity toward savagery.

"I followed you."

She blinked. "How did you know?"

"I watched your abigail leave you. When I entered your rooms in her stead, you were not there. It was easy to deduce how you made your egress since I'd had the door in sight. A quick glance from your balcony revealed your direction."

Maria halted so quickly, she stirred up the gravel. "You entered my rooms? Half dressed?"

He faced her, his gaze moving over her slowly and with rapidly building heat. As if nothing untoward had happened, he withdrew a kerchief from his pocket and rubbed the blood from his hands. "Oddly, I am more aroused by your masculine attire then I was when I pictured you naked in bed."

When their eyes met, she saw a darkness within that even the questionable light of the moon could not hide. There was a betraying tightening to his lips and fierceness to his stance that made her shiver. Her nostrils flared and her heart rate picked up once again as her sense of preservation asserted itself. Her instincts urged her to flee from the predator that stood before her.

Run. He hunts you.

"I told you I was unavailable," she said, her hand curling around the hilt of her weapon. "I am not known for tolerating those who meddle in my affairs."

"Do you refer to your unfortunate spouses?"

Maria moved on, walking with quick strides toward the manse.

"You should not have been out alone, Maria, and you should not have scheduled such a meeting here."

"And *you* should not seek to chastise me."

He caught her arm and pulled her to him. His hand stayed hers when she moved to withdraw her sword, catching it and settling it over his heart. It beat as fast as hers, and the gesture was telling, revealing that he was not made of stone as most believed him to be. Her other arm was rendered harmless, held to the small of her back by his grip around her wrist.

The result was highly intimate, her chest pressed to his, her nose in his throat. She briefly considered struggling, and then decided she would not give him the satisfaction. Besides, it was wonderful to be held after the events of only moments ago. A tiny bit of comfort she never allowed herself to seek.

"I intend to kiss you," he murmured. "Restraining you was necessary since you are once again armed and I've no wish to be run through. The weapons you carry grow larger with every encounter."

"If you think the only weapons I have are ones I carry upon my person," she countered, her voice soft, "you are sadly mistaken."

"Fight me," he urged in a husky whisper, staring down into her upturned face with tangible, unadulterated aggression. "Make me take you kicking and scratching."

Christopher St. John was ruthless, determined. She could feel the simmering hunger and need within him. It encircled her as surely as his arms did.

He had killed a man for her.

And it obviously brought out the devil in him to have done so.

She stared up into his hard, savagely beautiful face and realized what was happening. He had fought for her, therefore she was his prize. A shiver moved through her and his mouth curved in a purely sexual smile.

Heat flared across her skin and then sank into her blood. Blood that had been chilled from the moment her mother had taken her last breath.

Was she mad to want him for having killed on her behalf?

Had Welton made her some aberration that she would find his protection arousing?

Christopher wrapped his much larger body around hers, surrounding her in the rich, spicy scent of his skin. "Private use," he warned again, then he took her mouth. Hard and deep. Blatantly possessive and demanding. Forcing her head back so that she had no balance, no way to refuse.

Save for one.

She bit his lower lip. He growled, then cursed into her mouth. "I would not have thought," he rumbled, "that I would find a woman so skilled in masculine pursuits so bloody desirable, but it is undeniable that I want you more than any other female in my recent memory."

"You cannot have me tonight. I am not in a mood to indulge you."

"I can put you in the mood."

Christopher swiveled his hips against her, making the rigid length of his impressive erection abundantly clear. The tightening of her sex deepened into an almost unbearable ache.

"Do it," she challenged, knowing he would not force her even if he could make her enjoy it, which she had no doubt he could. The need in him was for her capitulation, her surrender. She knew this as only an intuitive woman would. Or perhaps only a woman who thought like him would.

His jaw clenched tight. Then he altered his hold, pulling the hand set over his heart to join its sister behind her back, freeing one of his hands to yank the scarf from her head and then pull on her hair.

She gasped at the pain, and he took advantage, pushing into her mouth with a sensual grace he had not bothered with a moment ago. Long, deep licks. Not thrusting, stroking. Rhythmically. Mimicking the sexual act, fucking her mouth with his tongue. Her knees weakened, making her sag into him until only his strength supported her. He urged her against him in strong nudges, rubbing his hard cock into the soft give of her belly. She grew damp between her legs, and then slick. Ready.

She whimpered, finding it impossible to stand firm against both his skill and his uncommon handsomeness.

He reacted to the sound in a way she did not expect, hitching her up, lengthening her legs to a standing position, so he could drag her back to the trellis. He left her there with an angry snort.

Maria bent over, hands on her knees, breathing hard. Her eyes squeezed shut as she collected herself. Every part of her body hummed with sensual energy, a vibrating coil of longing and loneliness that urged her to cast aside her pride and go after him. There were a multitude of reasons why she wanted him, not the least of which was Welton's edict, but she also knew that sometimes denying a man what he wanted was more effective than giving it to him outright.

Blowing out her breath, she climbed the trellis and jumped to the balcony as quietly as possible. She began to disrobe, her thoughts leaping from why she should not accept St. John to why she should. A knock came to the door and she tensed until she realized it did not originate from the gallery.

She called out, and her abigail entered with her customary efficiency, collecting the discarded garments. Dayton had engaged the maid's services, and Sarah had proven to be the soul of discretion, dealing with bloodstains as well as she dealt with wine stains.

"We leave for Dover in the morning," Maria said, her thoughts turning to the journey ahead. Though St. John had told her little, she understood the message.

Sarah nodded, accustomed to hasty departures. She assisted Maria with the donning of her night rail, then she departed.

Moving toward the bed, Maria paused, staring at the turned-down sheets. In her mind's eye, she pictured Simon as he would be at this moment—laughing, rolling about a bed in all his glorious nakedness, easily obtaining all the information he desired without his partner suspecting his perfidy.

She sighed, envying him that closeness. Though it was only physical, it was more than she'd had in over a year. The search for Amelia competed with the need to be available for Welton, leaving her no time to see to her own needs.

Welton. Damn him. He wished for her to do as Simon was doing, growing close to St. John, earning his trust, discovering his secrets. She had no notion how long she would be in Dover. No more than a sennight or Welton would grow suspicious. But with a man like St. John, a week apart might be too long. He might very well find his fancy caught by some other female, and she would have to wait for that to run its course. Even then, she knew from her own experience that once interest was lost, it was rarely regained. Somehow, she had to take him from raging desire to true bewitchment, and she had only hours in which to do it.

Assuring herself that it was only necessity that forced her hand, Maria opened the hall door, looked both ways, and moved stealthily down the gallery until she reached the suite of rooms she had previously ascertained were being used by St. John. She paused there on the threshold, dressed scandalously in only her gossamer-sheer night rail, her hand lifted to knock but arrested in the air. That damned sense of walking into a lion's lair was back.

Suddenly the door swung open and she found herself confronted by a completely, wonderfully, sinfully nude pirate of infamy. Golden skin and hair were seductively backlit by candlelight, bringing the hard lengths of beautifully delineated muscle into splendid relief. He filled the doorway with his size and strength; he filled her senses with awe and pulsing desire.

He scowled. "I will fuck you in the hall, if you wish, but you will be more comfortable in my bed."

Maria blinked, her gaze dropping and finding even more to covet. She struggled to find something witty to say, but her tongue was stuck to the roof of her mouth. She wanted him, all of him, everything she could see and the backside as well.

Christopher raked her from head to toe in a similarly thorough perusal. His gaze heated, became dark, and a low rumble that sounded deliciously like a purr rose up from his powerful chest.

Before she could find her wits, he caught her hand still held in midair and yanked her in.

Chapter 5

"**A**re you *daft?*" Christopher slammed the door closed, then glared down at the brazen temptress before him and bit out, "You cannot wander about dressed in that manner!"

The filmy feminine concoction presently touching the curves he desired was alarmingly transparent, revealing every bit of Maria's abundant charms—long, lithe legs, full hips, trim waist, and ripe, lush breasts. The shadowed juncture between her thighs and the dark circles of her areolas were plain as day.

His jaw clenched until his teeth ground audibly. In the candlelight, her olive skin shone like silk and he would wager it was of similar softness. To think of her traversing the gallery where any of the many bedroom-hopping guests could have stumbled across her . . .

She gave an elegant shrug. "You should not open doors naked."

"I am in my rooms."

"I am in your rooms also," she replied evenly.

"You were not a moment ago!"

"Are you going to hold my past against me? If so, I have far worse offenses."

"Bloody hell, that was only a minute past!"

PASSION FOR THE GAME   53

"Yes, and only a minute past you were standing naked in the hall."

She arched a brow, her deportment every inch the Wintry Widow. He might have believed the façade if not for her eyes and bared body, both of which exuded sensual heat. Besides, she was here, ready for sex.

"I personally think your offense is greater," she continued. "I, at least, have a garment on."

Christopher growled. Catching her shoulders, he tugged her close and heard a rip. The sound only goaded his anger. Whatever she was wearing, it offered less protection from a man's hands than it did from his eyes. "This is not a garment! This is a temptation, and what you are tempting *with* belongs to *me*."

Her mouth fell open. "Beast! Tearing my clothes and handling me in this manner."

She stepped back, shrugged off his hands, and slapped him. Across the face.

The action so startled him, Christopher could scarcely process it. No one dared to assault him. Even those who had a wish for death chose to find it in a more peaceful manner than by provoking him—

He faltered, unsure of how he felt about her actions. The near-painful throbbing of his cock answered that question, and before his mouth could ruin it for him again, he lunged after her retreating form with such force they both tumbled to the ground. It was only by the grace of God that he managed to jerk himself to the side before crushing her.

"*What are you—*"

"*Oompf!*" The impact of hitting the floor with only the rug to soften the blow jarred every bone in his body.

"By God!" Maria cried shrilly, turning her head to gaze at him with wide eyes. "You, sir, are certifiable!"

Her prone body wiggled delightfully beneath the arm and leg he pinned her with. She was as soft and lush as he had imagined she would be. She also smelled delightful, that sweet smell of things both fruity and floral that teased with its promise of innocence, a promise her appearance could never deliver upon.

Part of him knew that he should say something, apologize for her torn gown or some such platitude that would soothe her, but damned if he could do more than grunt and try to push up her hem with his knee.

When her elbow connected with one of his ribs, a low, warning rumble rose up from his chest. It was a sound that struck terror in most. In Maria, it inspired rage.

"Do not growl at me!" she snapped, struggling with such strength he doubted his ability to restrain her without hurting her.

It was then he gave up his attempt to be gentle, knowing it was hopeless, understanding that he had regressed to some primitive frame of thought that cared only about how desperately aroused she made him.

Catching both of her wrists in one of his hands, Christopher slid over her, then forced her legs apart by settling between them.

Maria paused for a moment, collecting his intent. Then she fought him as he had urged her to do earlier—like a feral cat. She struggled, attempting to crawl across the English rug to the sitting room door but not budging an inch. "Oh no! You will *not* have me!"

He snorted, then tore her night rail in his impatience to bare the beautifully rounded curve of her derrière. This time he managed a sound that resembled something vaguely apologetic.

She was not impressed. "I would sooner share the bed of Lord Farsham than I would yours."

That comment earned her a slap to the ass, which made her yelp. Farsham had two score years, at least, and was said to be impotent, neither fact mitigating Christopher's rising agitation at the thought of any other man seeing her thusly.

In retaliation, Maria sank sharp teeth into his forearm with vicious fervor. He roared in pain and felt a trickle of moisture slide down the crown of his cock. He thrust his hand between her legs and found her cunt slick, hot, and ready. Studying her features, he noted her state of arousal reflected in her passion-dazed eyes and the flush of her skin.

Thank God. He was nigh undone, his seed leaking in its eagerness to flood her with his lust.

Maria stilled for a moment, her gasp the only sound in the room, his own breath trapped in his lungs at the feel of her beneath his touch. He stroked through the lips of her sex with trembling fingers and closed his eyes. Without forethought, his head dipped, his lips pressing against the curve of her shoulder.

His hand moved, leaving her, aiming his aching erection at her creamy opening.

"*Maria.*" Finally. A word. Squeezed out of his clenched throat by the fisted grip of her cunt around the flared head of his cock.

She whimpered and arched her hips upward as much as his weight would allow her, altering the angle with which he pressed into her. He slipped a fraction deeper.

Christopher's breath hissed out between his teeth. Christ, she was fevered inside, hot as hell, and so exquisitely tight . . .

"How long?" he bit out.

She threw her hips at him impatiently.

He nipped her earlobe with his teeth. "How long?"

"A year," she said, her voice low and breathless. "But continue with this pace and it may be two. Did you forget how to have sex when you forgot your manners?"

"Maddening. Contrary. Vexing wench." He punctuated each word with a thrust of his hips, working his way into her, forcing her thighs wider with his own.

"That. Is. *My lady.* To you," she retorted with gusting breaths.

Then he hit a spot deep inside her that made her moan and

writhe in a completely different fashion than she had before—in sensual invitation, not anger.

"Like that?" he murmured, his mouth curving lazily. Her sudden capitulation soothed him immeasurably. Being inside her helped also. From the moment he first touched her in the theater, this was where he wanted to be. "A little more?"

Christopher clenched his buttocks and slid deeper, dizzy with the feel of her beneath him, clasped around him.

Her cunt rippled hungrily, sucking him deeper, the sensation so intense he shuddered against her.

"Maria," he breathed, his head hanging down next to hers. "You . . ."

With his brain presently wallowing in sexual madness, he could think of nothing to say to describe . . . whatever it was he wished to describe. Instead, he pulled free of her, groaning at the caress of her soft, silky tissues on his withdrawal.

"Damn you," she muttered, rolling to her back when he slid off her. She glared at him, her beautiful face betraying her frustration and renewed anger. Oddly, the sight of a furious woman did not make him wish to be rid of her. Just the opposite with Maria.

She was not cowed by him and made no attempt to hide who she was—his equal. Her response made him ache from head to toe with the need to spread her wide and sink his hard cock into her. Over and over again.

"Not here," he growled, rising to his feet and yanking her up with him. When she tripped, Christopher caught her and tossed her over his shoulder.

"Brute!"

"Witch." He watt her again. Then, unable to help it, he rubbed the firm flesh with the palm of his hand.

"Craven! Fight me face-to-face. Instead you strike when my back is turned."

He smiled, adoring the sound of her voice, filled with such challenge. Leaving the sitting room, he entered his bedchamber.

He crossed the large space and threw her down upon the mattress.

She bounced, then kicked out at him, slapping at his grasping hands while heaping a thousand curses upon him. None of which was able to save her night rail. He tore it from her and tossed the remnants aside.

"I shall *fuck* you face-to-face, my passionate heathen," he purred, pinning her down with his much larger body. "Hence the necessary change of venue. We shall be at this for some time, and I've no desire for burns on my knees or on your luscious breasts."

Her nails dug into the backs of his hands as he laced his fingers with hers. With a strong push of his knee, he spread her wide and then thrust into her. The sound that left his throat as he sank to the hilt was harsh and visceral. Inwardly startled by it, he lowered his lips to her bared breast and sucked her nipple into his mouth.

"Yes!" she hissed, wiggling madly under him.

"Stop that," he admonished, lifting his head to look into her dark eyes. "You shall exhaust me before I have the chance to ride you properly."

Maria bucked. "Move along with it, damn you."

He laughed, the sound swelling to fill the intimate space created by the canopy above them.

She blinked and went still, watching him. "Do that again," she urged.

Christopher's brows rose, and he flexed his cock inside her. The soft pant that left her parted lips made his balls draw up. "I can laugh or fuck, but not both at the same time. Which would you prefer I do first?"

The instantaneous sexual tension that gripped her was palpable.

"Good," he murmured, licking her bottom lip. "That was my choice, too."

He moved then, pulling their joined hands down to her

shoulder level, using his elbows to support the weight of his torso. His hips lifted and fell slowly, dragging his cock out, then pushing deep again. Maria whimpered and he nuzzled his cheek against hers.

"Let it out," he whispered, his lips to her temple. "Tell me how much you enjoy it."

She turned her head and bit his earlobe. *Hard.* "You can tell me how much *you* enjoy it, if you ever start the business!"

He growled and stepped up the pace, knowing he was mere moments away from a brilliant orgasm of epic proportions. It could be nothing else. Because of *her*, and her blasted mouth and her temper that drove him insane. He intended to occupy that mouth with a much more pleasurable task. Later. At the moment, he was so bloody aroused, his cock and balls were pained with it, his skin coated in perspiration, his exhales bursting from his lungs as he rode her lush body with hard, deep plunges. All the while, he tried to make it good for her, a concern he had never had before, but one that goaded him fiercely now.

Maria took his lust and gave it back in like measure, her legs locked around his hips, her lithe thighs working with equal fervor. Her nipples were hard, and every thrust he made brushed his chest across them, making them both moan. All the while she whispered in his ear—naughty things, sexual things, tiny barbs and insults that drove him to the edge of reason.

Christopher lunged into her, balls deep, and rolled his hips, glaring down at her. He watched her eyes widen, her lips part, her neck arch as his pelvis circled against her clitoris. He watched the orgasm take her, move through her. Saw it darken her eyes and soften the tension that always bracketed her mouth.

The word "beautiful" was incapable of describing her. Maria was far beyond that, so stunning that he noted it even within the throes of his own building climax. He felt her cunt ripple along his cock, squeezing, sucking, drawing him deeper, until he could not hold back.

The pressure built at his shoulders, poured down his spine, pooled in his testicles, and burst from the end of his cock in a stream of white-hot semen. How he managed to keep from roaring out his relief, he would never know. He knew only that he was held tight against soft curves, tiny hands cupping his buttocks, a breathless voice crooning, anchoring him in the midst of a toe-curling orgasm.

And a kiss. Feather light in the crook of his neck.

Lost to a violent climax, he still felt that kiss.

Maria stared up at the shadowy recesses of the canopy above her and shifted restlessly. Christopher mimicked her pose an arm's distance away. The silence between them stretched out uncomfortably. Had she been in bed with Simon, he would have glasses of wine in their hands and some inane tale to tell her that would make her laugh. With Christopher there was only this damnable tension. And an all-encompassing tingle that thrummed through her entire body.

She sighed, reexamining the night's events.

Christopher's laughter had caught her off guard. How wonderful the sound how been, how delicious it had felt vibrating against her. It had transformed his features, making her heart stop altogether. On the whole, the entire encounter had been . . . *intense*, as she had known sex with him would be. His dangerous edge excited her, made her reckless, urged her to goad him into a fine temper. It was thrilling to push such a controlled man beyond his limits, to make him lose control. He fucked with such passion, such strength, his body a finely honed instrument of pleasure.

She shivered with renewed desire and turned her head to find him watching her. He canted an eyebrow and then yanked her closer, tugging her body to drape over his side.

It was nice to be held so tightly to him, his long legs tangled with her much shorter ones, his powerful arms wrapped around her torso. Remnants of perspiration made their skin cling together. Maria closed her eyes and breathed in his scent, now intensified by his exertions. It was obvious such tenderness was unknown to him. His hands moved over her hesitantly, as if he were unsure of what to do.

"Are you sore?" he rasped softly.

"We can have sex again, if you wish. Or I can retire, if you would lend me a robe."

His grip tightened. "Stay."

It was nearly dawn. She would have to leave soon, regardless—both his room and this manse. Dover and the possibility of finding Amelia was a strong lure. Optimism was a luxury, but if she had no hope at all she could not go on.

Christopher's hand stroked down the length of her spine, arching her into him, an action which revealed the hard length of his renewed erection against her thigh. Arousal, more languorous than the fever they had experienced earlier, moved through her veins. It made her breasts swell into his chest and her nipples harden next to his skin.

"Hmm . . ." he purred, drawing her completely on top of him.

She stared down at her fallen-angel lover, gifted with the beauty of the heavens on his exterior but the conscience of a predator on the interior. Her hands shifted through his golden hair, making his eyelids lower with pleasure and his pupils dilate with desire.

"I do not find blond men all that attractive," she said, mostly to herself.

In response, he laughed that rich deep laugh that made her belly warm. "I am grateful other parts of you disagree."

Snorting, she rose up to a seated position.

"I do not like shrewish women." The curve of his mouth deepened. "But I do like you. God only knows why."

His praise, offhand as it was, pleased her. In the distance, she heard a timepiece sounding out the hour.

Christopher's smile faded. "A pity we are not at home," he said, his sapphire gaze intense. "I dislike being rushed."

Maria shrugged, refusing to acknowledge that she felt the same. Neither of them knew how to deal with the other, but the level of awareness between them was so high, she knew she would feel its lack.

Arching her hips, she found the hot length of him with the lips of her sex and glided along his cock, the movement aided by the slickness of their mingled release. His large hands gripped her thighs and urged her to repeat her actions. She did, then paused.

His eyes never left her. The intensity of his perusal was unique, and she could not decide if she liked it or if she did not. So she reached between them, aiming him skyward, and gloved him with her body, effectively scattering her thoughts.

A harsh inhale and the tightening of his frame was his reply. Maria felt the same brutal rush of sensation. It had been a long time since her last sexual encounter, too long. But Christopher was a well-endowed man in addition to that, and his possession of the tight space inside her stretched her deliciously. She quivered around him, starting from deep inside where she hugged him and then spreading outward.

"Damnation," he hissed, throbbing and growing in girth within her. "How could I ever think you were cold?"

Intrigued by his possible meaning, she stilled just shy of engulfing the root of him.

A muscle in his jaw ticked violently. "Your cunt is burning hot and greedy. It sucks at my cock. The sensation is incredible."

She smiled and lowered, taking him completely inside her. She knew in that moment that she had his attention. He would desire her while she was gone, and that impatience would serve her well. Pleased, Maria leaned over him, pausing with her mouth hovering just above his. "May I kiss you?" she asked.

His head lifted, his mouth taking hers, his tongue plunging deep and then thrusting rhythmically, licking, stroking. Making her shiver.

"Yes," he whispered darkly, breathing hard, his hands cupping her spine. "Do everything to me."

She rose for leverage and gasped at the feel of his mouth latching onto her nipple. As he began to suck, her eyes slid closed. She grew wetter, more aroused, the weight of her torso balanced on the hands she had rested next to his shoulders. He drew on her with long, deep pulls that were echoed in the tremors her body made around his cock. He flexed inside her and she moaned a low, plaintive sound.

"This is how we will start the day." Christopher's raspy voice was a tactile caress across her fevered skin. "Don't move. I will suck you to orgasm, and your cunt will do the same for me."

If she could have spoken, she would have told him that was impossible, but then he would have proven her wrong. His mouth was enchanted, tugging firmly in a timed rhythm, his tongue stroking back and forth across the underside of her nipple. First one, and then the other. His large hands with their tantalizing calluses soothed her as she became more agitated, her body writhing over his in its quest for orgasm.

When she climaxed, he followed her, her cunt grasping at his cock, luring his seed, spasming as he flooded her with a guttural cry. Maria was held taut, suspended, caught in a grip of brutally fierce pleasure.

He caught her close, engulfing her in warm arms, his lips pressed tightly to her forehead. He fell asleep that way.

But even in slumber, he did not let her go.

Maria entered her rooms with a sigh of relief. She had not been seen by anyone, a miracle made possible by pressing herself into recessed doorways to avoid detection by industrious maids.

In another part of the manse, Christopher slept on. He had

frowned when she pulled away from him, but he did not wake.

Shutting the gallery door, Maria moved through the sitting room toward her bedchamber and stopped midstep, startled by the large form that filled the doorway.

"*Mhuirnín.*"

Simon leaned against the doorjamb, his body fully clothed and beautifully attired in rose-colored breeches with matching coat. One heeled foot crossed over the other, but the artless pose was unable to hide the tension of his frame.

"You gave me a fright," she admonished, her hand pressed over her racing heart.

His gaze started at the top of her head and dropped all the way to her bare feet. She was drowning in Christopher's robe, so there was not much of her to see, but she knew the night's lascivious activities could not be disguised.

"You slept with him," he noted. Straightening, Simon came to her with his leisurely, seductive stride and cupped her face in his hands. "I do not trust him. Because of that, I do not trust you with him."

"Do not think about it."

"Easier said than done. Women often find their feelings tangled with sex. That concerns me."

"Aside from you, I have never had that problem."

His mouth twitched. "I'm flattered."

"No," she said wryly, "you're arrogant."

"That, too." His half smile widened into a grin.

Maria shook her head, yawning. "I need sleep. After I bathe, we will be departing. I think I will nap in the carriage."

"Dover. Sarah informed me." He pressed a quick, hard kiss to her forehead. "She has nearly finished packing. My trunks are already on the coach in the drive."

"I will not take long." The scent of Christopher clung to her skin and made her stomach quiver. He had killed for her, then made passionate love to her, and then held her with such tenderness . . . The multiple sides to him took her by surprise, rocking the very foundations of the image of the pirate she had once entertained.

Simon stepped back and then moved to the sideboard to pour a glass of water. "I urge you to haste, *mhuirnín*. We do not want any unpleasant scenes."

Maria hurried to the bedroom door, then paused on the threshold. "Simon?"

He looked at her with brows raised in silent query.

"Do I tell you often enough how much I appreciate you?"

"You love me," he replied with a wicked grin. "There is no need to say it, I know you do." He tossed back his drink and poured another. "But feel free to tell me as often as you like. My ego can bear it."

Laughing, Maria shut the door.

Chapter 6

"You knew she would be departing this morn," Thompson said, his face impassive.

"Yes, yes." Christopher sat on a wooden chair, his body canted to allow his arm to drape along the top. He was bereft of waistcoat and coat, and yet he was still overly warm. His body longed to be in motion, to chase after the woman who left him without so much as a fare-thee-well, and the effort he exerted to remain seated was not insignificant.

His valet moved with quiet purpose, preparing the items needed to shave his master's morning whiskers. "The knowledge of the men you set to follow her coach does not alleviate your concern?"

Christopher snorted. Concern. Was that what this feeling was? Why did he feel it, when he knew Maria was capable of caring for herself?

Perhaps it was because Quinn was with her.

His teeth clenched.

Quinn.

"Angelica, love." His voice was low and direct, his head turning to find her finishing her morning tea by the window. "You learned nothing?"

She shook her head, her mouth curved downward. "I did try, but he has a way with . . . distractions."

He arched a brow. "How much did you tell him?" He

knew little of Quinn, but he recognized the man as one who lived by his wits.

The blush that spread across her cheekbones made Christopher curse under his breath. "Not so much," she said hastily. "He was mostly curious as to your interest in Lady Winter."

"And how did you answer?"

"I said you kept your business to yourself, but if you had your eye on her, you would have her." She blew out her breath and leaned backward, the dark circles under her eyes betraying a night spent much like his.

The memory of Maria, soft and open to his desire, made his blood heat. Scratches marred his back and arms, teeth marks decorated the tops of his shoulders. He had shared his bed with a delectable hellion and he was marked by the encounter. In more ways than one.

"Quinn's reply?" he asked softly.

Angelica winced. "He said possession is nine points of the law."

Christopher showed no outward sign of the effect of that statement, but it prodded him with the same intensity as a blow from a horsewhip. Quinn was correct. It was he who shared Maria's home, her life, her confidence, and Christopher had nothing of her but a few hours of pleasure.

"Go pack," he said, watching as the former light o' love rose and did as he bid.

"Will you seek her out?" Thompson asked, straightening from his task and stepping back so that Christopher could take his seat in the appropriate chair.

"No. The men I assigned to watch her will handle the matter. What I need to learn of her will be found in London, and the sooner I return, the swifter that is accomplished."

Blowing out his breath, Christopher inwardly acknowledged that he wanted her again. He liked the woman in all the ways men liked most women, but then he also liked her in ways he rarely liked anyone—he admired her, respected her, and saw her as a kindred spirit. Because of this, he could not trust her. Survival was his goal and he knew it must be hers as well.

Then there was the small matter of his need to sacrifice her for his freedom. Wanting her was damned inconvenient and in direct opposition to the agency's aim.

But there were other considerations beyond his lust and the agency. Quinn was not taking care of Maria properly. Sending her alone to meet with Templeton and leaving her available for Christopher's use were perilous risks.

As he contemplated what manner of mischief she was set upon now, his fingers curled around the arms of his chair.

He remained seated by dint of will alone, the urge to take off after her nearly too much to resist. Maria lived a dangerous life, a fact that bothered him like a sore tooth.

His eyes slid closed as Thompson plied the blade against his cheek. Sadly, despite his desire to keep her safe, the truth was that the greatest danger to her at the moment was him.

Maria leaned against the slatted back of her wooden chair and glanced around the intimate private dining room she occupied. Across from her, Simon watched the flirtatious serving wench with a lascivious gaze. The inn they chose to spend the previous few nights in was comfortable and warm for a variety of reasons beyond the merry fire and worn English rugs.

"She returns your interest," Maria noted with a smile as the servant departed.

"Perhaps." He shrugged. "Under the circumstances, however, I cannot indulge. We are close, *mhuirnín*. I can feel it."

After four days of searching and querying, he had located a merchant who knew of a governess recently come to town. Just that afternoon they had discovered her place of employment. No one knew anything about the young girl the woman had been hired to instruct, but Maria hoped desperately that it was Amelia. Information gathered over the last few weeks suggested it was.

"You have worked tirelessly these last days, Simon love. You deserve a respite."

"And when will you rest?" he asked. "When will you have a respite?"

She sighed. "You have given enough—your time, your energy, your support. You do not need to deny yourself what pleasure you can find for my sake. That will not give me comfort. That will distress me further. I am happy knowing you are happy."

"My happiness is inextricably bound to yours."

"Then you must be miserable. Cease. Enjoy yourself."

Simon laughed and reached across the table to set his hand atop hers. "You asked me the other day if you tell me often enough how much you appreciate me. I must ask the same of you. Do you know how desperately I welcome your affection? In all of my life, you are the only person—female or otherwise—who wishes unselfishly for my happiness. I do the things I do for you out of gratitude and a reciprocal desire to see you happy."

"Thank you." Simon was fiercely loyal and direct, two traits she admired and needed desperately. She understood how he felt. Simon fulfilled a similar role in her life. He was the only person who cared for her at all.

He patted her hand and settled back in his chair. "The men who arrived from London this afternoon are watching the house now. Tomorrow, we will utilize the daylight and go ourselves."

"I agree, the morning is soon enough." She smiled wide. "Which means the night is yours to do with as you will."

At that moment, the serving girl returned bearing a fresh pitcher. Maria winked at Simon, who then tossed his head back and laughed.

Affecting an exaggerated yawn, she said, "Forgive me. I believe I should retire. I am overly fatigued."

Simon stood and rounded the table, pulling the chair out for her and lifting her hand to his lips. His blue eyes sparkled with amusement as he wished her good night. Content in the knowledge that he would enjoy the rest of his evening, Maria departed to her room, where Sarah waited to assist her disrobing.

Pleased as she was for Simon, there was an unfortunate aspect to being without his company: she no longer had a distraction from memories of a raspy voice and hard body that had wrested pleasure from her against her will.

And made her love it.

It was becoming ridiculous how often she thought of St. John. She told herself it was simply due to her prior long abstinence. She was thinking of the sexual act itself, not her partner.

"Thank you, Sarah," Maria murmured as the maid finished brushing out her hair.

After a quick curtsy, the abigail prepared to depart, but a sudden knock on the chamber door arrested her egress. Maria dissuaded her from answering with a raised hand and collected her dagger from the table by the bed. Then she took a position to the side of the door and nodded her permission for Sarah to proceed.

"Yes?" Sarah called out.

When the visitor spoke, Maria recognized the voice as belonging to one of her outriders. Instantly relaxing, she dropped her arm to her side. "See what he wants."

Sarah stepped out into the hall and a few moments later returned.

"That was John, my lady. He says you and Mr. Quinn might wish to go with him now. There is activity at the house, and he fears they are readying to flee."

"Dear God." Her heartbeat faltered. "Go below and see if you can find Mr. Quinn. I doubt it, but try."

After Sarah left, Maria moved to her trunk at the foot of the bed and began to change garments again. Her thoughts raced ahead of her, considering various scenarios and how best to manage them should they arise. She had only a dozen men with her and she would need to assign the majority of them to guarding the perimeter. At most, she could keep two outriders with her to see to her safety.

A soft knock was immediately followed by the opening of the door. Sarah entered shaking her head. "Mr. Quinn is no longer downstairs. Should I go to his room?"

"No." Maria belted her scabbard to her hips. "But after I depart, you may inform his valet."

Once again dressed in breeches and boots with her hair hidden beneath both scarf and hat, she was passable as a young boy at far distance, a ruse that would waylay any talk of suspicious women riding at night.

With a reassuring smile at the clearly worried abigail, Maria stepped out into the hall where John waited. Together they descended the rear steps to the waiting horses outside.

The delivery door of Maria's London townhouse opened, and Christopher stepped silently into the kitchen. His man stood there waiting, having established residence inside the Winter household a few days before in the guise of a footman. If Maria were home, he would not have been selected, but she had been gone for nearly a fortnight. Christopher lured away three of her previous footmen with better-paying positions elsewhere, and desperation had forced her housekeeper to act without guidance.

With a slight nod, Christopher acknowledged a job well done. He collected the single taper his man held aloft, and then took the winding servants' staircase to the upper floors. The gallery was well appointed, the runners thick and beautifully colored, the alcoves decorated with presently unlit gilded sconces.

Wealth. The home reeked of it. Two noble husbands dead, leaving behind settlements that afforded Maria the means to maintain an affluent existence.

He'd investigated her marriages because the men she had chosen were a source of great interest to him. The elderly

Lord Dayton had retired with her to the country, where they stayed the entirety of their short marriage. The younger Lord Winter had kept her in Town and flaunted her shamelessly. It was Winter's demise that first fueled speculation of Dayton's. Winter had been a man in his prime, a burly sportsman with hearty appetites all around. Death by malady had been inconceivable for so bold a man.

Christopher's teeth clenched tightly at the thought of Maria as the possession of another, and he furiously shoved the notion aside.

Nearly a sennight had passed since the night he'd spent with Maria, and he had yet to go more than a few hours without being plagued by thoughts of her. One report had arrived, detailing a thorough inquiry into the location of the governess. Why Maria wished to find this woman, he still did not know. Who was she that the likes of Templeton would be engaged to find her?

Opening the first door he came to and then continuing on, Christopher memorized the interior of the house and the positioning of the rooms. He wasn't pleased to find that Quinn occupied the suite adjoining Maria's. It revealed the depth of Maria's attachment to the man that she gave him so important a place in her household.

Christopher *knew* they were no longer sharing a bed. She had admitted it had been a year since her last sexual encounter, and the tightness of her body gave proof to the claim. Still, he was irritated by Quinn, and worse than that, he did not understand why.

As he rifled through the other man's drawers and armoire, Christopher found his mood worsening. The proliferation of weapons, letters of a cryptic nature, and a drawer of garments one would wear in disguise hinted at a man who was not the simple paramour he appeared to be.

Christopher exited Quinn's room through the connecting door, crossed the shared sitting area, and entered Maria's boudoir. Immediately he was struck by the scent of her, which permeated the air with its gentle fruit undertones. His cock twitched and then swelled slightly.

He cursed under his breath. He had not been afflicted with an unwanted erection since his youth. Then again, as fate would have it, it had been that length of time since he found his sexual affiliations lacking, as had been the case this past week.

None of the women in his household had been sufficient to take him to the level of satisfaction he had achieved with Maria. A level he now hungered for. Two visits to Stewart's, run by the delectable Emaline Stewart, had proved to be of little help. Three of the madam's most popular girls had worked him until morning two nights in a row. He'd ended up exhausted, spent, and still craving. He wanted a woman who made him fight for her attentions, and in all of his life, he had crossed paths with only one who could.

Lifting his arm higher to spread the reach of the candle-light, Christopher spun in a slow circle, admiring the varying shades of blue with which Maria had decorated the room. Oddly, compared to the rest of the chambers, this one was much more understated. Nothing adorned the striped damask walls except a portrait of a couple that graced the space above the mantel.

He stepped closer to it, his heels silent as he crossed the rug. With narrowed eyes, he studied what he knew must be Maria's parents. The resemblance was such that it could not be mistaken. He wondered at the location. Why here? A place where no one but her would see it.

Something niggled at the back of his mind. She kept her true father's image so close to her, and yet she was said to be close to her stepfather, Lord Welton, as well. Christopher knew of Welton. That man lacked the warmth that radiated from the eyes of Maria's father. The two men were not cut of the same cloth.

"What are your secrets?" he asked before turning away to begin his search of Maria's adjacent bedchamber.

His man could easily have done this for him with far less risk, but the thought of Maria's intimate belongings and garments being handled by a lackey prevented that course of action.

She was his equal, and he would give her the respect of treating her like one. When it came to Maria, he would do everything personally, the highest compliment he could bestow.

After tying their horses to a neglected length of fence, Maria and two outriders moved away from the beasts like shadows in the darkness. They were dressed all in black, which made even John's great size of nearly six and a half feet difficult to detect.

Tom gestured to the left and then moved in that direction, his short, slim form melding with the saplings around them. Maria followed, with John bringing up the rear. With only the moonlight to assist their progress, the distance to the home was slowly traversed.

Every step closer made Maria's heart race faster until she was softly panting, her anxiety and eagerness a heady combination. The wind carried a slight chill, but sweat misted her skin as the hope she told herself not to feel refused to be denied. Despite the disappointment that intensified with every near miss and dead end, she wished desperately to succeed, her heart aching with longing.

The home was simple and the gardens untended, but the property held on to an artless charm. Fresh paint, clean brickwork, and cleared pathways showed the care of a loving hand, despite what appeared to be a lack of servants. A book left on a marble bench hinted at leisure time spent outdoors.

The welcoming scene made Maria's throat tight. How she longed to live such a carefree life such as the setting before her promised.

Her thoughts were filled with dreams of a tearful but joyous reunion when John's meaty hand gripped her shoulder and shoved her down roughly. Startled, but experienced enough to keep her silence, Maria dropped to her knees and shot him a questioning glance. He jerked his chin to the side and her gaze followed, watching with a frown as four horses were led out of the stable and hitched to a waiting traveling coach.

"Our mounts," she whispered, her gaze riveted to the industriously working stable boys. Tom rose and hurried back the way they had come.

Panic assailed her, making her palms so damp she had to wipe them dry on her breeches. With highwaymen a very real hazard, no sane traveler set out at this hour. Something was amiss.

At that moment, two cloaked figures appeared, both so slight of frame they could only be women. Maria's heart caught in her throat. She willed the smaller of the two to look her way.

Look at me. Look at me.

The hood turned toward her, the wearer's gaze wandering to where they hid. In the faint light from the lanterns, Maria could not make a firm identification. A tear fell, and then another, coursing hotly down her cheeks.

"Amelia," the taller figure said, her voice carrying across the field in tones muted by distance. "Step lively."

For a moment, Maria was arrested. Her heart stopped, her lungs seized, and blood roared in her ears. *Amelia.* So close. Closer than she had been in years. Maria would not lose her again.

She leapt to her feet, her muscles tensed to run. "John!"

"Aye, I heard." His sword whistled its freedom as he withdrew it from its scabbard. "We can take her."

"Look at what we 'ave 'ere."

The singsong voice at their backs startled them both. Spinning, they faced a group of seven men swiftly closing in from the forest behind them with various weapons in hand.

"A big 'en and a lil 'en." The man laughed, his greasy hair

glistening as brightly in the moonlight as his eyes. "'ave at 'em, mates."

Maria barely had time to withdraw her foil before a melee ensued. Outnumbered, she and John nevertheless leapt into the fray with confidence. In the quiet of the country night, the clashing of steel was a bold cacophony. Their opponents shouted and laughed, seeming to believe their victory was assured. But they were fighting for coin and sport. Maria was fighting for something far more precious.

She thrust and parried against two men at once, her steps hampered by the uneven ground, her sight hindered by the darkness.

All the while she was achingly aware of the carriage behind them, her brain ticking off the time it would take to hitch the equipage. The fighting would be audible and the nearby danger would urge them to greater haste. If she could not break free quickly, she would lose Amelia again.

Suddenly, more combatants joined the fracas, fighting not against her, but at her side. She had no notion who they were, she was simply grateful to be freed. Leaping back from a thrusting small sword, Maria parried, then spun on her heel and ran for her life toward the coach yard.

"Amelia!" she cried, tripping over a rut but maintaining her footing. "Amelia, wait!"

The small form paused with one foot on the step, one hand shoving back her cowl to reveal a dark-haired young woman with bright green eyes. Not at all the child Maria remembered, but it was Amelia regardless.

"Maria?"

Struggling against the taller figure, her sister tried to step down but was shoved inside.

"Amelia!"

The opposite door opened and Amelia fell out, scrambling to find her footing amidst the jumble of her skirts.

Maria ran faster, finding some source of strength she hadn't known was in her. She was almost there, the edge of the coach yard only a few feet away, when a powerful force struck into her back and took her to the ground.

Crushed beneath the weight of a man, her foil knocked away, she couldn't breathe, the air forcibly expelled from her lungs by the blow. She clawed at the ground, her nails breaking in the dirt, her gaze riveted to Amelia, who struggled as she did.

"Maria!"

Desperate, Maria kicked at the man whose legs were tangled with hers, and then pain unlike she'd ever known tore through her shoulder. She felt the flesh rip beneath the plunging blade. Not once but twice.

Then, mercifully, the weight was lifted from her. She gasped her sister's name and tried to move, finding herself pinned to the ground by the weapon that bore through her. The pain of her wrenching movement was too much.

One moment there was agony. And then nothing.

Chapter 7

"We are bringing a ship into Deal tomorrow night." Christopher stared out his black velvet–framed study window at the street below, his fingers rubbing into the sore muscles of his neck. Hackneys rattled by in haste, as no one wished to spend more time in this area of town than was absolutely necessary. "Is everything in readiness?"

"Yes," Philip assured behind him. "The lander has already arranged the carts and mounts, so transportation will begin posthaste."

Christopher nodded wearily, suffering from lack of deep sleep. Driving himself to physical exhaustion would not cure the restlessness caused by his current predicament, and Maria's place in it.

"This cargo is an impressive haul, I've heard," Philip said, his tone lined with the inquisitiveness Christopher fostered.

"Yes. I'm pleased."

Diluting of the over-proof spirits and packaging of the contraband tea would take some time, but his men worked industriously, and his goods filtered into the retail market much quicker than competing smugglers and gangs.

A knock came to the door and he called out permission to enter. The portal swung open and Sam entered, his hat pressed against his chest in a gesture Christopher had come to recognize as a nervous one. Because Sam had been one of the four men assigned to follow Maria, Christopher was immediately set on edge.

"What is it?" he asked.

Sam winced and ran a hand through his red locks. "There was a skirmish two nights ago and—"

"Was she hurt?" Every muscle tensed, his mind flooding with memories of her sweetly curved body straining beneath his. She was so tiny, so slight of frame . . .

"Aye. Knife wounds to the left shoulder, one clean through."

Christopher's voice became even more controlled, a sure sign of his growing irritation. "The entirety of your purpose was to see to her safety. Four of you, yet you all failed?"

"She was set upon! And there were more of them than there were of us!"

Christopher glanced at Philip. "Have the coach hitched."

"She's here," Sam offered quickly. "In Town."

"Say that again." Christopher's heart raced. "She traveled in that condition?"

Sam cringed and nodded.

A low growl rumbled up from the depths of Christopher's chest.

"I will have your horse brought round," Philip offered, retreating hastily.

Christopher's gaze never left Sam's flushed face. "You should have kept her abed and sent for me."

"'Tis a blessing I can tell the tale!" Sam held out his hands defensively, the brim of his hat crumpled in his fist. "When we took her back to her inn, the Irishman went bloody mad." He scratched furiously at his head and blurted, "He frightened Tim! Tim was quaking, I tell you, and Tim could look the devil in the eye and laugh."

"Quinn was not with her when the attack occurred?"

Sam shook his head.

His hands fisting at his sides, Christopher left the room with rapid strides, forcing Sam to leap out of the way. Crossing the hall, he paused at the door to the parlor, where a dozen of his lackeys were engaged in a card game. "Come along," he said before taking the stairs to the street level.

The men scrambled to their feet behind him.

He collected his coat and hat and swept out the main door. Within moments, he was mounted and the others were galloping around from the mews where their horses were always at the ready for whatever task he might send them on.

As they rode from St. Giles to Mayfair, beggars and prostitutes gave way to vendors and pedestrians, but all called out to him, waving hats and arms in cheerful greetings. Christopher tipped his brim as necessary, but the movement was habitual, his thoughts fully focused on Maria.

Later, once he'd assured himself that she was well, he would hear reports of the incident in minute detail from each of the four men who had been present. There would be discussion, and the point of error would be discovered. The other men would hear of it, and the failure would be used as a teaching tool. The four men would most likely never be given so important a task again.

Others in his position would take more brutal measures of discipline, but a maimed man was less efficient than a whole one. And loss of privilege would teach the same lesson. When violence was necessary, it was quite simply necessary, but he had no need of it to control those under his command.

Arriving at Lady Winter's townhouse, he dismounted as two of his men detained the startled groomsmen. Entry to the house was gained by simply swarming in past the outraged butler, and Christopher shoved his hat and gloves at the blustering servant before taking the stairs two at a time.

Altogether the time between his learning of Maria's injuries and his arrival at her bedroom was impressively short, but not swift enough for him. He pushed the door to her bedchamber open at the same moment Quinn entered the sitting room from his own suite.

"By God!" the Irishman roared. "Step one foot in there and I shall kill you with my bare hands."

Christopher waved his hand carelessly at the men who followed at his heels. "Take care of that," he drawled, shutting out the scuffle that ensued with a firm click of the latch.

Breathing deeply, he pulled the scent of Maria deep into his nostrils and thumbed the lock, surprised to find himself somewhat hesitant to turn about and face her. The thought of her wounded did odd things to his equanimity.

"Be grateful I am too weary to give you your due, Mr. St. John."

He smiled at the breathy sound of her voice. It was weak, yes, but it challenged him just the same. Turning, he found her lost in her large bed, her olive skin pale and her brows furrowed with pain. Dressed in a thin cotton night rail with lace at the throat and wrists, the infamous Lady Winter looked as innocent as a schoolgirl.

His gut clenched.

"Christopher," he corrected hoarsely, the betraying rasp forcing him to clear his throat. Shrugging out of his coat, he took a moment to collect himself.

"Make yourself comfortable," she whispered, watching him.

"Thank you." He draped the garment over the back of a slipper chair and moved to her side, sitting on the edge of the bed.

Her head turned to keep their gazes locked together. "You do not look well."

"Oh?" Both brows rose. "I think I look better than you."

The corner of her mouth lifted. "Nonsense. You are pretty, but I am far prettier."

He smiled and caught up her tiny hand within his own. "I will not argue with that."

A loud crash in the next room followed by a curse made her wince. "I hope you have enough men out there. Simon is in a mood, and I have seen him dispatch a small army by himself."

"Forget about him," he said curtly. "I am here. Think about me."

Her eyes slid closed, revealing delicate lids darkened by tiny purple veins. "I have done nothing else for a few days now."

He was startled by the statement, and confused as to whether he could believe it or not. Which led him to wonder about how he would feel if it were true. He frowned down at her. "You have been thinking of me?"

Without thought, he lifted his hand and brushed loose tendrils of her unbound hair behind her ears. His fingertips returned to her cheek, caressing feather light over the satin-smooth skin. The tenderness he felt took him aback. It made him wish to stand up and back out of the room, return to his home, where everything was familiar and ran like clockwork.

"Did I say that aloud?" she murmured, slightly slurred of speech. "How silly of me. Pay me no mind. It is the laudanum, I'm sure."

The withdrawal of her admission pulled him forward, urging him to lean closer. He paused with his lips a breath away from hers, the scent of her skin so strong it made his loins tighten.

"Do it," she breathed, goading him even in her vulnerable state.

The way she pushed him made him smile, and his smile set off hers. Satisfaction flared that he could lift the weight of pain that shrouded her.

"I am waiting for you," he murmured.

There was a slight, telltale moment of hesitation. Then Maria's head moved slightly, closing the tiny distance between them until her lips pressed gently to his. The soft, innocent kiss arrested him, froze him in place, his heart lurching from its normal steady beat into a breakneck race.

Unable to resist, he licked along the seam of her mouth, collecting the flavor of opium, brandy, and pure delicious

Maria. She gasped, opening the sweet depths to his tentative thrust, her hand clutching at his. When the tip of her tongue ventured in return, Christopher groaned.

Even helpless, she undid him.

Then her free hand moved between his legs, slender fingers stroking the rigid length of his cock. He jerked back violently from the caress, a curse gritted out between clenched teeth.

She cried out softly in pain as the force of his movement rocked her.

"Maria. Forgive me." Contrite, he lifted her hand to his lips. "Why touch me in that manner when you haven't the wherewithal to follow through?"

It took her a moment to reply, her eyes squeezed shut as she appeared to recover from the hurt he'd unwittingly caused. "You did not say you thought of me during our separation. I wished to know."

Some object made of glass broke in the room next door, and then something heavy thumped against the wall. Quinn yelled and someone retorted.

Christopher growled low. "My siege today is insufficient proof of my desire to be with you?"

Her lids lifted, revealing fathomless dark eyes that seemed so desolate to him, far beyond what he would expect from a battle wound. The hopelessness he saw was soul deep and bleak.

"Sieges are a way to defeat an enemy," she said simply. "Though your haste *is* flattering."

"And the kiss?" he asked. "What was that?"

"You tell me."

He stared at her, his chest lifting and falling. Frustrated with his lack of control, Christopher pushed to his feet and began to pace, something he never did.

"Would you like some water?" he asked a moment later.

"No. Go away."

He paused midstride. "Beg your pardon?"

"You heard me." Turning her head, Maria rested her cheek against her pillow. "Go. Away."

Giving in to his desire to depart, Christopher moved toward his coat. He did not need this aggravation, and he was not the type of man to woo women. They either wanted him or they didn't.

"I am not sure how I feel about your men following me," she murmured.

His hand stilled atop his garment. "Grateful?" he suggested.

She waved him away.

The dismissive gesture rankled. Here he'd waited impatiently for her to return and then, because he did not give her the platitudes she desired, she sent him away.

"I thought of you," he grumbled.

Her eyes did not open, but one dark brow rose. Only Maria could make that tiny movement convey icy disdain.

Because he felt as if he'd revealed something he should not have, he said, "I was hoping we would stay a day or two in bed when you returned; however, I had envisioned the time spent more strenuously than merely lying about as you are doing."

Her returning smile was knowing, as if she collected his need to reduce his statement to physical hunger and nothing more. "How often?"

"The sex? As often as I recovered."

She laughed softly. "How often did you think of me?"

He growled. "Too often."

"Was I unclothed?"

"Most of the time."

"Ah, well."

"How often was I unclothed?" he asked hoarsely, thoughts of her possible musings renewing his hunger.

"All of the time. It seems I am more lecherous than you."

"I think it's far more likely that you and I are evenly matched."

Opening one eye, Maria glanced at him. "Hmm . . ."

Leaving his coat, he returned to her. "Who is this governess whom you seek at such cost?" He resumed both his seat on her velvet-draped bed and his possession of her hand. It was then he noted how short her nails were, nails that had once been long enough to do damage to his back. His thumb rubbed over the tips.

"She is not the one I want."

"Oh?" Christopher lifted his gaze to search her pale features. Even with her unhealthy pallor, he found her beautiful. Certainly he knew many lovely women, but there were none he could imagine who had the strength to bear the pain Maria had to be in. "Who, then?"

"Did you not question your men?"

"There was no time."

"Now I am truly flattered," she drawled, smiling in a way that hit him with the force of a blow. Had he ever seen her smile before today? He could not recall.

"I am questioning *you* instead."

"You look dashing in that shade of brown." Once again she touched his thigh, caressing his breeches. The muscle tensed beneath her fingertips. "You dress beautifully."

"I look better naked," he said.

"I wish I could say the same. Sadly, I bear a few holes."

"Maria." He spoke low and earnestly, his grip on her hand tightening. "Allow me to assist you in your endeavors."

She gave him her full attention. "Why?"

Because I must betray you. Because I need to redeem myself in some way before I do. "Because I can help you."

"Why do you want to help me, Christopher? What do you gain?"

"Must I benefit in some way?"

"I think you must," she said, wincing as her bedroom door rocked in its hinges.

"Maria!" Simon shouted through the door, followed immediately by a grunt and a thud.

Christopher had to admit, he was impressed at the other man's ability to persevere.

"They won't harm him, will they?" she asked with a worried frown. "A little rough play is one thing, but I will not tolerate anything beyond that."

Her concern for the other man was an irritant.

"All I ask of you," he said tightly, "is what I asked before—I want you available for my use. No haring off. I want you when I want you, not a sennight later and too ill to take me."

"Perhaps I prefer to decline and manage my own affairs."

He snorted. "Perhaps I might have believed you if you had not admitted to thinking of me."

"I am no man's mistress."

"I offer the same level of convenience to you. I will come when you call for me. Does that put the arrangement in a more agreeable light?"

Maria's fingers stroked across his palm. It was an innocent caress, one given almost without thought. Her gaze was distant, her mind occupied elsewhere, her lower lip worried between her teeth. He lifted his free hand and stroked his thumb across the plump curve.

"When we first met in the theater, you mentioned an agency," she reminded, her breath hot against his skin.

"*The* agency." Christopher fought the urge to tell her to keep her silence, to tell him nothing that he could use against her.

"Is that the true purpose behind this offer?" Her head tilted to the side as she studied him. "Because you have need to use me in some way beyond warming your bed?"

"Partly." His thumb left her lip to brush along the curve of her cheekbone. "I do want you, Maria. I do want to help you."

Her eyes closed again on a sigh. "I am weary, Christopher. It was a hard journey in this condition. Later, I will consider your proposal."

"Why did you risk returning?" He sensed there was more

than weariness involved. She seemed disheartened and deeply melancholy.

Her eyes blinked open and the way she clutched at his hand conveyed urgency. "Welton is not aware of my . . . interests or travels. If you truly wish to help me, I have a task for you."

"What can I do?"

"Where were you two nights past when I was injured?"

He was at Emaline's attempting to convince himself that one cunt was as good as another, but damned if he would say so. He scowled at her.

"Are your whereabouts that night well known?" she revised.

Afflicted by guilt—an emotion he so rarely felt that it took him a moment to recognize it—he said hoarsely, "No."

"Would you say I was with you if asked?"

"Hmm . . . I might. With the right persuasion."

"If you were with another woman, I'm not inclined to persuade you about anything. I shall find another alibi."

"Are you jealous?" He smiled, warmed by the thought.

"Should I be?" Maria shook her head. "Disregard. Men do not tolerate jealous women."

"True." Christopher pressed a chaste kiss to her lips, then deepened it when she did not pull away. Instead, she shivered and opened wider. His tongue stroked deep, his blood simmering instantly at her response. Hurt and in pain, she still accepted his amorous attentions as if unable to resist.

He whispered against her mouth, "But *this* man likes the thought of a jealous Maria."

A knock came to the door that led to the gallery, forcing them apart.

"Rest," he said when she opened her mouth to reply. "I will make myself useful."

Rising to his feet, Christopher moved to the door and opened it, finding a sheepish-looking Tom.

"Lord Welton is in the parlor," Tom said. "Philip has asked for you."

Christopher was immediately on his guard, his face impassive but his thoughts awhirl with possibilities. He nodded, then retreated back into the room and collected his coat.

"What is it?" Maria asked, dark eyes wide with concern. "Is Simon well?"

It took a moment for him to squelch his urge to retort rudely. "I will see to him, but tell me this: would you show such concern if it were I in Quinn's place?"

"Are *you* jealous?"

"Should I be?"

"Yes. I hope you squirm with it."

A bark of laughter escaped—part humor, part disgust with himself for being enamored with a beauty infamous for her history with men. When she offered up another smile, he settled into resignation and nursed a faint hope that his enchantment with her would pass.

"Give me a moment to handle an unexpected matter, my lovely savage," he murmured, shrugging into his coat. "Then we will speak further on the terms of our association. I will check on Quinn, as well."

She nodded and he departed through the sitting-room door, pausing a moment on the threshold to take in the destruction of the furnishings and the struggling, gagged Irishman tied to a gilded chair in the corner. Furious mumbling and violent thrashing accompanied Christopher's appearance. Quinn rose to his feet, hunched over by the shape of his chair, and two of Christopher's battered and rumpled men shoved him back down.

"Gentle with him, lads," he admonished wryly, noting the half dozen men sprawled about the wreckage in varying degrees of pain. "The lady insists, though it appears her fear is groundless."

He managed to quell his laughter until he reached the

stairs. Then he gave it free rein until he reached the foyer. Thankfully, he discovered the lower floor in much better order than the upper.

Philip met him at the bottom step. "I sent the housekeeper to speak with Lord Welton in the parlor," the young man explained, leading Christopher to his command position in the lower study. "She told him the lady is indisposed. Apparently, the news was not well received. The housekeeper asked for you."

Christopher turned to the woman who stood tall and proud by the front window. "What can I do for you, Mrs . . . ?"

"Fitzhugh," she replied with a lift of her chin. Gray strands of hair curled by the heat and humidity of the kitchen surrounded a face lined with age, but handsome in its features. "'e asked me if she was ill or injured. I doona like 'im, Mr. St. John. 'e pries."

"I see. I take it you would prefer he not learn of your lady's condition."

She nodded grimly, reddened hands twisting in her apron. "'er ladyship gave strict orders."

"Send him away, then."

"I canna do that. 'e settles the accounts."

Christopher paused, his niggling sense of suspicion flaring into absolute certainty of something amiss. Maria should be settled in her own right, not dependent upon the largesse of her stepfather. He shot a side glance at Philip, who nodded his silent understanding. The matter would be investigated thoroughly.

"Have you any suggestions?" Christopher asked, returning his attention to Mrs. Fitzhugh and considering her carefully.

"I said you were coming to call. That you were expected and Lady Winter was indisposed."

"Hmm . . . I see. So perhaps I should arrive at the scheduled time, yes?"

"You wouldna want to be late," she agreed.

"Of course not. Step out in the foyer, Mrs. Fitzhugh, if you would please."

The housekeeper hurried out and Christopher arched a brow at Philip. "Send for Beth. I wish to speak to her this evening."

"I will see to it."

Christopher left the room and traversed the short distance to the front parlor, where he entered behind Mrs. Fitzhugh as if he'd only just arrived. He feigned surprise. "Good afternoon, my lord."

Lord Welton glanced up from the act of pouring a libation and his eyes widened. Satisfaction flared in the emerald depths but was quickly masked. "Mr. St. John."

"A lovely afternoon to call, my lord," Christopher said smoothly while surreptitiously examining the fine quality of the other man's garments. Despite a mode of living reported to be excessive in all vices, the viscount looked the picture of health and vitality with his raven tresses and cunning green eyes. He bore the appearance of a man who felt so secure of his place in the world, nothing concerned him.

"Yes. I agree." Welton's throat worked with a large swallow, then he said, "Though I had heard that my stepdaughter is ill."

"Oh? She was vibrant when I saw her only two nights past." He sighed in mock disappointment. "Perhaps she will withdraw from our plans for the afternoon. I'm crushed."

"Two nights past, you say?" Welton asked, frowning suspiciously.

"Yes. After our fortuitous introduction at a weekend gathering at Lord and Lady Harwick's, she graciously accepted my invitation to supper." Christopher said the last with a hint of male satisfaction in his tone.

The subtle implication was not lost on Lord Welton, who smiled smugly. "Ah well, sounds as if this rumor is as worthless as most." He tossed back the contents of his glass and set it on the nearest side table before standing. "Please give her my regards. I've no wish to intrude on your appointment."

"Good day to you, my lord," Christopher said with a slight bow.

Welton grinned. "It already is."

Christopher waited until the front door closed behind the departing viscount and then returned to the study. "Have him followed," he said to Philip.

He took the stairs back up to Maria.

Robert Sheffield, Viscount Welton, descended the short steps to the street and paused a moment to look up at the home behind him.

Something was wrong.

Despite the apparent facts to the contrary—the governess's oath that the attackers were unknown to them and St. John's assurance that he was with Maria the night of the attack—Robert's gut told him to be wary. Who else would want Amelia besides Maria? Who else would be so bold? He would not have believed Amelia's claim that her assailants were unknown to her, but the governess had corroborated the tale and she had no reason to lie to the person who paid for her services.

Robert paused on the threshold of the carriage door and glanced up at his driver. "Take me to White's."

Vaulting into the interior, he leaned back against the squab and considered the alternatives. Maria could have sent men in her stead, freeing her to meet with St. John, but where would she gain the coin to finance such a venture?

He rubbed the space between his brows to ward off a headache. So ridiculous, really, this constant push and pull. The wench should be grateful. He'd rescued her from certain rotting in the countryside and seen her married to titled and wealthy peers. Her lavish home and envied mode of dress was due entirely to him, and yet had she ever thanked him?

No. Therefore, he would keep her in mind as the prime suspect, but he was no fool. He also had to consider the possibility that someone else had a grievance with him, someone who knew his fortunes rested with Amelia. He hated to expend funds that could be used for his pleasure on a fruitless search, but what choice did he have?

Robert sighed, realizing that he would need more money if he wished to maintain his present style of living. Which meant he needed to search for a generous admirer for Maria.

Chapter 8

"**A**melia, do not cry any more. I beg you."

Amelia pulled the damask counterpane farther over her head. "Go away, Miss Pool. Please!"

The bed sagged next to her and a hand came to rest on her shoulder. "Amelia, it breaks my heart to see you so distressed."

"How else should I feel?" She sniffled, her eyes burning and gritty, her heart broken. "Did you see what she went through? How she fought to come to me? I do not believe my father. Not any longer."

"Lord Welton has no reason to tell you untruths," Miss Pool soothed, her hand stroking down her spine. "Lady Winter does have a somewhat . . . fearsome reputation, and you saw her garments and the men at her service. To me it appears that your father is correct."

Tossing back the blanket, Amelia sat up and glared at her teacher. "I saw her face. That was not the look of a woman who gleefully accepts coin to stay away from me. She did not look like a conscienceless monster who wishes to train me into the life of a courtesan or similar such nonsense as my father has accused."

Miss Pool frowned, her pale blue eyes filled with confusion and concern beneath her blond brows. "I would not have stopped you from speaking with her if I had known she was your sister. I saw only a young boy running toward you. I thought it was a lovelorn swain." She sighed. "Perhaps if you had exchanged words, you would not hold these illusions about her strength of character. Also, I'm not certain lying to Lord Welton was wise."

"Thank you for saying nothing to my father." Amelia caught up her teacher's hand and squeezed. The coachman and footmen had also kept their silence. Having been with her from the beginning, they had a *tendré* for her, and while they stopped short of allowing her to leave, they did their best to make her as happy as possible. Except for the grooms- man Colin, the object of her affection, who spent all of his time either avoiding her or glaring at her.

"You begged me," Miss Pool said with a sigh, "and I was not strong enough to refuse."

"No harm was done by keeping the knowledge from him. I am here in Lincolnshire with you." Deep in her heart, Amelia suspected strongly that if her father learned of Maria's ac- tions, everything in her life would change. She doubted it would be for the better.

"I read the papers, Amelia. Lady Winter's mode of living is not one that would be conducive to your instruction in lady- like pursuits. Even if everything else your father said was . . . *embellished*—which I doubt after seeing what I saw—you must agree that the chances of her being a suitable influence are very small."

"Do not insult Maria, Miss Pool," Amelia said briskly. "Neither of us knows her well enough to cast aspersions upon her character."

Amelia's voice broke as she recalled the sight of the large ruffian who had crushed Maria to the ground and then pierced her with a knife. Tears hung on her lower lashes and then fell to water the flowers that decorated her muslin gown. "Dear God, I hope she is well."

All this time she had thought her father was protecting her from Maria. Now she was at a loss. The only thing she knew for certain was that her sister's voice had carried a note of desperation and longing that would be impossible to feign.

Miss Pool pulled her closer and offered a shoulder to cry on, which Amelia gratefully accepted. She knew Miss Pool would not be with her for long. Her father changed her governesses every time he moved her, which was no less than twice a year. Nothing in her life was permanent. Not this new house with its charming garden pathways. Not this lovely room with its floral décor in her favorite shade of pink.

Then her thoughts paused.

Siblings were permanent.

For the first time in years, she realized that she was *not* an orphan. There was someone in this world willing to die for her.

Maria had risked life and limb in an attempt to speak with her. What a drastic difference that was from her father, whom she heard from only through third parties.

Suddenly, she felt as if something she had been waiting for had finally come to fruition, though she did not understand why. She would have to explore it, come to terms with it, then decide how she would act upon it. After years of days that blended one into another with nothing new to offer, a mystery had been revealed, one that offered the hope to end her loneliness.

The tears that fell next were tinged with relief.

Maria stared up at the canopy above her bed and attempted to find the fortitude within her to bear the pain of moving. She needed to see to Simon. She knew he was capable of taking care of himself, but she also knew he would be worried about her and she could not allow him to fret unnecessarily.

She was about to slip out of bed when the door from the gallery opened and St. John returned. Once again, her breath caught at the sight of him. He was beyond uncommon handsome, yes, but it was the absolute confidence with which he carried himself that she found most attractive. Simon also bore the trait, but in Christopher it was packaged differently. Where Simon exploded in Irish passion, Christopher coiled tighter and became more dangerous.

"Move and I will turn you over my knee," Christopher rasped.

A smile hovered, but she held it back. The fierce pirate was something of a mother hen. She found it rather charming. It balanced out his otherwise overbearing and curt deportment. She could tell she set him off kilter. It was a simple joy to tease him, knowing that she was able to penetrate beneath his skin.

"I must show Simon that I am well."

A low growl rumbled through the space, then he stalked to the adjoining door. Opening it, he said loudly, "Lady Winter is well. Do you understand this, Quinn?"

Grunts and incensed mumbles accompanied Christopher's statement. He turned to look at her and asked, quite arrogantly, "Do you feel better now?"

"Simon, love?" she called out, wincing as the expansion of her lungs caused her shoulder to burn.

Violent thumping of chair legs against the floor was her reply.

Christopher stood there with one brow arched, waiting.

"Must you restrain him so?"

The other brow rose to match the first.

"I feel as if I should do something to save him," she murmured, chewing on her lower lip.

Slamming the door shut, Christopher shrugged out of his coat and returned to his spot on the bed. She took note of how the stricture of his garments seemed to irritate him. Then she imagined him in only shirtsleeves and breeches on the deck of one of his ships and she shivered.

His mouth lifted at the corner, as if he knew her thoughts. "I've no wish to be courteous to him. He should have been watching you. He failed in that task."

"He was unaware I was leaving."

"You snuck out?"

She nodded.

He snorted. "More fool he, then, for not anticipating such an action on your part. He should know you better than I, and yet even I would have expected you to run off."

"I would not have gone had I anticipated danger," she argued. But then she would have missed that sighting of Amelia. While the outcome was heartrending, it gave her some hope. Amelia was healthy and still in England.

"Those who live as we do should always anticipate danger, Maria," he said softly, stroking the back of her hand with his thumb. "Never lower your guard."

As she struggled with her response to his gentleness, her gaze shifted to the door, seeking escape.

"Lord Welton was here."

Her gaze flew back to meet his. Dark blue and fathomless. The man was an expert at keeping his thoughts to himself. She, however, was almost certain he could read her panic. "Oh?"

"He was under the impression that you were injured."

Maria winced inwardly.

"But I assured him that two nights past we shared a repast and you were in excellent health."

"Two nights past," she parroted.

Christopher leaned closer, his free hand lifting to brush across her cheek. He could not seem to stop touching her in some fashion, a foible she found vastly appealing. She had been taking care of herself for so long, it was lovely to feel cared for.

"I told you I would help you," he reminded softly.

But there was something she sensed churning beneath the surface masculine perfection. More than mere unease with new territory. Until she knew what it was, she could not trust him with simple truths, let alone with something so vital as the reclamation of Amelia.

So she nodded to signify her promise to consider his request, then closed her eyes. "I am truly weary." The left side of her body throbbed from her head to her hip.

She sensed him lean closer, felt his breath brush across her lips. He was going to kiss her again, one of those light but utterly delicious meldings that made her blood thrum. Because she relished those kisses, she opened to him. He laughed softly, a throaty sound she adored.

"Can I trade a kiss for a secret?" he asked.

She opened one eye. "You put too much stock in your kisses."

His grin stole her breath. "Perhaps you put too much stock in your secrets."

"Oh, go away," she said with a wide smile.

Instead he kissed her senseless.

"Amelia?"

Christopher settled farther into the window bench, resting his forearm atop his bent knee as he looked out at his rear garden below. It was after nightfall, but his home and its surrounding exterior were brightly lit and well guarded. Hedges were trimmed to prevent the creation of any hiding places. Like his life, the necessities were there, but there was no room for comforts or extravagances.

"Yes, that's what she was saying."

"And it was the girl who replied, not the governess. You are certain?" He shot a sidelong glance at the four men who were lined up a few feet away.

They all nodded their agreement.

"Why did no one go after the coach?" he asked.

All four men shuffled uncomfortably.

Sam cleared his throat and said, "You told us to watch the lady. When she was injured . . ." He shrugged lamely.

Christopher sighed.

A knock came to the door and he called out. Philip entered and said simply but gravely, "Lord Sedgewick."

"Show him in." Christopher waved the other men out,

and a moment later Sedgewick entered. Tall, pale, and attired in a profusion of lace, jewels, and satin, Sedgewick was the epitome of aristocratic foppishness. That the man thought he could dictate to Christopher was so absurd it was laughable. That the man was actively hunting Maria was infuriating. And Christopher was not a man one wished to infuriate.

"My lord." He rose to his feet.

"How is life without shackles treating you?" Sedgewick asked with a mocking smile.

"I do not recommend feeling too smug, my lord." Christopher gestured toward the green settee which waited opposite the one he sank into. "Your position is as precarious as mine."

"I have every confidence that my methods, while unorthodox, will lead to laudable results." The earl adjusted his coat tails before sitting.

"You have kidnapped a false witness from the government and are using him to extort my cooperation. If the truth of your witness came to light, the uproar would be . . . messy."

Sedgewick smiled. "I am well aware of your popularity with the people. My witness is safe. In any case, you can reclaim your freedom at any time by delivering Lady Winter. The conditional pardon you hold assures it. We are simply waiting to see if you shall fail and return to prison, or succeed and give us the lady. Either outcome is an agreeable situation for me. I must say, at present, it looks as if the first scenario is the most likely."

"Oh?" Christopher studied the earl with narrowed eyes. "And how, pray tell, did you reach that conclusion?"

"A fortnight has passed and you've yet to be seen with Lady Winter. It appears you are making little to no progress."

"Appearances can be deceiving."

"I was hoping you would say that. Therefore, I have invented a way for you to prove you are not wasting our time." Segdewick smiled. "Lord and Lady Campion are holding a masquerade the evening after next. You will attend with Lady Winter. I've made certain she is expected."

"The notice is too short," Christopher scoffed.

"I am prepared to take you into custody should you fail to appear."

"Good luck to you, my lord." But while the words were spoken lightly, inside Christopher was not amused.

"I can magically reproduce the witness," the viscount said while fluffing the lace at his wrists, "for a steep price. Steep enough to override fear of reprisal."

"Neither of you would pass under close examination."

"Once you are jailed, your chances of survival will diminish greatly. After your passing, whether or not the witness is viable will be moot."

Though he remained outwardly impassive, inside Christopher's gut twisted with fury. Maria was injured and in great pain. It would take her some time to recover. How could he ask her to attend a social function in her present condition?

"Would correspondence suffice as proof of our connection?" he asked.

"No. I want to see you and her together, in the flesh."

"Next week, then." Even that would be too soon, but better than two days. "Perhaps a picnic in the park?"

"Have I called your bluff?" Sedgewick taunted. "And to think I called you 'frightening'. Ah well, I suppose even I must err occasionally. I am not dressed to return you to Newgate, but I will make an exception in this case, since I am already here."

"You think you can take me from my own home?"

"I came prepared. There are a number of soldiers and two Runners in the alley by the mews."

That the Viscount truly believed he could enter St. John's house by force made Christopher smile, and gave him an idea. As he said recently, appearances could be deceiving. Perhaps a masked Angelica could be made to pass as a decoy for Maria. It was worth considering.

"Lady Winter and I will see you at the Campion masquerade two days hence, my lord."

"Lovely." Sedgewick rubbed his hands together. "I am breathless with anticipation."

"I will kill him, Maria."

Watching Simon pace at the foot of her bed was making her head ache, so Maria closed her eyes. She was also feeling a fair measure of guilt for Simon's treatment at St. John's behest, which exacerbated her discomfiture. Sporting a bruised right eye and swollen upper lip, Simon certainly looked the worse for wear.

"At the moment, I need him, Simon love. Or at least information about him."

"Tonight I meet with the young man who has secured a position in the St. John household. He works in the stables but has started a liaison with a chambermaid. Hopefully, he has managed to learn something of import from her."

"Why do I doubt the likelihood of that?" she scoffed. She could not imagine St. John having any loose-tongued servants.

Simon cursed in Gaelic. "Because you are wise. All new servants to St. John's household spend a minimum of two years in his service before they are allowed into the main house. It is one of the ways St. John controls the loyalty of his lackeys. Anyone who has a secondary purpose, as we do, usually finds the wait to be too long. Also, it is said that St. John provides so well for his underlings that those who come to him with a nefarious agenda are quickly lured into his fold."

"It is easy to see how he is so successful, yes?"

"Do not ask me to admire him. Already my patience is stretched thin."

Moving slightly in an attempt to find a position of greater comfort, Maria whimpered as white-hot shards of agony pierced her left side.

"*Mhuirnín.*"

The next moment, strong hands were positioning her as carefully as possible.

"Thank you," she whispered.

Firm lips brushed across hers. Her eyes opened and her heart ached at the concern she saw in Simon's beautiful eyes.

"It pains me to see you this way," he murmured, leaning over her with a lock of black hair draping his brow.

"I will be well in no time at all," she assured him. "Hopefully, before Welton comes to call again. We can only pray that the sight of St. John here yesterday will be enough to keep him at bay long enough for me to heal properly."

Simon moved away and sat in the nearby slipper chair. On the low table before him, the day's post waited on a silver salver. He began to shift through it, muttering to himself as was his wont when agitated.

"There is a missive here from Welton," he said at length.

Maria, nearly asleep, blinked sleepily. "What does it say?"

"Just a moment." There was a long pause and the sound of parchment rustling, then, "He says he has someone whose acquaintance he wishes you to cultivate. Tomorrow evening at the Campion masquerade."

"Dear God," she breathed, her stomach roiling. "I must decline, of course. I cannot go about in this condition."

"Of course not."

"Have my secretary draft a reply. Tell him I am previously engaged at his behest, and St. John would not be welcome at such an event."

"I will see to it. Rest. Don't worry."

Nodding, Maria closed her eyes and moments later, sleep claimed her.

She awoke some time later to the smell of dinner. Turning her head, she saw darkness beyond the sheer curtains.

"How are you feeling?" Simon asked from his seat in the chair by her bed. Setting his book on the floor, he bent over, his forearms coming to rest on his knees.

"Thirsty."

He nodded and rose, pivoting in a soft swirling of his black robe, returning a moment later with a glass of water. Supporting her head, he brought the glass to her lips and watched as she drank greedily. When she finished, he resumed his seat, the empty glass rolling between his moving palms, his legs bared by the parting of his garment.

"What is it?" she asked, noting his agitation.

His lips pursed before he said, "Welton replied."

As the memory of his request returned to her, Maria winced. "He would not accept no for an answer?"

Simon shook his head grimly. "He prefers that you attend alone."

In pain, disheartened, and desperate to be left in peace, Maria began to cry. Simon rounded the bed and crawled into place beside her, carefully tucking her against his warm body. She cried until she could not cry any more, and then she sobbed without tears.

All the while Simon murmured to her, held her, put his cheek next to hers and cried with her. Finally there was nothing left, all of her hopes drained away, leaving her empty.

But emptiness held its own comforts.

"I cannot wait for the day Welton meets his reward," Simon said vehemently. "Killing him will bring me great pleasure."

"One day at a time. Can you select a gown that hides my shoulder and neck?"

He exhaled harshly, resigned. "I will take care of everything, *mhuirnín*."

Maria mentally began the process of filling the depleted stores of hope within her with a sense of renewed purpose.

Welton would not tear her down. She would not afford him the pleasure.

"Do you prefer this one?" Angelica asked, spinning prettily in her silver shot-silk taffeta gown.

"Hold still," Christopher admonished, studying the gown and her figure in it as the hem and panniers settled into their proper places.

Angelica was slightly taller than Maria and her figure was not as lush, but clever staging could hide those discrepancies. This gown did a better job of that than the others she had tried. The color enhanced the olive skin tone he found so appealing on Maria and the bodice was such that it flattened Angelica's breasts slightly, making them swell. With the right hair arrangement and a full face mask, they might be able to manage the ruse.

"You mustn't speak," he warned. "No matter what is said to you by anyone." Angelica's voice would never pass for Maria's. Neither would her laugh. "And do not laugh. It is a masquerade. Be mysterious."

She nodded vigorously. "No talking, no laughing."

"I will reward you well for this, love," he said gently. "Your cooperation is greatly appreciated."

"You know I would do anything for you. You gave me a home and a family. I owe you my life."

With a careless toss of his hand, Christopher waved away her gratitude and his discomfiture with it. He never knew what to say when people thanked him, so he preferred they not do it. "You have been of great help to me. There is nothing to repay me for."

Angelica smiled and danced closer, lifting his hand to kiss the back. "So is this dress the one?"

He nodded. "Yes. You look stunning."

Her smile widened, then she retreated to the dressing room.

"I would not have the courage to attempt this deception," Philip said from his seat by the fire.

"It would not be wise to antagonize Sedgewick now," Christopher explained, lighting a cheroot off a nearby taper. "Until I know what my next move will be, it's best to leave him with his illusions of power. It will set him at ease, per-

haps make him complacent, freeing me to work on a permanent solution without his interference."

"I have seen only renderings of Lady Winter, but from the
tales I have heard she sounds quite unique. It is hard to imi-
tate the incomparable."

Christopher nodded, his gaze resting briefly on the reflection of light in Philip's spectacles. The young man had cut his
brown hair short that morning, unfashionable as the style
was. It made him look younger than his ten and eight years.

"Very hard, but Maria is too ill to attend, there is no skirt-
ing around that fact. The risk to her health outweighs my
need at the moment. If Sedgewick were to detect the ruse, I
could explain it in some fashion. There is no denying that
Maria and I are . . ." Christopher exhaled, releasing a puff of
fragrant smoke. "Whatever in hell we are, she would acknowledge me if I asked."

"I hope you are correct in assuming that no one will notice
the differences between the two women."

"It is much easier to disclaim a fraud when one compares
the original to the fake. In this case, Maria has been out of
Town for a fortnight. The guests will have to rely upon their
memory of her, as she will be home in bed. Angelica and I
will make certain we are seen by Sedgewick posthaste and
then we will depart quickly."

Philip lifted his brandy-filled glass. "May your plan succeed flawlessly."

Christopher grinned. "They usually do."

Chapter 9

As they waited in the line of carriages approaching the Campion manse, Maria breathed in and out with a measured rhythm. Every bump in the road brought her such pain she felt nauseous. The constriction of her corset did not help matters and the weight of her elaborate hair arrangement made her neck ache.

Simon sat across from her, his garments far more casual, his gaze glittering in the semidarkness created by the turned-down carriage lamps.

"I will be waiting for you," he murmured.

"Thank you."

"Despite the circumstances, you look ravishing."

She managed a wan smile. "Thankfully, Welton and I never speak for long. I anticipate a half hour, though the actual assignation may take up a bit more time than that."

"I will send a footman after you if an hour passes. You will be called away. Say it is St. John who seeks your company."

"Lovely."

The carriage rattled over the cobblestones of the circular drive and then stopped again. This time the door was pulled open and her footman extended his hand to assist her down. He was careful, but not obviously so. Maria rewarded his concern with a soft smile, then she took the steps and entered the manse.

The subsequent wait in the receiving line was torture, as was managing to sound gay when speaking to the beaming Campions. It was with great relief that she was freed from the formalities, and with a quick adjustment of her feathered half-mask, she entered the crowded ballroom.

Her lovely gown of pale pink with its silver ribbons and lace was hidden beneath her black domino. Nothing she owned was capable of hiding her injury, leaving her no other recourse. Because of her lack of options, Maria wore her garments with aplomb, but kept a discreet profile. She moved carefully around the perimeter of the room, weaving between guests, sending out a silent signal to stay away that, thankfully, was effective.

Her gaze drifted from one side of the vast space to the other, searching for Welton. Overhead, three massive chandeliers were ablaze with countless candles, lighting up the ornate ceiling with its elaborate moldings and colorful murals. The orchestra played and guests spun about on the dance floor in a profusion of lace, impressively styled coiffures, and floral fabrics. Numerous conversations coalesced into a single hum of sound, the noise somewhat soothing because it meant that no one was paying attention to her.

Maria was beginning to think she might survive the excursion when she was bumped by a careless guest. Pain lanced down her left side and she gasped, her body turning away in self-defense.

"Forgive me," a low voice said behind her.

Spinning to face the offending person, she found herself standing before a man whose eyes widened as if he knew her.

"Sedgewick!" a portly man called out. Maria knew him to be Lord Pearson, a man who spoke and imbibed far too much. Since she had no wish to speak to him or to be delayed by an introduction to the graceless Sedgewick, she hurried away.

It was then that she saw him, her faithless paramour, his

golden hair glinting beneath the candlelight, his powerful form resplendent in cream silk accented by beautiful embroidery. Despite the mask that hid his features, she knew it was Christopher. He was leaning over a dark-haired woman attentively, his pose betraying his affection.

His promise of exclusive use was a lie.

The throbbing in her shoulder faded as a different feeling of hurt took over.

"Ah, there you are." Welton's voice behind her made her stiffen. "Must I send the modiste to you again?" he asked as she turned to face him. "Have you nothing more fetching to wear?"

"What do you want?"

"And why are you so bloody pale?"

"New powder. You do not find it attractive?" She batted her lashes at him. "I think it shows my patches and rouge to better advantage."

He snorted. "No, I do not like it. Throw it out. You look sickly."

"You wound me."

Welton's glare spoke volumes. "Your worth in this world is based entirely upon your appearance. I would not be so quick to devalue it."

His insult affected her not at all. "What do you want?" she repeated.

"To make an introduction." His smile made her skin crawl. "Come along." He collected her right hand and led her away.

After a few moments of silence while traversing through the crush, Maria found the courage to ask, "How is Amelia?"

The examining glance he threw over his shoulder revealed a great deal. He did not discount her as a possible instigator of the recent attack. "Wonderful."

She hadn't truly expected that he would rule her involvement out. Still, her spirits plummeted as she realized how he would respond. Security would be tighter, his movements more wary. Her work to find her sister would be harder.

"Ah," Welton murmured, his tone smug. "There he is." He jerked his chin toward the man who stood a few feet away. Maria knew to whom he referred despite the crowd because of the intensity of the stare directed at her from the eyes of the mask. The man leaned insolently against the wall, his long legs crossed at the ankle, his pose seductively arrogant.

"The Earl of Eddington," she breathed. A libertine of the first water. Handsome, wealthy, titled, and reputed to be quite accomplished in every activity he set his mind to—including bedsport.

Coming to an abrupt halt, Maria released Welton's arm and turned to face him with a scowl. "What the devil do you want with him?"

"He asked for an introduction."

"You know very well what he wants."

Welton's smile widened. "And he would pay handsomely for it. If you decide to indulge, it would line your purse nicely."

"Have you fallen into debt so soon?" she snapped.

"No, no. But my expenditures are about to increase, which means your allotted share of Winter's settlement is about to decrease. I thought you would appreciate my assistance in shoring up your finances."

Stepping closer, she lowered her voice, a gambit that did nothing to hide her revulsion. "I appreciate nothing about you."

"Of course you wouldn't, ungrateful child," he said smoothly. He lifted his hands in mock defensiveness, but nothing could add warmth to those vacuous eyes. "I am facilitating an introduction, not a tryst."

She glanced at Eddington and he bowed slightly, his mouth curved in a smile that had brought ruin to many women. Besides making her teeth grit together, it did nothing for her. "You pulled me away from St. John for this?"

"I saw St. John," he dismissed. "He is besotted. A night without you will only increase his enchantment."

Snorting, Maria applauded St. John's ability to deceive. Of course, Welton preferred to see things in the most beneficial light, which was not always the way things actually were.

"Do not glare at me," he admonished. "It is not attractive." He sighed as if dealing with an unreasonable child. "It is the hint of your unavailability and insatiability that makes you so sought after. Why do you think I allow you to keep that Irish lover of yours? If he did not increase your appeal I would have rid you of him long ago."

It took her a moment to rein in the fury that gripped her at his carelessly tossed threat to Simon. Finally, she was able to say, "Shall we move along with this, then? I've no wish to be here all night."

"You truly must learn to enjoy yourself more," Welton murmured, reclaiming her hand.

"I will enjoy myself well enough when you are dead," she retorted.

Her stepfather viscount threw his head back and laughed.

"This is a palace," Angelica whispered, her eyes wide behind her mask.

"The peerage lives well," Christopher agreed, searching the room for Sedgewick.

"You are wealthier than most."

He looked at her with a slight smile. "Are you suggesting a man with my proclivities live in something so ostentatious?"

"Perhaps it is not the most practical—"

He lifted a hand to cut her off. "Coin can be put to much worthier uses. What use have I for ballrooms? More ships and lackeys would benefit us better."

Angelica sighed and shook her head. "You should try to enjoy life more. You work too much."

"That is why I am wealthier than most." He pulled her to the edge of the room and began to stroll. "I appreciate how unique this evening is for you, but we are wasting too much time. The longer we dally, the higher the risk of discovery."

They were attracting attention he did not want. There was no help for it. Angelica was lovely, and he had mistakenly attended without a wig. He had hoped the lack would facilitate Sedgewick finding him. Instead, he feared everyone recognized him except for the one man he sought.

As his gaze continued to roam across the room, Christopher noted those who shielded their identities with dominos and wished he had done the same. Of course, what he truly wished for was to be elsewhere. Anywhere but here, but most especially with Maria.

He paused a moment, his attention caught by Lord Welton and the female with whom he conversed. Her shoulders were set rigidly, her chin lifted high. Whatever they were discussing, it was not pleasing to her.

Philip was actively searching the viscount's past, but such inquiries took time. Christopher could be supremely patient when necessary. However, this time, he felt a peculiar urgency to know all that he could about his current paramour.

"Beth says Lord Welton is charming, though he is sometimes too rough with her." Angelica's gaze followed his.

"Welton is self-centered in all things, love. I've spoken with Bernadette. She will see to it that Welton takes his darker urges away from our Beth."

"She told me you gave her leave to be done with him."

Christopher shrugged. "I am not a purveyor of flesh, as you well know. I will ask for favors, but I will not force them. If Beth is unhappy, I would not want her to remain that way." He looked back at the man in question and then paused midstep, the hairs on his nape rippling with awareness.

The woman speaking with the viscount struck a deep chord of recognition. She was of familiar stature. The glossy, upswept hair and determined cant of her bearing made his heart rate pick up.

"Bloody hell," he muttered, inwardly certain that Welton was speaking with Maria. He was, however, a man who required absolute proof.

He stepped forward again, his pace as rapid as the crush would allow. He ceased looking for Sedgewick, instead focusing on finding the best viewing angle to confirm his suspicions. Welton began moving forward again, pulling the woman with him, leading her toward . . .

Christopher looked ahead of them slightly and found a man who stared boldly at the pair. The Earl of Eddington. A man widely pursued by women of all ages for both his title and lauded fine features.

By God, was it Maria's intent to speak with him? Was that who she intended to lure to the altar? Eddington was a perennial bachelor, but Maria could tempt a monk to break his vows. Her allure was a point of wager, with many freely admitting that the excitement of marriage to such a woman would outweigh the risks to their longevity.

The thought made his jaw tighten.

Increasing his pace further, Christopher was nearly plunging through the thick crowd, Angelica bringing up the rear and clinging desperately to his hand. He was almost close enough to attempt a proper identification when his path was suddenly blocked.

"Move," he growled, craning his neck to keep Welton in view.

"In a rush?" Sedgewick drawled.

Christopher cursed under his breath, watching Eddington lift the woman's gloved hand to his lips before leading her away.

Leaving Christopher and his desperate curiosity behind.

"Lady Winter," Eddington murmured, his dark eyes locked to Maria's as he kissed the back of her hand. "A pleasure."

She managed a brief smile. "Lord Eddington."

"How is it that we have not managed to speak before now?"

"You are quite sought after, my lord, leaving you scarcely any time to waste on one such as me."

"Time with a woman so lovely could never be a waste." He studied her carefully. "If you would indulge me a moment, I wish to speak with you in private."

Maria shook her head. "I cannot think of anything we would say to each other that could not be said here."

"You think I mean to ravish you?" he asked with a half smile that was quite charming. "What if I promise to stand arm's distance away?"

"I am still declining."

He leaned closer and his voice lowered to a whisper. "The agency has become quite interested in you, Lady Winter." His face was impassive as if he had commented on nothing more shocking than the weather.

Maria's gaze narrowed.

"Would you consent to speak privately with me now?" he asked.

Unable to do otherwise, she nodded and allowed him to lead her out of the ballroom and down a long hall. They passed a number of guests as they went, but the crowd thinned the farther away they traveled. Finally, they turned a corner and with a quickly tossed glance over his shoulder to be certain they weren't followed, Eddington pulled her into a darkened room.

It took a moment for Maria's eyes to adjust to the reduced light. Once she could see, she realized they were in a large sitting room populated with a number of settees, chairs, and side tables.

"What are you?" she asked, turning to face him as he shut the door with a soft click of the latch. His pearl gray garments melded in and out of the shadows, but his eyes caught the pale moonlight and glittered dangerously.

"After the deaths of agents Dayton and Winter," he said, ignoring her question, "you came under suspicion of treason."

Swallowing hard, Maria was grateful for the darkness that hid any telltale sign of guilt. "I know."

"And you remain a suspect," he continued.

"What do you want?" She lowered into a nearby wingback chair.

"I was speaking with Lady Smythe-Gleason last evening. She briefly mentioned seeing you conversing with Christopher St. John at a recent gathering at Harwick House."

"Oh? I converse with many people. I forget most of them."

"She said the heat between you was palpable."

Maria snorted.

Eddington took the seat opposite her. "The disappearance of the witness against St. John precipitated his release. The agency suspects St. John is to blame, but I think it was someone within. An agent either aligned with the pirate, or one who wished to use the informant as a leverage. The man was too well guarded. St. John is accomplished, but even he has his limits."

"If the agency suspects St. John, may I assume that you are alone in your suspicions about another agent?"

"You should worry less about my interests and more about your own."

"What are you saying?"

"You could use a . . . *friend* within the agency. And I could use a friend of St. John's. That makes us uniquely suited."

"You wish to use me to learn information from St. John?" she asked incredulously. "Are you jesting?"

"At the moment, you and St. John are the two most closely examined individuals on the agency's list of most wanted criminals—you for the suspected killings of two well-respected agents, and the pirate for a variety of sins."

Maria could not decide whether she wished to laugh or

cry. How had her life come to this? What would her parents think if they could see how far she had fallen?

Eddington leaned forward, setting his forearms on his knees. "Welton arranged both of your marriages, and saw a marked increase in his fortunes after your husbands' deaths. He was quick to introduce you to me after I settled his markers the other evening. Your stepfather has quite a mercenary interest in you. Winter said the same to me once."

"I fail to see why that is of any interest to you."

"You know what I believe?" he said softly. "I believe Welton has something he is holding against you, something he has used to gain your cooperation. I can free you from him. I do not expect you to help me without any benefit."

"Why me?" she asked herself wearily, her gloved hands stroking absentmindedly along the edge of her domino. "What have I done to deserve this misery?"

"The question, I believe, is what haven't you done?"

How true that was.

"Ascertain what happened to the witness," he urged, "and I will secure your freedom from both the agency and Welton."

"Perhaps my soul is black as sin, and I will sell word of your curiosity to the men you seek." Sometimes, she wished she had no soul. She suspected her life would be much easier if she were as conscienceless as the men who used her.

"It is a risk I am willing to take."

The earl waited a moment and then rose to his feet. He held out his hand to her. "Think on it. I will call on you tomorrow as an ardent swain and you may give me your answer then."

Resigned, Maria placed her hand in his.

"My lord," Christopher greeted tightly. "Lady Winter, may I present to you Lord Sedgewick. My lord, the incomparable Lady Winter."

Angelica dipped into a lovely curtsy as Sedgewick bowed.

"A pleasure to make your acquaintance," the viscount said. "I apologize again for my carelessness earlier."

Christopher stilled a brief moment. What were the odds?

"Please forgive me," Sedgewick continued when Angelica said nothing.

Maintaining his composure, Christopher lifted a finger to his lips in a gesture that conveyed silence. "Lady Winter is incognito this evening, my lord. You understand, perhaps, how that enlivens the festivities."

"Ah, of course." Sedgewick's smile was broad and smug, his shoulders held back with cocky pride. "I applaud your decision to discard the domino, my lady. A gown as lovely as yours should not be hidden."

Maria was here. "If you will excuse us, my lord."

Sedgewick lifted Angelica's hand to his lips, said some platitudes to which Christopher paid no mind, and then the viscount stepped out of the way.

Freed from his lone duty for the evening, Christopher pulled Angelica out of the ballroom and strode swiftly down a long hall. He had no notion if he was heading in the right direction to find the woman in the black domino or not, but it was the way to the rear garden. From there, Angelica could skirt the house to the front, where she would await him in the coach.

"Thank you, love," he said, kissing her cheek before seeing her out a set of French doors. He whistled low, calling his men who surrounded the perimeter of the manse to watch her safely to his carriage. Then he turned about . . .

. . . in time to see Welton's companion emerge from a room with Lord Eddington exiting directly behind her. That they'd had a liaison was obvious.

More secrets. Would there be more lies?

Christopher took a risk and called out. "Maria."

The woman lifted her chin and untied her mask, revealing the features he craved to look upon. She met his gaze directly.

"Enjoying your evening?" she asked coldly, every inch the Wintry Widow.

Apparently, she had seen him with Angelica and did not like it. Good.

He removed his own mask, allowing her an unhindered view of his own displeasure. He waited for her explanation.

Instead, she turned on her heel and walked away.

Enraged, he gave chase.

Chapter 10

Maria heard Christopher exchange curt words with Eddington as she fled down the hallway. She stepped up her pace. It hurt to run and she quickly grew dizzy, but her carriage was waiting. With haste she could reach it and make her escape.

"Departing so early, my lady?"

Startled, she slowed and turned her head to see the man Lord Pearson had identified as "Sedgewick" approaching from an opposite hallway.

He frowned and looked over her shoulder. "Where is your companion?"

She blinked, her steps faltering.

"Ah, there he is," Sedgewick murmured.

Glancing over her shoulder, she saw Christopher approaching with rapid strides. Lacking the luxury of time to puzzle out the cryptic comments, she resumed her flight.

Her footsteps padded softly along the runner and then grew louder as she crossed the marble-lined foyer. Brushing past a startled footman and several late arrivals, she descended the front steps to the crowded drive and weaved between the many carriages, her gaze darting amongst the liveried drivers and footmen in search of her own.

"Maria!"

The call came from before and behind her, the two male

voices distinctive in accent and tone—one clipped and angry, the other lower and urgent. She turned quickly to the right, rushing headlong toward Simon, who caught the elbow of her uninjured arm and thrust her into the waiting carriage.

"Better luck next time, old chap!" he crowed to Christopher and then he vaulted up behind her as the equipage lurched into motion.

Christopher's string of curses made her smile grimly. She hated that the sight of him with another woman had affected her so strongly, and she relished the tiny victory of thwarting his attempt at excuses. That he had hovered over the silver-clad figure so affectionately and kissed her so chastely spoke of much care and also reminded Maria of his recent visit to her home. He had displayed similar affection for her, though his kisses had been far from chaste.

"Care to explain?" Simon asked, studying her intently.

Maria relayed the events.

"Good God," he muttered when she finished. "What are the odds that you would land in this predicament with Eddington?"

"Has my life not always been a series of unfortunate events?" Closing her eyes, she leaned her head back against the squabs.

"And Sedgewick's behavior is a puzzle?"

"Delve into him. He approached me as if we had met at some point, yet I'm certain I have never made his acquaintance. Did he mistake St. John's companion for me? Also he appeared unconcerned to find the pirate in attendance. Very odd."

"I will investigate both peers." There was a pause, and then Simon said softly, "Eddington's offer—if it is sincere— would be a godsend, *mhuirnín.*"

"How can I trust him beyond a doubt? Eddington desires two things—the capture of St. John and the identity of the killer responsible for the deaths of Dayton and Winter. He is ambitious. What a coup it would be for him to capture me in the bargain, yes?"

Simon tapped one booted foot restlessly against the floor-boards. "I agree. I feel as if a net is closing around you, yet I can do nothing."

She felt the same.

The ride to Mayfair was lamentably long, and after the night's exertions, her injury throbbed and tormented her. Battered by her roiling thoughts and confusion, her equanimity was askew. Once again, she was reminded that she was a pawn and valued only for her usefulness. But one day she would be rid of all of the people who chose to exploit her. She and Amelia would leave, start anew, find happiness.

Once they reached home, Simon escorted her up the stairs. He dismissed Sarah, preferring to undress Maria himself, his large hands gentle and mindful of the ache the permeated every cell in her body. He tucked her gently into bed and then changed her dressings, murmuring his concern at the fresh blood that stained the cloths.

"At least it is a clean wound," she whispered, her eyes closing in relief as she settled back into the down-stuffed pillows.

"Here."

A spoon was placed at her lips and a moment later laudanum slipped down her throat. It was quickly washed down with water, and soon the potent effects were evident by the easing of the pain that plagued her.

"How do you feel, *mhuirnín*?" Simon's fingers drifted across her brow and kneaded gently into her temples.

"Grateful for you." Her words slurred together, ending in a soft purr as his lips brushed across hers. She inhaled deeply, absorbing the beloved scent of his skin deep into her lungs. Her hand caught his and squeezed.

"Rest now," he admonished, "so you can heal. I need you well."

She nodded, and drifted into sleep.

Her dreams were unpleasant, her heart racing with distress as she chased after an elusive Amelia while Welton's laughter echoed through her mind. Maria thrashed, which aggravated her shoulder. With a whimper, she awoke.

"Easy," rasped a voice beside her.

Turning her head, she found her cheek pressed to a warm, nude chest. Coarse hair cushioned her head and strong arms held her as immobile as possible without hurting her further. Moonlight poured in through the windows, revealing the one sash that was pushed upward, inviting in a cool evening breeze—as it had apparently invited in the man who shared her bed.

"Christopher," she breathed, finding comfort in the familiarity of his embrace.

He exhaled as if the sound of his name affected him, his chest falling and then rising beneath her. The room was dark, and though she could not see the clock, she knew that hours had passed since she'd first fallen asleep.

"Why are you here?"

He was silent for a long moment, then, "I don't know."

"How did you slip past my men?"

"With great difficulty, but obviously, I managed the task."

"Obviously," she said dryly. Her fist, which rested over the taut cords of his stomach, relaxed, opening to press her palm against his skin. Her touch slid downward, reaching his waistband.

"So you are not entirely undressed," she noted.

"Would you wish me to be?"

"I admit the thought of you caught without your breeches does have its amusements."

"Bloodthirsty vixen." His raspy voice was tinged with affection. He pressed a hard kiss to her forehead and pulled the dislodged counterpane over her injured shoulder. "I came to berate you for leaving me as you did. My temper was high and in need of release."

"Are you enamored with me?" she teased, hiding the strength of her anticipation for his answer.

"I expect the promises made to me to be kept." The warning was clear.

"You made a like promise to me."

"I kept mine," he murmured. "Can you say the same?"

Maria leaned back to look up at him. "What sexual feat can I perform in this condition?"

"A touch, a kiss." He stared down at her with glittering eyes. "A suggestive glance would be too much."

Maria considered him a moment, carefully taking stock of her reactions to this man. She wasn't quite certain why he appealed to her so strongly. As much as there was to like about him, there was even more to be wary of. "You kissed a woman."

"It was worth it to see your reaction."

A soft laugh escaped her, a sound both wry and derisive. A heartbeat later he joined her, the rumble of his merriment a joy to hear.

"We are an unfortunate pairing," he said.

"Yes. If we had the option, I would suggest we stay far away from one another."

Christopher's hand stroked down her back. "The woman you saw was Angelica. Quinn knows her quite well."

"Ah." Maria nodded.

"Quinn occupies the room next to yours. If his position in your household is so important," he asked gruffly, cupping her chin and forcing her to once again meet his gaze, "why is he not at your side?"

"You should not care about Simon or Eddington. I should not care about Angelica. What we do when we are apart should be of no consequence to any business between us."

His lips firmed. "I agree that is the way it should be. But that is not the way it is."

"It was sex between you and me. If we indulge again, it would remain nothing more than sex."

"Very good sex," he corrected.

"Did you think so?" She studied what she could see of his features in the darkness.

He smiled and her breath caught. "I knew it before the fact." His fingers drifted across her lips. "You need to heal so we can resume our bedsport. In the meantime, tell me. What did Welton want of you that forced you to go out in this condition, rather than recuperating as you should be?"

"Why did Sedgewick approach me as if he knew me and assume that you were my escort?"

They stared at each other in silence, neither willing to make an admission. Finally, she sighed and snuggled tighter against him. How she missed the feel of a man in her bed, the comfort of a strong embrace and the warmth imparted by a handsome man's desire. Somehow the things left unsaid brought her closer to Christopher. There was no denying that they were impossibly alike.

"My brother was an agent," he said suddenly, his breath blowing warmly into the hair at her crown.

Staring out the window at the starry night, Maria blinked and held her breath, wondering why he would reveal such a thing to her.

"He learned information," he continued, his voice devoid of emotion, "and shared it with me. You see, he needed funds quite desperately and I acquired them the only way I could."

"Illegally." Suddenly, the occasional sightings of goodness she had witnessed in him became explainable. She, too, functioned outside of the law for the welfare of a sibling.

"Yes. When he learned of my activities, he was furious. It did not sit well with him that he benefited at the risk of my neck."

"Of course not."

"So he came to London to assist me, which spared me many times. I was always aware of traps before they were sprung."

"Dastardly," she whispered, her hand running down his side. "And quite brilliant."

"We thought so. Until his actions were discovered."

"Oh."

"Our cooperation was then extorted using my brother's safety as leverage. It was messy, and in the end, deadly. Nigel wanted to save me and he did, but it cost us his life."

"I am sorry." She pressed a kiss to his chest, her lips clinging to his skin. How well she knew what it was like to lose a sibling. At least she had a chance of recovering Amelia. Christopher's brother was lost forever. "I trust you were close to one another?"

"I loved him."

The simple statement rocked her to the core. The words detracted not at all from his seeming invincibility. They were imparted with such strength that the admission could never be construed as a vulnerability. "Is that your grievance against the agency?"

"In part. There is more."

"You tell me this to gain my sympathy and my assistance?"

"Partly. And partly because if we cannot discuss the present, that leaves us with only our pasts."

Maria closed her eyes, her equilibrium unbalanced by the laudanum and Christopher, whom she could not understand. "Why discuss anything? Why not leave it with sex and the bare minimum required to achieve your ends?"

She felt the impact of his head falling back into the pillows. The action was rife with frustration.

"I find myself in bed with an invalid, a woman I cannot trust in any fashion. If I sit here in silence, I shall go mad attempting to reason out why I am here and not elsewhere. Since fucking is out of the question, another activity is required to distract me."

"Is that all I need to do to extract information from you?

Deny you my body? Then you will spout secrets to entertain yourself?"

He growled low, and she shivered. Not with fear, but with a tiny flare of desire. The man had no notion of what to do with her or with himself while he was around her. Since she knew exactly how he felt, she sympathized.

"I loved Dayton," she offered, her tone so low it was scarcely more than a breath.

Christopher's large frame stilled beneath her.

"He was a good man, and I made every attempt to be good to him in return. I was so young and untried, and he was accomplished and worldly. He made it possible for me to survive. And I repaid him by costing him his life." Although she tried to hide it, there was an aching note of loss in her words.

"Maria." His hand slid into her hair and cupped the back of her head. He said no more than that, but he didn't have to.

She'd shared very little, but Maria felt as if she had revealed her deepest self. It was not a feeling she welcomed. As if he knew her turmoil, Christopher adjusted her so that her face tilted up to his, enabling him to take her mouth.

It started with a soft swipe of his tongue along the curve of her lower lip. Then a press of his lips, so different from Simon's—thinner, firmer, more demanding. His head tilted and he fit his mouth over hers, stealing her breath, making it his own. Even as she struggled with the change, she understood it. Physical interaction was something they both felt comfortable with.

She opened to him, their movements controlled and leisurely, every touch of their tongues thought out and considered. It was a calculated encounter, one planned and executed with a purpose. This was not foreplay or a prelude. It was the finale. *No more emotion.*

Then she ruined everything by reaching for his hand and lacing her fingers with his. Their grips tightened, and an edgy sound filled the shared space of their kiss. Whether it was his or hers, she could not tell. Unnerved by the sudden intimacy, she pulled away, turning to hide her face in the space between his shoulder and throat. He breathed harshly in the silence, his chest rising and falling rapidly against hers, which heaved similarly.

Eddington would come tomorrow with the offer to rid her of Welton and thereby give her Amelia. And all she had to promise was Christopher, served up on a silver salver.

She inhaled his scent, her breath still shaky.

"Maria."

Her name. Spoken hoarsely. He said no more than that, but again, he didn't have to.

Amelia exited the small manse in her temporary home of Lincolnshire and sucked fresh air deep into her lungs. Every home they occupied was in some state of disrepair—this one seemed clogged with dust—and each was a distant holding of someone her father knew. How he managed to secure use of the properties was a mystery to her, but then everything about her life was an enigma. No one told her anything, aside from the insistence that her sister Maria was a degenerate.

Pausing on the side of the house, Amelia looked over at the stables, her gaze searching for the tall, lean form of Colin and the reassurance the sight of him would bring. The handsome groomsman was the nephew of her coachman, and he'd been with her since they were children. He was three years older, yet he seemed much older than that. They'd been friends once, playing together in the moments when he was free from work, running through the fields and pretending they were people who lived in far different circumstances.

That seemed so long ago. Colin had matured and grown away from her. His free time was now spent with women his age or older, or with the other servants. He avoided her now and was curt and ill-tempered the rare times he was forced to speak with her. She was an annoying child of ten and six to a young man of nineteen. Despite this, she was quite besotted with him. Always had been. Prayed she would not always be. She had her pride, and being shunned by the object of her affection was so miserable she prayed for the day he affected her not at all.

Silently chastising herself for looking for him, Amelia turned away and found the unkempt pathway that she wandered along daily for exercise.

"You will grow out of it, too," her last governess had said, when Amelia had cried over a particularly hurtful dismissal from Colin. She hoped that was true, that she would eventually grow out of her childish infatuation.

Soon. Please, God, make it soon.

Swinging her bonnet in her hand, Amelia circumvented the estate, jumping over raised tree roots and piles of fallen leaves with nimble, boot-clad feet.

When she reached the wooden fence that separated her from freedom, Amelia paused and for the first time considered what it would be like to flee. She'd never entertained the thought before, but now her thinking was altered by Maria's attempt to retrieve her. What was out there? What adventures waited beyond her minute existence that consisted of servants and a governess and a life on the road?

"Ah, the pretty lass strays."

Startled by the coarse masculine voice behind her, Amelia spun too quickly and nearly fell over.

"Heavens," she cried breathlessly, her hand placed over her racing heart. She recognized the freckled young man who stood a few feet away as one of her father's new lackeys. The ones he had hired to replace those lost in the altercation with Maria. "You gave me a fright."

"Sorry," he offered, smiling apologetically. Short and sinewy, the brown-haired boy was the youngest of the crew whose livelihood it was to keep her safe. Of course, she was beginning to suspect that they were supposed to keep her *in*, rather than keep others *out*.

She noted the long pole in his hand. "What are you doing?"

"Going fishing." He gestured to the other side of the fence with a jerk of his chin. "There's a stream over there."

"Oh." She didn't mean to sound disappointed.

"Do you like fishing?" he asked, studying her curiously with pale blue eyes. Dressed in woolen breeches and coat, his overly long locks sticking out from beneath his cap, he didn't look dressed for fishing, but what did she know?

"I've no idea," she admitted. "I have never been fishing."

He grinned, looking so boyish that she suspected he was the same age she was, maybe even younger. "Would you like to try it?" he offered. "I wouldn't mind the company."

Amelia frowned, curious but wary.

"The fish might bite, but I won't," he teased.

She chewed her lower lip.

"Come on, before Dickie comes around this way and keeps you from leaving." He walked past her and hopped over the low fence. Then he held his hand out to her. "It's not far. If you don't like it, we can come right back."

Knowing she probably shouldn't go, Amelia went anyway, enjoying the rush of excitement she felt at doing something so completely out of the ordinary, something new and different.

"What is your name?" she asked, as he helped her over.

"Benedict. But everyone calls me Benny."

"Hi, Benny." She smiled shyly. "I'm Amelia."

He released her, then tipped his hat in a grand bow before collecting his pole from where he'd set it aside to assist her. They walked without speaking for a few moments, moving through the thick grouping of trees until the sound of rushing water could be heard.

"How is it that you came to work for Lord Welton?" she queried, studying him with a sidelong glance.

He shrugged. "I heard there was work to be had and I showed my face at the spot I was told to."

"What kind of living is this?" she wondered. "What skills will you gain? What will you do when you are no longer needed?"

He smiled, his eyes sparkling from within the shadow cast by the brim of his hat. "I'm earning my way down to London, you see. By the time I make it, I'll have experience. Then I plan to work for St. John."

"Who is that? What does he do?"

Benny stumbled to a halt, gaping at her. He blinked and then whistled low. "Yer green as grass," he murmured, shaking his head, then he continued on.

"What does that mean?" she griped, stumbling after him.

"Never mind."

They emerged from the coppice and approached a small but rapidly moving stream. The bed was rocky and the water shallow, a lovely place that carried the feeling of innocence, as if the area was rarely breached by anyone. Amelia plopped onto a fallen log and began to untie her boots, impatiently pushing her waist-length hair back over her shoulder. Benny moved to the shore and shrugged out of his coat. While he settled himself comfortably, she shucked her stockings. Then, lifting her skirts, she moved to the water and stepped carefully into it. Her breath caught as the water chilled her feet.

"Yer scaring off all the fish!" Benny complained.

"Oh, this is wonderful!" she cried, filled with memories of hunting tadpoles and sloshing through mud with Colin. "Thank you!"

Benny frowned at her. "For what?"

"For bringing me here. For talking to me." Laughing, she spun about, then cried out in surprise as she slipped on a smooth river rock and tumbled. Gallant Benny leapt to his feet and tried to catch her, only to land flat on his back, half in and out of the water, with her atop him.

Unable to help it, Amelia laughed out loud, and once she started, she couldn't seem to stop.

"My sire always said the Quality was daft," he muttered.

Amelia was in the process of pushing herself up when scuffed boots came into view and she was ignobly hauled up by the scruff of her flowered gown.

"What in bloody hell are you doing?" Colin growled, glaring down at her.

Her laughter choked into silence, her eyes wide at the vision before her. Colin was dark haired, dark skinned, and dark eyed with a big-boned build that made her mouth dry. Gypsy blood, her last governess had said.

When had he grown so tall? He towered over her, his hair falling over his brow as he stared down at her so intensely she squirmed. There was nothing boyish about him, not with that chiseled jaw and knowing eyes. What had happened to the friend she had once loved?

Sadly, she realized he was gone forever.

Her head fell forward in an effort to hide her grief over the loss. "I was enjoying myself," she said softly.

A long moment passed when she could feel his gaze boring into the crown of her head. Then a low, agitated sound rumbled in his throat.

"Stay away from her," he bit out to Benny, who had pushed up to a seated position at their feet.

Colin grabbed her elbow and pulled her away, catching up her boots and stockings as he passed them.

"Stop it." Amelia struggled, her feet crunching on dead leaves. Without missing a beat, he tossed her over his shoulder and strode into the trees like a conquering warrior.

"Put me down!" she cried, mortified, the cascade of her hair pouring over her face to nearly drag along the forest floor.

But he ignored her, carrying her into a tiny clearing before he set her down and dropped her belongings.

She swallowed hard and lifted her chin. "I am not a child! I can make my own decisions."

His gaze narrowed and he crossed his arms, revealing the powerful muscles he built with hard labor. Dressed in breeches and sweater, he looked rough and ready for anything. His appearance intensified the strange feelings she'd begun having for him, flutters that started in her lower belly and radiated outward.

"I suggest one of those decisions involve wearing your hair up," he said coldly. "You are too old to wear it down any longer."

"I will do what I please."

A muscle in his jaw ticked. "Not when what pleases you is cavorting with the likes of him." He gestured behind him.

She gave a harsh, derisive little laugh. "Who do you think you are to order me about? You are a servant. My father is a peer of the realm."

He inhaled harshly. "You don't have to remind me. Put your shoes on."

"No." Crossing her arms beneath her recently acquired breasts, she arched a brow and hoped she looked haughty.

"Don't push me, Amelia." His gaze dropped, and he made an edgy sound. "Put your damn shoes on."

"Oh, go away!" she cried, tossing up her hands, thoroughly sick of the new Colin and slowly giving up hope for the old one. "What are you doing out here? I was having fun for the first time in ages, and you had to come along and ruin it."

"You were gone longer than usual," he accused gruffly. "Someone had to fetch you and keep you out of mischief."

"How would you know how long I was gone? The only time you notice me is when you're surly and wish to vent on someone." She tried to tap her foot, but the gesture lost impact when done with bare feet. "And I hardly call making friends an undesirable activity."

"You don't wish to befriend those of his ilk."

"I wish to befriend someone! I have no one since you grew to hate me."

The line of Colin's lips tightened, then he ran both hands through his thick hair and groaned. She was jealous of his hands, wanting to feel those glossy strands slipping through her own fingers.

"Stay away from the men," he ordered, in a tone that brooked no argument. She was preparing to argue anyway when he walked right past her and headed toward the manse.

Amelia stuck her tongue out at his broad back and struggled with the ache in her chest. He talked to no one else like he did to her, so curt and nasty. It hurt, and it fueled her dreams of running away and leaving him behind.

As she sank to the ground and retrieved her stockings, she lamented her existence. But soon she would go to London for her presentation to the court. Then she would wed and forget about Colin.

Her jaw tightened. "I will forget about you, Colin Mitchell. I *will*."

Chapter 11

When Maria woke, Christopher was gone. She lay there a moment, staring up at the canopy, attempting to make sense of their mutable association. He was waiting. Waiting for her to admit some connection to the agency that he could use. She had no notion if her admission of love for Dayton would alter his thinking. Of course, she had loved her first spouse like a favored uncle and he had looked fondly upon her as one would a favorite niece, but she thought it best to mislead the pirate on that point.

Why? she'd asked simply when the Earl of Dayton had paid Welton a small fortune to have her.

My Mathilda is gone, he answered just as simply, his kind eyes filled with pain. *I have since found little to live for. Assisting you will give me a purpose.*

They wed and retired to the country, where he used his considerable knowledge of subterfuge and combat skills to train her. Most days they were up at dawn, and the sunlit hours were occupied in physical pursuits such as fencing and marksmanship. The evening hours were spent discussing topics such as cryptology and ways to hire men of dubious skill sets. There was nothing he left to chance, knowing she would do whatever was necessary to reclaim Amelia.

"How are you feeling this morn?" Simon asked as he stepped into her room. He was dressed for riding, in breeches and polished Hessians. His windswept hair and the scent of horseflesh told her that he was returning, rather than leaving. "Did you sleep well?"

She considered that question a moment, pushing fond memories of Dayton aside. "I did," she noted with some wonder. Last night was the first occasion since seeing Amelia that she had managed to sleep without bad dreams. It was due to Christopher, she knew. The man was prepared for anything, and that made her feel safe. Odd, considering how dangerous he was.

"I went to Bernadette's last night and spoke with Daphne." He helped her sit up and arranged her on the pillows. "It appears we've had a stroke of luck. He had a favorite, a new girl named Beth. Apparently, she had a disliking for some of his carnal proclivities, so he has begun to spend more time with Daphne, whose tastes are more diverse."

Maria smiled. "I am in need of good luck."

"Truer words were never spoken." He studied her carefully. "You look different this morning."

"Better, I hope."

"Much." His smile was breathtaking. "I will order tea and breakfast for you."

"Thank you, Simon." She watched him as he walked away. "Eddington will come to call today," she called after him.

"I haven't forgotten," he tossed over his shoulder.

Alone again, she considered her predicament. There had to be a way to delay all of them—Christopher, Welton, and Eddington. Her brain was still sleep fuzzy, but given the proper amount of time and clear thought, she knew there had to be a way to position the three men to assist her. They all had something she wanted, and if she was clever, she could see her ends met.

With this in mind, Maria spent the morning lost in thought, absentmindedly completing the steps required to prepare herself for Eddington's visit. She dressed carefully in a cream-colored day gown and settled a fichu over her shoulders to disguise her bandages. By the time the earl was announced, she had settled upon a temporary plan. She felt confident enough in her idea to have him shown into her lower parlor rather than her study, where she usually conducted business.

"Good morning to you, my lord," she said with exaggerated civility.

"My lady." He bowed. Dressed in fawn-colored breeches and a dark green jacket, he cut quite a dashing figure. Every inch the lauded rakehell, he winked at her before settling in the pale blue settee on the other side of the low table.

"Tea?" she inquired.

"Yes, thank you."

She was deliberately casual and unaffected in her preparation of the beverage, her hands moving with deliberate gracefulness. Twice she glanced aside at him with a secretive smile. The returning indulgent curve to his lips told her he knew her game, but still wished to play.

"You are a vision this morning," he murmured as he accepted the cup and saucer from her.

"I know."

Eddington laughed, his handsome features softening from their usual predatory alertness. He hid it well with his heavy-lidded gaze, but she knew his kind.

"A joy to meet a woman without artifice," he said.

"I took pains to appeal to you, my lord. I would not live up to my reputation if I failed to know when I was most attractive."

"Do you wish to bed me, then?" Both brows raised. "Insatiability is also something I admire."

Maria laughed. "I've quite enough men in my life at the moment, thank you. Still, women's wiles are a powerful tool, yes?"

His voice lowered. "Especially when they are wielded by a woman as seductive as you."

"I've reached a decision regarding your proposal," she

said, her tone clipped to signal the end of their banter and the beginning of business.

The earl smiled against the rim of his cup. "Excellent."

"It will cost you more than the removal of Welton and the agency from my life."

"Oh?" His gaze narrowed.

"Much more," she warned.

"How much more?" he demanded gruffly.

She waved her hand carelessly and smiled. "I refuse to discuss monetary matters with anyone other than my solicitor. I find it quite vulgar and oftentimes unpleasant. I will give you his direction and you can settle my accounts with him."

Eddington set his cup down with undue care. "Coin?" He blew out his breath. He was an intelligent man. He knew she would be expensive. "Perhaps I do not think St. John is worth that much."

"You have one witness, if he is even still alive. If not, you have nothing. Except for me."

"You will testify against him?" Eddington asked, his alertness intensifying.

She nodded.

"What about the deaths of Dayton and Winter?"

"What about them?"

"You are the prime suspect."

Maria smiled. "Perhaps I did murder them, my lord. Perhaps not. I give you leave to prove it, one way or the other."

"How can I know if you are trustworthy or not?"

"There is no way to know that. Just as I cannot know whether this is merely an elaborate ruse designed to implicate me in the deaths of my husbands." She shrugged. "You said I was a risk you were willing to take. If you've changed your mind, you may leave."

He considered her for a long moment. "I cannot tell whether you are a demon disguised as a temptress, or a victim of those around you."

"I ask myself the same every day, my lord. I suspect I am a

little of both." She rose to her feet, forcing him to rise as well. "If you find the answer with any certainty, please let me know."

The earl rounded the table and came to a halt before her. He stood close, too close. He meant to intimidate her with his greater height and physical strength, but she wasn't cowed. In their association, she held the power. He had nothing without her. Only conjecture, with no way to penetrate St. John's defenses.

"Tread lightly," Eddington warned, his voice low and filled with danger. "I leave Town this evening and will be gone a fortnight, but I will know what you do."

"Of course."

A few moments after the earl departed, Maria rose and moved to her study, where she penned a missive to Welton and sent it off. A knock came to the open study door, and she smiled as Simon entered.

"You look like a cat with cream," he said.

"I have convinced Eddington to fund my search for Amelia."

He arched a dark brow. "You told him?"

"No." She grinned.

Walking toward her, Simon sank into one of the two chairs before the large desk. "Eddington wants the same information as Welton. Who do you intend to share it with?"

She blew out her breath. "I haven't yet decided. If I tell Eddington, he might help me with Welton and then I could find Amelia. But Christopher would hang."

"*Christopher,* is it?" he asked tightly.

"If I tell Welton," she continued as if he had said nothing, "he will attempt to extort either St. John or whoever else may have been involved. I would be no further ahead than I am now, but St. John would live. Of course, St. John might then dispatch Welton and save himself the annoyance. Having become somewhat acquainted with the pirate, I can say for certain that Welton has overstepped himself this time."

"Or you could tell St. John about Welton and Eddington

in return for help with finding Amelia," Simon suggested. She knew how much it cost him to say such a thing, to admit that St. John could help her in a way that he himself had been unable to. It was a testament of his affection for her that he would set aside his masculine pride to see her happy.

"I thought of that." Maria stood and went to him, cupping his face in her hands and kissing his forehead in gratitude. "But until I know the reason why he was released and what role he intends for me to play, I cannot trust him."

Simon tugged her gently into his lap. "So what will we do now?"

"I have sent for Welton. I intend to tell him that I am retreating on holiday. I need to heal, and it's time to make inquiries outside of London. We have the funds to expand our search. Truly the best course for us would be to find Amelia before I have to make a decision. Having her in my possession will change everything."

He nodded. "I will see to the necessary preparations."

"How long has this been going on?" Christopher asked curtly.

"A few weeks," Philip replied, pushing up his spectacles. "I learned of the situation this afternoon and promptly brought it to your attention."

Leaning his hip against his study desk, Christopher crossed his arms and inhaled deeply before replying. "Why wasn't I told about this immediately?"

"The lander felt that he could handle the matter."

"When a rival gang encroaches on my territory, I will handle it. By God, you give them an inch and they will take the entire length of the shore."

A knock came to the door and Christopher bade them to enter. When he saw his valet, he said, "We leave in a few hours and will be gone for a fortnight at least."

"Yes, sir." The servant bowed and retreated.

"May I accompany you?" Philip asked. He stood a few

feet away, his stance tall and proud as Christopher had taught
him when he was a boy.

Christopher shook his head. "Gang wars are bloody and
not for spectators. Your skill lies with the brain in your skull,
not with your sword arm. I will not risk you merely to satisfy
your curiosity."

"You are far cleverer than I, and your loss would be felt
more keenly. Why risk yourself when you have men who
could see to the matter with similar results?"

"They cannot see to it." Christopher straightened and retrieved his coat from where it hung over the back of a chair.
"This is not simply about prime coastal space. This is about
me and mine. They want both. Until I confront them, they
will not back down. Why do you think my enemies haven't
shot me dead? Unless they best me face-to-face, they cannot
truly take the reins. Their power would always be in question."

"Damned if that isn't primitive," Philip muttered.

Snorting, Christopher shrugged into his coat. "Humans
are animals, after all."

"Do you ever contemplate leaving this life?" the young
man asked, his head canted to the side. "You've coin aplenty."

Christopher paused and stared at his protégé. "What
would I do with myself?"

"Marry. Raise a family."

"Never." He fluffed the lace at his neck and wrists. "The
only way out of this livelihood is death. If it wasn't me they
were after, it would be those closest to me. If your end aim is
to be a family man, move along now, young Philip. The deeper
entrenched you become, the further away that goal will be."

Philip followed him out to the foyer. "Where are you going
now?"

"I must bid Lady Winter farewell."

As soon as the words left his mouth, they struck Christopher
wrong. Always in times like this he acknowledged the possibility of his demise. He had safeguards in place to protect the

members of his household, which allowed him to leap into the fray with the gusto of a man who accepted death. Now, however, he found himself hesitant, less willing to make the journey to hell. He wanted to see Maria again, to feel her beneath him arching in pleasure, to hear her throaty laughter as she teased him. He wanted her to prick his temper as only she could until he was hard as a rock and hot to ride her all night.

Damn it, base as it was, he wanted to fuck her again and the craving was such that he wished to live long enough to manage to task. A harsh bark of laughter escaped him as he collected his hat and gloves from his butler and left his house. Primitive animals, indeed.

It was absurd to want a woman this badly. He could have anyone, from a duchess to a fishwife. Women lusted for him, always had. But as he pulled his mount to a halt before Maria's home and tossed the reins to the waiting groomsman, the anticipation that coursed through him was a unique product of only one female.

When the butler opened the door to find him on the stoop with calling card in hand, the servant could not hide his look of dismay.

"Take the card," Christopher drawled, "and we can avoid a siege."

Sniffing, the servant did as he suggested and led him to the same parlor where he had previously spoken with Lord Welton. Once he was left alone, Christopher took note of the room in daylight, noting the elaborate gilded moldings that decorated the pale gray walls. He hated waiting, and he hated the way his impatience made him pace. Some men paced. Christopher was generally not one of them.

Finally the door opened and Maria stepped into the room. He paused midstep, staring, startled by his reaction to her in casual attire. It seemed oddly intimate, reminding him of the night before and the way she had felt in his arms, lush and warm. He could not think of one thing he would rather have done than lie abed with her, feeling her lips wet and soft and clinging to his.

He reached her shortly, his stride swift in his eagerness to take her mouth and relive the delights of the previous evening. Cognizant of her delicate condition, Christopher cupped her spine with great care and tilted his head to kiss her as he wanted. Maria stood rigid for a moment and then yielded sweetly.

He licked, nibbled, and ate at her as if she were a dessert he could not consume enough of. His skin grew hot, then damp with perspiration, every muscle tense with need and desire. From *a kiss*, and he did not even really enjoy kissing, considering it a needless distraction from the good part of sex.

But *by God* . . . Maria's kisses were sexual acts in and of themselves. He withdrew only because he needed to breathe. Certainly that was the only reason he felt dizzy.

Maria's eyes opened, revealing dark and dazed depths. "Hmm . . ." she murmured, licking her lips. "Delicious."

The throaty way she said the word aroused him further. He growled his frustration and cupped her face in his hands. "Listen. I must depart today. There is a matter of some urgency that requires my attention. Tell me now if you are intent on another harebrained scheme so I can assign some men to protect you."

She smiled. "I am going on holiday, to rest and recuperate."

"Good." His fingers tightened their hold and then he released her, backing away quickly. There was something about her bearing that made him suspicious. He would keep additional guards on her anyway. "Where are you going?"

"I have yet to decide."

"When are you departing?"

"Today."

"When will you be back?"

She laughed, her dark eyes bright. With her kiss-swollen

lips and black-as-pitch hair, she was beyond beautiful. "Will you miss me?"

"I hope not," he muttered, feeling surly for no reason he could recognize.

"I shall miss you."

Alert, he studied her. "You will?"

"No. It seemed like the thing to say."

"Witch." He knew she was toying with him, could see it in the way she looked at him, and yet part of him wished she were sincere.

"Christopher?" she prodded, when the silence stretched on. "You do not seem to be yourself today."

"It is you who is different," he accused. She seemed . . . lighter in mood than usual. He wanted to know why. Who had wrought this change in her?

Maria sighed audibly and walked to the settee. "So we part ways here." She sat and patted the space next to her in silent invitation.

He did not move.

She settled her hands primly in her lap and arched one brow expectantly. Belatedly Christopher understood that she was waiting for him to say something.

"I have to go," he said. *To kill, and perhaps to be killed.*

She nodded.

"If you have even the slightest desire to kiss me good-bye," he said gruffly, "you should do so now."

"I see." Her lips pursed. "Why do I have the feeling that a flippant remark here would ruin the moment?"

He turned on his heel and walked out.

"Christopher! Wait."

He paused on the threshold and turned, his mien one of patent boredom.

Maria was standing again and appeared to have taken steps to follow him. "I slept better last night than I have in a long while."

It was some sort of olive branch, so he stepped back into

the room and closed the door. She was either the best trick-ster in the world or she was growing soft on him. Masculine satisfaction warred with guilt.

Then she crossed the room to him with an enticing sashay and set her hands on his chest. She tilted her head back and looked up at him. He stared down at her, waiting, needing her to be the one who closed the distance between them.

"I should have allowed you to leave," she complained, shaking her head.

Stepping away to collect a footstool, Maria then set it down before him. She climbed atop it, which still left her short of eye level but brought her much closer to his mouth. "Tell me again why I am exerting myself in this manner."

He smiled, content now to leave and do what he must. "For this."

And then he kissed her ardently.

Chapter 12

"Feeling better?" Miss Pool asked, glancing aside at Amelia as they walked through the village on their return trip home.

Amelia nodded. "I am, yes. Thank you."

Ever since the night Maria had come for her, she'd grown more and more restless. When it became obvious that she couldn't concentrate on the day's lessons, Miss Pool had suggested they set the work aside in favor of a day outdoors. Parasols in hand, they had ventured out with no particular destination in mind but had found themselves drawn to the nearby market town. Amelia enjoyed the afternoon stroll, appreciating the opportunity to see others industriously going about their daily business. Other people had full lives, even if she did not.

"The body needs as much conditioning as the mind," Miss Pool said in her soft, sweet voice.

"I have always thought so, too." Of course, she'd grown up alongside a physically active boy and had learned to relish hard play. She also relished a dimpled smile, but she had not seen that in years.

"I do like your hair worn up." The governess smiled. "You look every inch the fine lady. I will write your father this evening and suggest the procurement of a proper abigail for you."

Amelia touched her hair nervously. Braided and then coiled into a bun, it was heavy and her neck ached with the unaccustomed weight. But if this was what was required to be considered a young woman and not a child, she considered the discomfiture worth it.

"Good afternoon, Miss Pool. Miss Benbridge."

They slowed and smiled at the young cobbler who had stepped outside of his shop to greet them. The handsome blond man smiled shyly through his beard and rubbed his palms nervously against his apron.

"Good afternoon, Mr. Field," Miss Pool greeted with a soft blush on her cheeks that didn't escape Amelia's notice.

The two appeared to like each other, with more than casual interest. Curious, Amelia studied them, wondering if she looked so obviously smitten when she crossed paths with Colin. How dreadful if she did, to wear that glowing look of hope and longing in the face of his curtness and obvious distaste for her.

Feeling both morose and embarrassed that she was intruding on an exchange that seemed intimate, she turned her back to the couple . . .

. . . and spotted a familiar set of broad shoulders and long legs walking away from her. At Colin's side was a blond girl who Amelia guessed was close to his age, if the ripe womanly curves were any indication. They were laughing, their eyes bright as they looked at each other. His hand was at her lower back, steering her around a corner so that they disappeared from view.

Unable to resist, Amelia moved forward, her movements jerky. Colin and the buxom girl had looked at each other much as Miss Pool and Mr. Field were. A look filled with promise.

Amelia rounded the same building, her steps slowing as she heard low murmured voices and subdued giggles. She passed barrels and crates, her focus so narrow that when a stray cat leapt to the ground with a meow it frightened her half to death. She fell back against the brick, her hand sheltering her racing heart, her eyes squeezed shut with dread. It was cooler back here, the pass-through shaded from the sun by the building.

She knew she should turn back. Miss Pool wouldn't be distracted long and then she would worry about her. But Amelia's heart ignored reason, to no surprise. If the stubborn thing listened at all, it would have ceased pining for Colin months ago.

Taking a deep breath of courage, she pushed off the wall and turned the corner to reach the back of the shop. There she stilled, her breath seized in her lungs, her open parasol first falling to her side and then falling from her fingers to thud on the soft earth.

Colin and his companion were too occupied to note the sound. The pretty blonde was pressed against the rear wall, her head tilted back to invite Colin's roving mouth, which moved across the swell of flesh exposed by her low bodice. He caged her in, his left arm bearing the weight of his torso, his right hand kneading the full breast the girl thrust wantonly toward him.

Pain stabbed deep into Amelia's heart, a wound so brutal she moaned with the agony of it. Colin's head flew up, his eyes widening as he saw her. He straightened instantly, thrusting himself away from the building and the girl he ravished there.

Horrified, Amelia turned and ran the length of the shops, leaving her parasol behind. Her sobs echoed off the rear of the stores, but she heard him calling out to her, regardless. That deep voice, so different from the boy she had known, the tone serrated and pleading as if he cared that he'd broken her.

Which he didn't, she knew.

She ran faster, the thudding of her panicked boot steps lost in the sound of blood rushing in her ears.

But even running her fastest, she could not outrun the memory of what she had seen.

"Will you please allow me to handle the matter?" Simon murmured, his head next to Maria's as they both stared out the small traveling coach window.

"No, no," she insisted, her foot tapping impatiently upon the floorboards. "It will be less messy all around if I do it."

"It's too dangerous."

"Nonsense," she scoffed. "If you approach the man, you will end up in fisticuffs, which will draw attention. In order for this to succeed, we will need to depart as quietly as we arrived."

He sighed audibly and fell back against the squabs with high drama, playing the part of the exasperated male to perfection. Maria laughed, then immediately fell silent as a large form appeared from the mews behind the St. John household. "Is that one of them?" she asked.

Simon looked out the window again. "Yes. But I suggest we wait for one of the smaller ones."

Maria considered that a moment, admitting to herself that she was quite intimidated by the man's great size. He was a giant. His long, unkempt hair and black beard only added to the image of a large troll. He walked away from them with a heavy, lumbering stride that she was certain shook the very ground beneath him.

She took a deep breath and thought of her sister. Maria had already questioned all of the men who had been with her the night she failed to retrieve Amelia. Sadly, there was very little useful information to be gained from them. They had been too intent on saving her. Christopher's men, on the other hand, might have been more inclined to absorb the whole scene. Therefore, she had to question at least one of them. Her sister needed her. Somehow, she would find the strength required to abscond with a behemoth.

Thrusting open the door, Maria stepped down before she could come to her senses. She hurried after the man, calling out for his assistance such as a helpless, needy female would.

The giant paused and turned with a scowl, which quickly turned to masculine appreciation, which in turn immediately grew into wariness as she pulled a pistol from behind her back.

"Hello," she greeted with a wide smile, aiming for his heart. "I would enjoy your company for a spell."

His gaze narrowed. "Are ye daft?" he rumbled.

"Please don't make me shoot you. I will, you know." She widened her stance in preparation for the resulting kick of the discharging weapon. It was all for show, of course, but he couldn't know that. "I would deeply regret putting a hole in you, as you helped to save my life recently and I do owe you a great deal for that."

His eyes widened with recognition, then he cursed under his breath. "They'll tease me for the rest of my life for this," he muttered.

"I am sorry about that."

"No, yer not." He stomped past her, proving her suspicion about the quaking earth. "Where?"

"My coach is around the corner."

He reached it and yanked the door open, revealing a wide-eyed Simon.

"Good God!" Simon blinked. "That was too easily done."

"I'd take 'er over my knee," the giant rumbled, "but St. John would 'ave my 'ide." He climbed into the carriage and took up an entire squab, causing the equipage to creak in protest. Crossing his arms, he griped, "Come on, then. Get on with it."

Maria handed Simon the gun and stepped up unassisted. "Your cooperation is greatly appreciated, Mr.—?"

"Tim."

"Mr. Tim."

He glared. "Just Tim."

She settled on the rear-facing seat next to Simon. She arranged her skirts as the coach lurched into motion and then beamed at her guest. "I hope you like Brighton, Tim."

"The only thing I'll like is to know that you torment St. John the same," he grumbled.

Bending over conspiratorially, she whispered, "I am much worse with him."

Tim grinned from the depths of his beard. "I like Brighton fine, then."

The setting sun cast the ocean in a reddish glow that turned the water to molten fire. Hard, heavy waves pounded onto the shore, molding it into shape, the rhythmic roar soothing Christopher as it always had. He stood on the high cliff, his stance wide, his hands clasped at his back. The salty sea breeze gusted against him, chilling his skin and tugging strands of his hair free of the queue that contained them.

Beyond the horizon one of his ships waited, its belly full of spirits and tobacco, rich materials and exotic spices. Once night fell, the vessel would draw closer, searching for the winking light his crew would use to signal them into the proper position.

It was then that his rivals would strike, disrupting the transport of contraband to the shore. Tonight they would receive what they had truly been spoiling for—a fight.

The anticipation for the confrontation ahead thrummed in Christopher's veins, but he was neither anxious nor eager. This was a necessary task, nothing more.

"We stand at the ready," said Sam, who took up position beside him.

Christopher's men were scattering everywhere, some along the cliffs and beach, others in the caves and village. His hands unclasped, allowing his shirtsleeves to flutter violently in the wind. He gripped the hilt of his foil and inhaled sea air deep into his lungs.

"Right," he murmured. "Let's go down, then."

He led the way to the beach below, his gaze directly meeting the eyes of his many men as he passed them. It was such a simple thing, those fleeting glances, yet they said so much to the men who risked their lives in service to him.

I see you. You are someone to me.

Over the years he'd watched others in command and noted how they walked the gauntlet with eyes set straight ahead, puffed up with pride as if they were too good to acknowledge their underlings. The only loyalty such men inspired was built on fear or love of coin. A shaky foundation, easily destroyed.

Christopher stepped behind a large boulder that rested partly in the water and waited. The sky darkened; the roaring waves lessened their fury. The lander moved into place to begin the well-organized task of hauling cargo from the ship to the shore.

The knowledge of what was to come coiled tightly inside Christopher. He watched the beach from his hiding place, emotionless, as he would need to be to survive the long night. Shadows flowed down from the village like smoke, betraying those who wished to usurp him. As he gestured for the lantern that was hidden to the side, the clash of steel and shouts of warning could be heard. The air changed, became charged, the scent of fear filling his nostrils. Christopher revealed himself, holding a lantern aloft to cast illumination upon his features.

"Ho, there!" he called out, his tone filled with such command that the battling men on the shore faltered. As he expected, one man separated himself from the many.

"About time you showed yer cowardly face!" the cretin shouted.

Arching a brow, Christopher drawled, "Next time you desire my company, might I suggest a handwritten invitation?"

"Quit yer riddles and fight like a man."

Christopher smiled coldly. "Ah, but I prefer to fight like a heathen."

A grouping of men rushed toward him and he tossed the lantern at their feet, spraying oil and flames, which quickly engulfed the lot of them and lit up the beach. Their screams of agony tore through the night, sending a ripple of terror and unease outward to engulf anyone within hearing distance.

Yanking his foil free of its scabbard, Christopher tossed up his left arm for balance and lunged into the ensuing fracas.

The night was long, the carnage plenty.

"Are you going to see Mr. Field?" Amelia inquired from her seat on Miss Pool's bed.

The pretty governess lifted her blue eyes to meet Amelia's in the vanity mirror's reflection. "Are you playing matchmaker?"

Amelia wished she could smile, but she hadn't managed that feat in days. "You look as lovely as a china doll," she said instead.

Miss Pool turned in her seat to study her for the umpteenth time. "Are you certain you won't come with me? You always love a trip into the village."

Painful memories flashed through her mind, and Amelia shook her head violently to rid herself of them. She would not cry in front of Miss Pool.

"Please know that you can talk to me about anything," the governess coaxed. "I kept your secret about your sister. I can keep others, too."

Pursing her lips, Amelia tried to keep her thoughts to herself but found herself blurting, "Have you ever been in love?"

The blue eyes widened, then Miss Pool admitted, "I fancied that I was. It ended badly, I'm afraid."

"Did you still love him? When it ended?"

"Yes."

Rising to her feet, Amelia moved to the window. It looked out toward the stream and away from the stables, so it was an innocuous view. "How did you recover?"

"I'm not sure that I did, until I met Mr. Field."

Amelia turned back at that. "How does he signify?"

"I am no expert, so I hesitate to speak about this, but I think perhaps a new romance can fill the void left by an old one." Miss Pool stood and crossed to her. "You will never have to worry about that. You are far too wonderful a person to ever lose your love."

"How I wish that were true," Amelia whispered.

A commiserating smile spread across the governess's delicate features. She set her hands gently atop Amelia's shoulders and asked, "You speak of first loves, yes? Those always end with heartache, Amelia. It is a rite of passage. The signal that you have grown beyond youthful fancy into the deeper knowledge of yourself. It is painful proof that you have left the tiny concerns of childhood behind and have grown into a woman's awareness."

Tears welled in Amelia's eyes. Miss Pool pulled her closer and offered solace in a warm embrace. Amelia accepted it gratefully, crying until she was wracked with hiccups, then she managed to cry some more.

Finally empty of tears, she reached deep inside herself and found a bit of strength she had not known she possessed.

"Go," Amelia ordered, blowing her nose into the handkerchief thrust at her. Miss Pool was always prepared. "I have held you here long enough."

"I will not leave you like this," Miss Pool protested.

"I feel better. Truly. I feel so much better, in fact, that I intend to go for a walk to clear my head."

It was Tuesday, the day when Colin and his uncle had the afternoon to themselves. They always ventured away, which meant the estate was safe to traverse.

"Come with me, then."

Amelia shuddered. She was not *that* strong. "No, thank you. I would much prefer to stay close to home today."

It took more assurances and cajoling before Miss Pool reluctantly left for the village. Then Amelia questioned the cook—who knew everything about everyone—to make certain Colin was gone. Still, the fear of seeing him again made her nauseated.

Taking a deep breath, she burst from the kitchen door, ran across the unkempt lawn, and plunged into the cover of trees. As she approached the small fence with the intent to climb over it, a movement in the trees drew her up short.

She ducked low and hid behind a trunk, watching as one of her father's lackeys made his rounds along the perimeter of the property. He was an older man, neat in appearance but too lean, causing his clothes to hang on his bony frame. His roaming gaze was hard and cold, and his hand gripped the hilt of a wicked-looking dagger.

He paused and glanced around suspiciously. Amelia held her breath, afraid to even blink as he craned his neck back and forth, searching the area. Forever seemed to pass before the guard moved on.

For a long moment, she waited, needing to be certain that he'd gone far enough away that she would not be seen climbing over the fence. Then she made her escape.

Amelia hopped over onto the neighboring property, slipping into the wooded area before blowing out the breath she'd been holding. "Heavens," she breathed, relieved beyond measure to have succeeded. "What a most unpleasant man."

"I agree."

Amelia jumped at the sound of the low, cultured drawl. She spun about, then gaped at the gentleman who stood nearby.

He was undeniably wealthy, as indicated by the fine quality of his garments and the craftsmanship of his wig. He was pale and slender, almost pretty. Despite the fact that he looked to be of similar age, he carried himself with a bearing that proclaimed clearly that his word was to be obeyed. A man of privilege.

He gave an elegant bow and introduced himself as the Earl of Ware. Then he explained that the stream she so enjoyed was on his father's land. "But you are welcome to it."

"Thank you, my lord." She dipped a quick curtsy. "You are most gracious."

"No," he said dryly. "I am most bored. I appreciate the company, especially when that company is the fair maiden freed from her turret prison."

"What a fanciful image," she murmured.

"I am a fanciful fellow."

Lord Ware took up her hand and escorted her to the stream. There she found Benny, who was working industriously with a long stick. He felt her gaze and looked up. "I'll make you a pole, too."

"See?" Ware said. "No more need for tears and reddened noses. After all, what could be better than an afternoon on the shore with an earl and an urchin?"

She glanced aside at him and he winked.

For the first time in days, Amelia smiled.

As the sun climbed steadily above the horizon, bringing with it a new day, the scene on the beach at Deal was revealed to those who still drew breath. Bodies littered the blood-soaked sand and floated in the gently lapping morning waves. The ship was gone, its cargo unloaded and placed on carts that had long since rolled away.

Christopher ignored the aches and pains that wracked every part of his body and stood still, his hands steepled together and pressed to his lips. To the ignorant, he might appear to be lost in prayer, but those who knew him knew that God would never deign to help a soul as black as his. At his feet lay the man who had challenged him, the ambitious fool's heart pierced with a foil, pinning the corpse to the beach.

An older man approached with a pronounced limp, his upper thigh sporting a bloody bandage. "A dozen lost," he reported.

"I want a list of their names."

"Aye. I'll see to it."

A soft touch came to his arm, and Christopher turned his head to find a young girl standing beside him.

"Yer bleeding," she whispered, her eyes big as saucers.

He lowered his gaze, noting for the first time that he had a deep gash in his biceps that bled profusely and soaked his tattered shirtsleeves.

"So I am," he said, extending his arm so that she could tie it off with the torn strips of linen in her hand.

He studied her as she worked, admiring how composed she was despite her youth. Grown men were vomiting over the scene before them, but she bore it stoically. Violence was not unknown to her.

"Did you lose anyone today, child?" he asked softly.

Her gaze stayed focused on her work. "My uncle."

"I am sorry."

She nodded.

He exhaled harshly and turned his head to watch the sunrise. Although his position here was once again secure, he would not leave immediately. He had known the battle itself would be short. The fortnight he anticipated was for the rest of it. It would take at least a sennight to visit every one of the families who had suffered a death today and ensure they would have the means to survive. A miserable task, with days on end of grief, but it had to be done.

Then, quite suddenly, the thought of Maria entered his head. Where it came from was a mystery. Christopher knew only that her memory straightened the weary curve of his spine and gave him a goal—a soft bed and her warm, curvy body pressed to his. To hold her, to relax with her, to experience that odd tightening in his chest that he found so discomfiting. It would be preferable to this . . . *nothing* he felt now.

Do you ever contemplate leaving this life?

He did not, even now in the midst of this ugliness. But for the first time, he contemplated a reprieve, one made possible by Maria.

It was God's punishment for his sins that in order to keep his life, he would have to extinguish his one pleasure in it.

Chapter 13

Maria tucked her legs up on the chaise and studied Tim as he drew pictures at the desk. The cottage Welton had secured for her was small but comfortable. Situated near the shore, it was a lovely retreat, the soft crashing of the waves an enchanting accompaniment to lazy activities.

Tim hummed some tune to himself as he worked, and Maria marveled again at how gentle he was in comparison to his massive size. He was kind and deeply loyal to St. John, a loyalty which he extended to her because he believed she was important to the pirate. It was that which most startled her. Yes, St. John had shown great interest in her, but she knew men well. Deep interest did not mean deep affection. She had something he wanted, and she placed no more stock in their relationship than that. Tim, however, seemed to think there was more to it, and something inside her longed to believe that was true.

She missed him, her pirate. How odd it was to care for him so quickly, but she did. At night she lay in her bed and longed for the feel of his muscled arms around her, his furred chest cushioning her cheek, his heated skin warming hers. Sometimes, if she closed her eyes, she imagined that she could smell him, that luscious scent of bergamot and virile, lustful male.

Most of all, she wished for the illusion of safety. Christopher made her feel protected. Simon, bless him, was content to allow her to rule everything. Sometimes, however, she wished to have someone else bear the burdens. Only for a little while. Not enough to make her dependent, but enough to give her a smidgeon of peace.

"Here," Tim said as he pushed heavily to his feet and lumbered toward her. He handed her the drawing and moved back to the desk to begin another.

Maria set aside the map she studied and the notes she made to Simon of where she wished him to search, and stared down at the sketch with awe.

"You have a gift," she said, admiring the beautiful lines and shadings that created a picture of an exceptionally handsome adolescent male. Exotic features and dark hair and irises gave him an alluring edge of danger that was obvious even with his youth. Thick hair grew too long and fell over his brow, framing those sensual eyes and a beautifully etched mouth.

"It's nothing," Tim dismissed gruffly, causing her to lift her gaze and catch his blush.

"And your memory is nothing short of miraculous. I noted this young man, too, and yet until I saw this likeness, I could not have described him to you. His features are too unique to make common comparisons, yet you captured them perfectly."

He growled his embarrassment, his gaze narrowing beneath unruly brows. She smiled and then looked at the pile of drawings beside her. Together, they created a tapestry of that night's events—the carriage, the governess, the groomsman, and the coachman. Next up was Amelia, and Maria was almost frightened to see it, uncertain of how she would react. She had seen her sister only a moment, and over the last three weeks, she'd found that the mental image of her was already dimming.

"You will fetch her back," Tim rumbled.

Blinking, Maria returned her attention to her guest. The fortnight was nearly over, much to her relief. Her injury had required inactivity to fully heal, but the indolent life was anathema to her. She'd paced the floor enough to circle the globe on foot. Distant command was not her style. She much preferred to be directing the action in the flesh. Thankfully, in two more days she would leave for London. Tim would then be returned to St. John, and she would recommit herself fully to her search. "Beg your pardon?"

"Yer sister," he elaborated. "You'll fetch her back."

Dear God. How did he know?

"Is St. John aware?" she asked softly, her mind racing at the possibilities. Amelia was her one vulnerability. Aside from Simon and Welton, no one else knew that.

"Not yet. You caught me before I had a chance to tell him."

She sighed with relief, though her heart still raced.

"I cannot take you back now," she advised.

Of course both of them knew that he could depart at any time he chose. Nothing short of leg irons would hold a man of his size against his will, and even that was uncertain.

"I knew that when I told you," he retorted simply.

"So why?" Maria frowned.

The giant tugged at his wiry beard and sat back in the chair that was nearly too small to hold him. "I was tasked that night with protecting you. I failed. If I guard you now, perhaps I can right that wrong."

"You cannot be serious!" But she could tell by the set of his shoulders that he was. "There was no way for us to know what would happen."

He snorted. "St. John did, or he wouldn't have sent us. He trusted me to act in his stead, and I wasn't worthy."

"Tim—"

Holding up a meaty hand, he cut her off. "There's no point in arguing. You want to keep me with you, and that's where I want to be. Nothing to piddle o'er."

Her mouth snapped closed. There was nothing she could say to that bit of logic.

"*Mhuirnín.*"

Maria looked over her shoulder to see Simon, who stepped into the room with his usual indolent grace. He was still dressed in his traveling clothes, having only recently returned from his long stay away. Under her detailed written directions, he'd taken a dozen men and swept the length of the southern coast, making the necessary inquiries in their search for Amelia.

"You have a visitor."

Immediately alert, she swung her legs to the floor and rose. She hurried to him and lowered her voice. "Who is it?"

He caught her elbow and led her out, tossing a guarded glance over his shoulder at Tim. Then he bent low and murmured, "Lord Eddington."

Her steps faltered and she gazed up at him with wide eyes. He shrugged to answer her unspoken question and continued to escort her to the parlor.

She was not dressed for visitors, but then, this was not a social call. Lifting her chin, she swept into the room with all the charm she possessed. She found she needed it as Eddington turned to her with a fulminating glare.

"You and I have much to discuss," he said in a clipped, angry tone.

Quite accustomed to overbearing males, Maria offered a brilliant smile and took a seat on the settee. "Lovely to see you, too, my lord."

"You will not think so in a moment."

"She walked up to him with a pistol, bold as you please, in the bright light of day."

Christopher grinned at the image Philip's words brought to mind of Tim being captured by the tiny Maria. In his chest, warmth spread along with his smile. Damned if he did not like the woman more and more each day. Even absence had not lessened his appreciation and desire for her. Her welfare was the first inquiry he had made that afternoon when

Philip arrived at the posting inn. There was much for him to be apprised of, too much to wait until he returned to London.

"It *was* quite amusing," Philip said, having taken note of Christopher's mirth.

"I wish I would have seen it." He lounged deeper into the squab, his gaze moving to the window where the scenery flew by. Crimson curtains were tied to the side, the deep red a touch of color in the otherwise black interior. "So Tim has remained with her."

"Yes, which is probably best. The Irishman has been absent since the second day of her holiday."

"Hmm . . ." The thought gave Christopher deep pleasure. It was unfamiliar, that writhing feeling of discontent he felt whenever he thought of Maria with Quinn. That she still cared for the Irishman was glaringly obvious. The only comfort Christopher had was her empty bed that she shared only with him.

The last thought heated his blood. There were times when he told himself that the sex could not be as good as he remembered. How could it be? Then there were times—in the evenings while lying abed—where he could almost feel her hands caressing his skin and hear her low voice purring provocative taunts.

"Are we close?" he asked, eager to reach his recuperating lover. If he were gentle, perhaps he could have her today. Lust rode him hard, goaded by his lengthening abstinence, but he could control it. He would not aggravate her healing injury.

"Yes, not much farther." Philip frowned, but said nothing, merely rubbed his palms against his gray velvet breeches. Christopher knew the boy well enough, however, to know something troubled him.

"What is it?"

Philip removed his spectacles and withdrew a kerchief from his pocket. While he cleaned non-existent smudges he said, "I am concerned about Lord Sedgewick. It has been over a month since he released you. Surely he will grow impatient with the mostly inane morsels we send to him."

Christopher considered Philip a moment, noting how much he had physically matured, a fact which was hidden behind his glasses. "Until I have that witness in hand, I can only bide my time. There is nothing I could have done differently that would have put me any further ahead than I am today."

"I agree. But how you proceed from here is what concerns me."

"Why?"

Philip returned his glasses to the bridge of his nose. "Because you have a *tendré* for the woman, I can tell."

"I have a *tendré* for a large number of women."

"But none of the others are in danger of losing their lives at your hands."

Christopher inhaled deeply and turned his gaze to the window again.

"And forgive me if I am wrong," his protégé continued, shifting nervously on the squab and clearing his throat, "but you appear to care more for Lady Winter than any of the other women you know."

"What gives you that impression?"

"All of the things you have done that have been out of character—the siege of her home, this trip to Brighton. Her household expects her home two days hence and yet you travel out of your way to be with her, as if you cannot bear to spend any more time apart than is absolutely necessary. How can you turn her over to Sedgewick under these circumstances?"

It was a question Christopher had been considering more and more of late. The woman had done nothing to him. She was simply a temptation he had approached in the theater and had pursued ever since. He knew nothing of her association with Lord Winter, but he knew she had not caused the death of Dayton maliciously. She grieved for the man, said she had loved him.

His throat clenched at the thought of Maria's affections engaged by another. What was she like when she loved? He had become deeply enamored with the woman who had put a footstool before him and kissed him with passion so hot it branded. Was that the Maria who had been wed to Dayton?

Lifting his hand to his chest, Christopher rubbed ineffectually at the tightness there. The woman had secrets, of that there was no doubt. But she was not evil and she meant him no harm. How, then, could he lead her to the gallows? He was not a good man. Regardless of his feelings for her, it disturbed him to exchange his life for the life of a person who was better than he was.

"Here we are," Philip murmured, pulling Christopher from his reverie.

He straightened, his sightless gaze focusing on the cottage they approached. They were still some distance away, far enough that the rolling of the carriage wheels could not be heard from the house but close enough for him to see the well-appointed equipage that waited in the drive.

Feeling that now-familiar sense of burning possessiveness, he rapped on the roof with his knuckles and called out to his coachman, "Stop here."

He descended and finished the journey to the house on foot, the rhythmically lapping waves on the nearby beach inciting an uncommon urgency in his steps. It was dusk, enabling him to hide his movements in the shadows. The low warble of a birdcall alerted him to the men he'd assigned to protecting Maria. He whistled back, but the sound cut off midway as he recognized the crest on the door of the coach.

Eddington.

A hundred thoughts ran through his mind at once. He paused a moment, breathing deeply to settle himself, then he circled the cottage, searching for a way to witness the activities inside.

Luck was with him. As he rounded the corner, light spilled

from an open window to illuminate the loam in a slanting pattern. He moved closer and found an unhindered view of Maria and Eddington engaged in what appeared to be a heated debate. Their enmity might have soothed him slightly had Maria been dressed appropriately. But she was not. Her gown was not one a woman would wear to receive a formal caller. And Quinn was not at home.

Christopher ran to the house, pressing his back to the wall and inching closer to the open sash.

"Must I remind you," Eddington bit out, his angry tones floating on the ocean breeze, "that I am paying you handsomely to provide a service to me. I am not paying you to take a holiday!"

"I have been ill," she said icily.

"So you cannot perform on your back, there are other ways to meet your obligation."

Fists and jaw clenched tight, Christopher experienced a raging of his blood such as he had never known. He'd felt murderous before, but never had the feeling been accompanied by pain in his heart and burning in his lungs.

"Don't be crude!" she snapped.

"I will be whatever I damn well please!" the earl roared. "I pay enough for the right."

"If it is so painful for you to part with coin, release me and find someone less expensive to see to your needs."

Despite the sounds of the surf, Christopher thought it might be possible to hear the grinding of his teeth, but he could not stop. It took every ounce of control he had to prevent entering through the window and beating Eddington to a bloody pulp. The only thing restraining him was the knowledge that Maria's trust could not be taken by force. She had to extend it freely.

He moved away, his mind rapidly disseminating his association with the notorious seductress. She was embroiled in something vastly unpleasant, seemingly against her will, yet she had not sought assistance. He was her lover, a wealthy one at that, and he would help her if she asked, but Maria was too accustomed to dealing with matters on her own.

Hardening his aching heart, Christopher refused to feel discarded or forgotten or to blame her for acting in self-preservation. She was an intelligent woman. She could learn, and he would teach her. Kindness. Tenderness. How much of either had she ever been shown in her life? He, perhaps, was not the best man to approach for such things, but he was capable of learning, too. He would find a way to open himself to her, so that she could feel safe opening herself to him.

So he departed as swiftly as he had come. He returned to his carriage as a different man than the one who had left—somber still, but now leaden with an introspective shroud that Philip was wise enough not to disturb.

Maria paced the length of her room with a swift, agitated stride, her dressing gown swirling around her legs.

"Where are you?" she grumbled, her gaze moving once again to the open window, waiting impatiently for her golden-haired paramour to appear. She had been home for two days now and knew from her spy in the St. John household that Christopher was at home as well, yet he did not come to her. She'd sent him a missive that morning to no avail. He had not replied, nor had he appeared.

Here she had rushed home and hurriedly bathed the dirt of travel away in preparation for his visit, only to cool her heels for days. Deep in her chest an ache blossomed and grew.

Christopher might have lost interest in her while she was away. While she had considered that possibility, the realization wounded her in a way she could not have prepared for.

She paused at the window, looking down, seeing no movement. Her eyes closed on a harshly indrawn breath. He owed her nothing, yet she was angered at the hurt he had inflicted. She was furious that he had not given her the courtesy of a simple farewell. Even one written on paper, rather than spoken in person, would have been preferable to this silent dismissal.

Damned if she would allow him to treat her like this! She had bared herself in that note, made it clear how she wished for his company. It pained her to think of it, how deeply attached to the man she had become. To seek him out, to beg his attentions.

To be discarded without a word.

Seething, Maria disrobed and then called for Sarah to assist her with re-dressing. She donned crimson silk and then took a moment to apply a heart-shaped patch just above the corner of her mouth. Slipping her dagger into the hidden sheath in her gown, she then ordered her carriage brought around. Every moment that passed intensified the burning in her blood. She was spoiling for a row, and by God, the pirate would indulge her whether he wished to or not.

Outriders surrounded her coach as they left the relative safety of Mayfair for the squalor of St. Giles, which served as home to beggars, thieves, prostitutes . . . and her lover. She sat in the unlit comfort of her carriage and felt her ire simmer dangerously. By the time she arrived at the pirate's home, she was a menace waiting to be unleashed, a fact that must have been obvious. Her calling card was accepted from her footman, and she was escorted from the carriage into the foyer without delay.

"Where is he?" she asked with ominous softness, ignoring the large group of both men and women who filtered from various rooms to watch her.

The butler swallowed hard. "I will inform him of your arrival, Lady Winter."

One finely arched brow rose. "I can announce myself, thank you. Tell me where to go."

The servant opened his mouth, shut it, opened it again, then finally said with a sigh, "Follow me, my lady."

Maria took the staircase like a queen, her head held high, her shoulders squared. She might be a lover scorned, but she refused to act the part.

A moment later she swept into the room opened by the butler and paused inside, her heart in her throat. A jerking wave of her hand to signal for the closing of the door was all she could manage.

Christopher lounged before the fire in a state of semiundress, his feet and throat bare, his torso free of both waistcoat and coat. His head was leaned back, his brilliant blue gaze hidden in repose. Such a beautiful yet deadly creature. Even now, furious as she was, he affected her as no other man ever had.

"Christopher," Maria called quietly, her throat so tight at the sight of him that her voice came out as barely more than a whisper.

A slow smile curved his lips, but his eyes remained closed. "Maria," he purred. "You came."

"And you did not come. Although I asked for you and I waited."

He finally looked at her, his gaze narrowed and considering. "Is it so terribly wrong for me to wish you to make the effort to reach out to me?"

"I no longer have time for your games, St. John. I came for what you owe me—a clean severance."

She turned to depart, only to find that she had miscalculated. Christopher moved swiftly, pinning her to the door with his body.

"This is no game," he rasped with his lips to her ear.

Maria made every attempt to ignore the longed-for feel of his hard, muscled frame. He towered over her, his heated breath gusting intimately against the crown of her head. When he rolled his hips against her, she collected what he was telling her. It was impossible to feel him through the masses of underskirts and skirts, but there was no doubt he was aroused.

She fought off the flare of pleasure the knowledge gave her and said coldly, "Why then did you not come to me?"

Christopher moved, his hands leaving the paneled door to boldly cup the upper swell of her breasts. His powerful legs kept her pressed to the door as he fondled her. "I always come to you, Maria. I needed to know that you would seek me out in return."

She sucked in a breath as desire, hot and insistent, flared at his words. But he had made a grave error in judgment by freeing her hands and a second later he knew it. She sank the veriest tip of her blade into his upper thigh.

He pushed away from her with a curse, and she spun to face him, her hand reaching behind her and thumbing the lock.

A tiny spot of blood spread around the hole in his breeches. "Do you draw weapons on Eddington, as well?" he asked softly. "Or does his coin spare him?"

Maria paused with her blade held in front of her. "How does Eddington signify?"

"That is my enquiry." He nonchalantly drew his shirt over his head, revealing the golden expanse of his rippling abdomen. His bare chest had healing cuts and his ribs bore yellowed bruises. Her throat tightened at the sight of his many injuries, her heart pained at her contribution to the marring of such masculine beauty. He tore at the linen, ripping a strip long enough to tie around his muscled leg. "Are we familiar enough yet to share such secrets?"

"Is Eddington the cause of your refusal?" she asked, her stomach churning at the knowledge that he was aware of her continuing association with the earl.

Christopher crossed his arms and shook his head. "No. I speak the truth to you, Maria, because that is what I want from you in return. I want to support you. Help you. If only you will allow me that right."

His tone was so low, his gaze so earnest that she was arrested by him and the feelings he was engendering. Her dagger fell from nerveless fingers to thud on the floor.

"And what rights will you grant me?" she asked, her chest lifting and falling rapidly.

"What rights would you prefer?" Christopher stepped close again, lowering his head to swipe his tongue across her parted lips. "You could have gone to Quinn or Eddington tonight. Instead you came to me despite your anger. I have something you want, Maria. Tell me what it is, so that I may give it to you."

The last was said with a distant ache in his tone, which he quickly covered by taking her mouth in a deep, possessive kiss. His hands came up to cup her shoulders, pulling her fractionally closer.

Yet even as Maria realized that she had the power to hurt him, she also understood that he had the power to wound her in return. And he was doing it so well, weakening her with his kindness and seeming lack of guile.

"Perhaps all I want from you is sex," she said coldly, her lips moving against his. "You have a body built for sin and a mind well-schooled on how to use it."

His grip tightened, betraying a direct hit. It was deeply unpleasant to know that she had deliberately hurt him in order to protect herself, but she could think of no other way to act. This side of Christopher was far too dangerous. She could manage herself around the coarse pirate. She was not confident in her ability to survive the charms of the impassioned, gentle lover who was appearing more often. The rough seduction of their first sexual encounter had softened to these liaisons of sweet kisses, intimate recollections, and admissions of yearning for the other's company. If she trusted him, it would be a romance. Since his motives were suspect, it felt like a siege, and she could not afford to be conquered when the safety of Amelia was the prize.

"You want my cock," he whispered, "so I shall service you

with it. You have only to ask for what you need. I am prepared and more than willing to provide it. In bed, or out."

Her eyes closed, shielding her thoughts. She wished she had
the strength to set aside her longing and focus solely on the task
at hand, but the quivering in her limbs told her it was best to
flee while she was still able. The information Welton and
Eddington wanted would have to be gleaned by other means.
She would find a way, she always had.

"Undress me," she whispered, firm in her intent.

"As you wish." His tongue traced the shell of her ear,
making her shiver. "Turn your back to me."

Maria took a deep breath, and did as he asked.

Chapter 14

Christopher's fists clenched tightly as Maria presented the row of tiny buttons that coursed down her spine. He fought with his hands, ordering them to cease their trembling. He ached for her tenderness, some sign that she cared for him beyond his sexual prowess.

Why had she come? Why send him that note, so sweetly worded? Perhaps he was indeed a pleasure to her. He hated the part of him that said, *That is enough. Take what she will give you.* Because it was not enough. It could no longer be merely sex between them. He could not share her bed knowing that he was excluded from sharing the rest of her life.

"Have you changed your mind?" she murmured, glancing over her shoulder when he hesitated too long.

He stared at the heart-shaped patch near her mouth and longed to kiss it. The scent of her filled his nostrils, more heady than liquor. "No."

Christopher began the difficult task of unveiling her lush body, peeling back the yards of material that separated them. He was accomplished in the art of undressing a woman, but never had his hands shaken during the task.

Slowly, he managed, and the back of the crimson gown gaped open, the rich color a stunning contrast to her olive skin. His head lowered, his tongue traveling along the top of her shoulder. He felt her shiver and knew he would perform the same service to the rest of her. He would tug on her nipples with the hot suction of his mouth, then spread her legs wide and lick inside her. She would beg for surcease, arching and writhing beneath him. By the time he was done with her, no other man would satisfy and she would know what he had felt these last days—starved before a banquet and yet unable to eat.

He pushed aside the left flap of the red garment, his gaze arrested by the puckered pink scar left by the knife wound. His eyes closed against the emotions that moved through him. Then he felt the raised line of flesh beneath his fingertips, his hand having lifted without conscious direction. Maria gasped at the touch.

"Does it still pain you?" he asked, opening his eyes to watch his movements.

For a long moment she said nothing, then she nodded.

"I will be gentle," he promised.

"No," she argued breathlessly, "you will be on your back."

The memories her words envoked were so powerful, he shuddered. How many times had he relived their one night together, her above him, her nipple in his mouth, her cunt sucking his cock until he came in a pulsating rush that left him gasping and drained. That he was moments away from experiencing the same ecstasy made his balls draw up tight and ache to be emptied. He was desperate to be one with her. In body, in passion. To fuck her harder, faster, and deeper than she had ever been fucked before and to have her pay him in kind. Have her respond with a similar wildness of need and hunger. For him.

Only him.

"Hurry," she urged, her body rigid.

Christopher paused, understanding that she felt vulnerable, knowing that the change in the rules of the game had her wary and slightly frightened. He was uncertain as well, taking tentative steps as he trod new ground, never having bared himself in such a manner before.

So he deviated slightly, gripping the back of her gown and rending it open with a quick, hard tear. She stepped out of the remnants and faced him, her waist hugged by a corset, her legs lost in her skirts.

"Discard your breeches," she ordered, "and lie on the bed."

He studied her as his hands moved leisurely to do as she bade. She wanted control. He would give it to her, showing her by example that he was willing to put himself in her hands, if she would do the same for him. "I want you naked, as well."

"Later."

Nodding, Christopher freed his cock and shoved his breeches down. Maria's gaze dropped to his erection, goading him to take it in hand and pump it, bringing his seed to slip out over the head.

"See what you do to me?" he asked, holding his cock out to her like an offering.

What looked like sadness drifted across her delicate features. A low moan escaped him as he continued to masturbate for her view. Pleasure coiled around his spine and made his cock swell further.

"I have been too long without you, Maria. Did you miss me the same?"

"I wrote to you."

"Will you punish me for desiring some sign of your affection? For wanting you to visit me in my bed, rather than the reverse?"

"Stop," she said hoarsely, her gaze riveted to his industrious hands. "I want you hard and thick inside me, not spent."

Christopher dropped his hands to his sides, leaving his cock reddened, weeping seed, and curving upward. This was entirely new to him, this forfeit of power. He doubted he could do this for anyone else. A lesser woman would not have the deep-rooted command required to take the control from him. Even Emaline, with all of her vast experience, hadn't been able to master him in the bedroom. It was why she some-times serviced him herself instead of granting him the use of one—or more—of her girls. She occasionally needed the lux-ury of simply being fucked rather than being the one to do all the work.

So he waited, his breathing harsh, his skin misted with sweat. The anticipation rose, charging the air, inciting him further. Sex could be boring if the action lulled. That was not the case now. The space between him and Maria filled with a palpable energy, just as it always had.

"Have you changed your mind?" he prodded, tossing her words back at her.

Her brow arched. "Perhaps I am not ready."

His brow rose to match hers; he knew she was lying by the high flush on her chest and cheeks, and the rapid lift and fall of her breasts. He knew she was wet, knew that watching him pleasure himself had also pleasured her. "I can make you ready," he offered solicitously.

For a moment she did not move, his dark-haired temptress with her creamy skin and deep red lips. Her chemise, corset, and underskirts were white, hinting at an angelic image that was ruined by those knowing eyes with their impossibly thick lashes. He could see her delicious nipples through the sheer cotton, and his mouth watered with the urge to suck on them. The tiny heart-shaped patch teased him to kiss that lush mouth, to slide his cock into it and thrust until he burst. More cum beaded on the tip of his cock and slid down the burning, pulsing skin of his shaft.

"Would you allow me to take you with my mouth?" he asked. "It would please me to make love to you that way."

Her gaze darkened at his choice of wording and her lips parted on panting breaths. She nodded and stepped past him, her skirts swaying with her agitated stride. There was no hes-itation in her. When she was decided, she never looked back.

He followed, his brain in a fog of lust and deep yearning. She took a seat on the settee, her back ramrod straight. The pose was prim, until she hooked one knee over the curved wooden armrest and pulled back the masses of white material, baring first her beautifully curved calves, then her lithe thighs, and finally, the silken heaven between her legs.

Christopher growled low in his throat, sinking to his knees without preamble, his large hands cupping her inner thighs and spreading her so wide that nothing was hidden from him. She was slick and hot, as he had known she would be. Luscious Maria, the Wintry Widow. Except when she was with him. Then she melted.

"I love to see you this way," he confessed. "Open to me, willing and craving."

Dipping his head, he licked up the seam of her sex, relishing the hiss of pleasure that escaped from between her teeth. After this night, she would never forget him. She would lie in her bed, remembering the feel of his mouth upon her, and long for the pleasure only he could provide.

He surrounded her with his lips, his tongue flickering over the tight knot of her clitoris with light, teasing strokes. Her fingers drifted into his hair, caressing the sweat-dampened roots, her back arching into the intimate caress with a startled cry. He held her hips down, the circle of his mouth creating a soft suction that intensified her thrashing and brought her to harsh, panting breaths.

"Christopher! Dear God . . ."

She bowed upward, her grip in his hair painful but welcome. He dipped lower, thrust his tongue inside her, felt how tight and drenched she was, how deeply he affected her. Grateful that he could, because he was undone, his body trembling with need and tortured desire.

He moved upward again, sucking the hard bed of nerves in an unfaltering rhythm, forcing her to take what he gave her, forcing her to see what they had—a deep affinity that grew more precious to him by the day.

Her orgasm nearly prompted his, her cunt clenching around

his tongue as he drove it into her repeatedly. He didn't stop, refusing her attempts to push him away, his mouth working her, taking her, making her cry out in climax again. And again, until neither one of them could take any more.

He rose, gripping the gilded lip of the settee back with one hand and aiming his cock at her slit with the other.

His penetrating lunge into her body rocked the settee to its rear legs, the brutal jolt wringing a curse from him and a breathless cry from her. Christopher paused a moment, his eyes squeezed shut as her cunt rippled around him in the final throes of orgasm. Only when she lay quivering in the aftermath did he risk looking at her.

"This is heaven," he gasped. "I want to live inside you, feel you suck me deeper and deeper until we are one."

Maria stared up at the golden god who caged her so thoroughly and wondered how the events of the evening had spun so far out of her control. She was tender and swollen, oversensitive and stuffed full of rock-hard cock. His hands gripped the sofa on either side of her head, his lean hips cradled in the apex of her thighs, his rippled abdomen clenched tight and dripping sweat onto the pile of skirts gathered at her waist.

He stared down at her with open lust and affection, shaking the very foundations of her life. How could she give this up? She whimpered as Christopher's cock throbbed inside her. In this position she had no leverage, and his impressive endowments felt almost too huge to be comfortable. He withdrew and she spasmed around him, her body unwilling to give up the pleasure of his. Then, using his muscular legs to push forward and his arms to pull the settee downward, he lunged into her again, hitting the end of her, his heavy balls slapping erotically against her bottom.

Maria moaned helplessly. Her only recourse was to clutch his waist and brace herself for his thrusts, which grew in strength and speed until the private sitting room echoed with the unmistakable sounds of hard fucking. Her cries rose in volume, competing with the rhythmic banging of the sofa legs against the floor and the curses that rasped from Christopher's throat every time he sank into her.

His cock was thick, long, and hot, and he conquered her with it, seduced her with it, giving her exactly what she wanted. And exactly what she could not have.

It was raw, passionate sex. Lust tempered by far deeper emotions. Her gaze was riveted by the display of his clenching abdomen and the glistening length of his cock as it worked in and out of her with brilliant precision. The question of whether the memories of their first night together were embellished or not was answered. Christopher St. John was an expert lover, even when rutting at a fevered pitch. He plunged high and hard, hitting that spot inside her that had her toes curling.

"Yes!" he growled when she whimpered in near delirium, his raspy voice filled with pure masculine satisfaction, his gaze hot as he watched her fall apart beneath him.

Dear God, he was devastating her, making her care when she couldn't.

"No!" she cried, frightened by the feelings he evoked, her hands pushing ineffectually at his straining shoulders. "Stop!" She beat at him with her fists until she penetrated his single-minded focus.

He thrust deep and stilled, his chest heaving, his thighs quivering between hers.

"What?" he managed between labored breaths. "What is it?"

"Get off me."

"Are you *insane*?" Then something flickered over his features, his gaze lowered. Before she knew his intent, his head dropped, his lips pressing a lingering kiss to her puckered scar. "Am I hurting you?"

Maria swallowed hard, her heart beating so desperately it

felt like it could burst. "Yes." He was killing her, breaking her.

"Christ." His sweat-covered forehead pressed to hers, his harsh exhales gusting across her face.

Inside her, he throbbed. Her body, uncaring about anything other than climax, sucked at his cock, luring it deeper.

He inhaled deeply, then knelt on the edge of the seat and thrust his arms beneath her back, embracing her. He struggled to his feet with her clasped tightly to him, impaled on his rigid cock. How he made into the next room and the bed, Maria would never understand.

Christopher sat on the edge and then fell back, keeping her atop him. "You ride," he said hoarsely. "Take your pleasure from me in a way that will not pain you."

Maria nearly cried.

Her fingers clenched convulsively into the velvet counterpane. Who knew the infamous pirate could be so sweet, so caring? The fierce look on his handsome face reminded her of who he was—a notorious criminal who survived in a brutal underworld by his wits and lack of conscience. But here he was, subjugating his raging needs for hers . . . offering himself to her, to do with as she willed . . .

"Maria," he breathed, his hands on her thighs, his eyes staring up into hers. "Take me."

Dazed by his generosity, Maria moved as if in a dream. She lifted, relishing the feel of the heavy length of his cock slipping wetly from her and the hiss of his breath between clenched teeth as she lowered again. Christopher remained still, as he had promised, giving her the lead. The only movement he made was the ticcing of a muscle in his jaw.

She watched him as she rode him, enamoured with the sight of him. How beautiful he was! Even bruised and battered, he was a woman's deepest, most wicked fantasy. His face—so angelic in its golden coloring and unrivaled perfection—looked enticingly devilish when unkempt. His body—

long and heavily muscled—looked no less appealing when leaner. His eyes—those deep blue pools—were irresistible when filled with sexual promises and heated affection.

Her fingertips drifted across his brows, then brushed lightly along the lines of cynicism that fanned out from the corners of his eyes and mouth.

"Yes," he crooned, holding her waist lightly to balance her. "Love me as you will."

Maria bent and pressed a lingering kiss to his lips, soaking up the low groan he gave. This was the last time she would have him like this. The last time she would touch him in this manner and admire him naked. Even as her heart ached at the loss of what she wished they could have, she felt warmth blossom in her chest at the opportunity to say good-bye to him properly. When she left here tonight, she would have closure. It was why she had come, and she was grateful to leave with it.

So she took her time, her lips following her fingertips as they brushed over every flaw. Every cut, scratch, and bruise. His big body twisted beneath her, the muscles in his arms bulging as his hands fisted in the counterpane, helpless to their passion. Just as she was.

"Maria!" he gasped as her tongue played with his nipple. "I must come, love. Come with me."

She nipped him with her teeth and he cursed.

"Please!"

Her mouth covered his, her lips wet and soft against the firm line of his. Christopher groaned and thrashed more, twisting.

"I want this to last," she breathed, never wanted to stop, never wanting to lose the feeling of him stroking inside her, plunging deep and hard.

"Take it," he urged, the crests of his cheekbones flagged with high color. "Take me."

After a moment's hesitation, she nodded.

Her eyes slid closed as she pumped faster and stronger, plunging her cunt up and down his thick cock.

Christopher's powerful body arched, his neck corded with strain, his hands steadied her as she fucked him frantically, his golden head tossing from side to side as she rode him to the finish.

"Maria," he moaned. "Maria."

Bending at the waist, she took his mouth again, kissing him ravenously, her eyes stinging with the fervor with which he kissed her back. Her skin was so hot, feverish, covered in a fine film of perspiration. She ached to climax, to hear his cries, to feel him explode inside her.

Settling her hands on his chest for leverage, Maria lifted and fell in measured rhythm, feeling his great size stretching her, forcing her slick tissues to part and accept him. Her passion rose, her climax primed from his mouth and his blatant expertise. She was so wet with pleasure and desire that soft sucking noises filled the air.

Christopher moved with her in perfect timing, his hips rising to meet her every descent, falling on every ascent.

"Yes . . . Maria . . . dear God . . . *yes!*"

He thrust upward hard, his pelvic bone hitting her swollen clitoris, and she cried out in orgasm, unable to stop it, her body quaking around his wildly pumping cock.

He growled his triumph, and the sound flowed through her, making her come harder, her cunt spasming desperately as he joined her, spurting his seed deep inside her in hot, hard bursts.

She fell over him in a tangle of sated limbs, whimpering as he held her hips slightly aloft and continued to stroke his cock inside her until he was emptied.

Finally, gasping, he released her waist to clutch her tightly to his sweat-slick chest.

Maria pressed her fist to her mouth and stifled the sob that fought to leave her. She feared her feelings had already progressed too far. She wanted to remain like this forever, warm and safe in Christopher's embrace. But how much of this was real? How much of this was simply an effort to achieve his goal? Was Christopher truly the haven he presented himself as? Or was he the means of her destruction?

There were too many questions and no definitive answers. With Amelia's life in the balance, Maria could not take the risk.

And so she waited until his breathing was deep and even beneath her cheek, betraying his slumber. Then she extricated herself from his embrace and left the bed.

"Farewell," she whispered, her gaze raking the naked, magnificent length of his frame before she turned her back to him and made her egress. The bedchamber door shut behind her with a soft click of the latch.

Stepping into her ruined gown in the sitting room with shaking legs, she collected her blade and donned Christopher's coat, refusing to breathe through her nose for fear of smelling him. She would cry if she did, and there was still some distance to be crossed.

She remembered nothing of her journey down the stairs and out the front door. Was she watched? Had she garnered an audience? Did Christopher's lackeys witness her dishabille? She did not know, and she did not care. She knew only that she maintained her pride.

Until she was safely ensconced in her carriage. Then she allowed her tears to fall.

The silence of the night was broken by the approaching clatter of horses' hooves and the rhythmic sound of carriage wheels across cobblestones. Mist hung low to the ground, chilling the feet and legs of the man who hunched his shoulders and held his threadbare jacket close to his neck for warmth.

As the equipage rolled to a stop, the man stepped forward

and peered inside. The interior of the unmarked coach was darker than the outside, effectively hiding the occupants.

"Two daughters," he whispered. "St. John's coves found the one. Young gel in Lincolnshire."

"I require the direction."

"When I works wiv a flash, I get paid."

The barrel of a pistol appeared.

"Right, then." He dug in his pocket and withdrew a grimy, folded sheet, which he held out. "If you read it, I'll tell yer if 'e got the way of it."

A moment later, he nodded. "That's it. Bobby is a peevy cull."

A bag of coin was thrust out and grabbed with similar swiftness. "God love yer!" he mumbled with a tip of his hat, then he melded into the shadows and was gone.

The coachman urged the carriage on.

In the darkness of the interior, Eddington settled pensively into the squabs. "Bring me that girl before St. John takes her."

"Yes, my lord. I will see to it."

Chapter 15

Amelia peeked around the corner of the house, her lower lip worried between her teeth. She searched for Colin in the stable yard, then heaved a sigh of relief when she found the area empty. Male voices drifted on the wind, laughter and singing spilling out from the stables. From this she knew Colin was hard at work with his uncle, which meant that she could safely leave the manse and head into the woods.

She was becoming quite good at subterfuge, she thought as she moved deftly through the trees, hiding from the occasional guard in her journey toward the fence. A fortnight had passed since that fateful afternoon when she had caught Colin behind the shop with that girl. Amelia had avoided him since, refusing to speak with him when he asked the cook to fetch her.

Perhaps it was foolish to hope that she would never see him again, given how closely their lives were entwined. If so, she was a fool. There was not an hour of the day that passed without her thinking of him, but she managed the pain of her grief as long as he stayed away from her. She saw no reason for them to meet, to talk, to acknowledge one another. She only traveled by carriage when moving to a new home, and even then, she could associate exclusively with Pietro, the coachman.

Espying the waited-for opening, Amelia hopped deftly over the fence and ran to the stream, where she found Ware coatless and wigless with his shirtsleeves pushed up. The young earl had caught some color to his skin these last weeks, setting aside his life of bookwork in favor of hard outdoor play. With his dark brown locks tied in a queue and his cornflower-colored eyes smiling, he was quite handsome, his aquiline features boasting centuries of pure blue blood.

He did not set her heart to racing or make her ache in unfamiliar places as Colin did, but Ware was charming and polite and attractive. She supposed that was a sufficient combination of qualities to make him the recipient of her first kiss. Miss Pool told her to wait until the right young man came along, but Colin already had, and had turned to another instead.

"Good afternoon, Miss Benbridge," the earl greeted with a perfect bow.

"My lord," she replied, lifting the sides of her rose-hued gown before curtsying.

"I have a treat for you today."

"Oh?" Her eyes widened in anticipation. She loved gifts and surprises because she rarely received them. Her father simply could not be bothered to consider such things as birthdays or other gift-giving occasions.

Ware's smile was indulgent. "Yes, princess." He offered his arm to her. "Come with me."

Amelia set her fingers lightly atop his forearm, enjoying the opportunity to practice her social graces with someone. The earl was kind and patient, pointing out any errors and correcting her. It gave her a higher polish and a deeper confidence. She no longer felt like a girl pretending to be a lady. Instead she felt like a lady who chose to enjoy her youth.

Together they left their meeting place by the stream and wended their way along the shore until they reached a larger clearing. There Amelia was delighted to find a blanket stretched out on the ground, the corner of which was held down by a basket filled with delicious-smelling tarts and various cuts of meat and cheeses.

"How did you manage this?" she breathed, filled with pleasure by his thoughtfulness.

"Dear Amelia," he drawled, his eyes twinkling. "You know who I am now, and who I will be. I can manage anything."

She knew the rudiments of the peerage and saw the power wielded by her father, a viscount. How many more times the magnitude was the power wielded by Ware, whose future held a marquessate?

Her eyes widened at the thought.

"Come now," he urged, "have a seat, enjoy a peach tart, and tell me about your day."

"My life is dreadfully boring," she said, dropping to the ground with a sigh.

"Then tell me a tale. Surely you daydream about something."

She dreamt about kisses given passionately by a dark-eyed Gypsy lover, but she would never say such a thing aloud. She rose to her knees and dug into the basket to hide her blush. "I lack imagination," she muttered.

"Very well, then." Ware situated himself on his back with his hands clasped at his neck and stared up at the sky. He looked as at ease as she had ever seen him. Despite the rather formal attire he wore—including pristine white stockings and polished heels—he was still a far more relaxed person than the one she met weeks ago. Amelia found that she rather liked the new earl and felt a touch of pleasure that she had wrought what she considered to be a positive change in him.

"It appears I must regale you with a story," he said.

"Lovely." She settled back to a seated position and took a bite of her treat.

"Once upon a time—"

Amelia watched Ware's lips move as he spoke and imagined kissing them. A now-familiar sense of sadness shivered through her, an effect of leaving her beloved romantic notions behind and embracing unfamiliar new ones, but the sensation lessened as she thought of Colin and what he had done. He certainly did not feel any sadness about leaving her behind.

"Would you kiss me?" she blurted, her fingertips brushing tart crumbs from the corners of her lips.

The earl paused midsentence and turned his head to look at her. His eyes were wide with surprise, but he appeared more intrigued than dismayed. "Beg your pardon. Did I hear you correctly?"

"Have you kissed a girl before?" she asked, curious. He was two years older than she was, only one year younger than Colin. It was quite possible that he had experience.

Colin had an edgy, dark restlessness about him that was seductive even to her naïve senses. Ware, on the other hand, was far more leisurely, his attractiveness stemming from innate command and the comfort of knowing the world was his for the taking. Still, despite her high regard for Colin, she could see how Ware's lazy charm appealed.

His eyebrows rose. "A gentleman does not speak of such things."

"How wonderful! Somehow, I knew you would be discreet." She smiled.

"Repeat the request again," he murmured, watching her carefully.

"Would you kiss me?"

"Is this a hypothetical question, or a call to action?"

Suddenly shy and unsure, Amelia looked away.

"Amelia," he said softly, bringing her gaze back to his. There was deep kindness there on his handsome patrician features, and she was grateful for it. He rolled to his side and then pushed up to a seated position.

"Not hypothetical," she whispered.

"Why do you wish to be kissed?"

She shrugged. "Because."

"I see." His lips pursed a moment. "Would Benny suffice? Or a footman?"

"No!"

His mouth curved in a slow smile that made something flutter in her belly. It was not an outright flip, as was caused by Colin's dimples, but it was certainly a herald of her new awareness of her friend.

"I will not kiss you today," he said. "I want you to think upon it further. If you feel the same when next we meet, I will kiss you then."

Amelia wrinkled her nose. "If you have no taste for me, simply say so."

"Ah, my hotheaded princess," he soothed, his hand catching hers, his thumb stroking the back. "You jump to conclusions just as you jump into trouble—with both feet. I will catch you, fair Amelia. I look forward to catching you."

"Oh," she breathed, blinking at the suggestive undertone to his words.

"Oh," he agreed.

By the time she headed for home, her belly delectably full of delicacies, she was confident in her decision to kiss the charming earl. He had agreed to meet her the next day, and she made mental preparations for the repeating of her bold request and then the result of it. If it went well, she intended to ask for another favor—the posting of a note.

To Maria.

"What mischief are you planning now?" Cook asked as Amelia snuck in through the service door in her continuing effort to hide from Colin.

"I never plan mischief," Amelia cried, settling her hands on her hips in a great show of affront. Why did everyone think she sought trouble?

Cook snorted and narrowed her wizened gaze. "Yer too old for troublemaking."

Amelia broke out in a wide grin. That was the first time anyone had told her she was too old to do something, rather than too young.

"Thank you!" she cried before kissing the servant's cheek and running up the stairs.

As far as days went, this one had been nearly perfect.

Christopher's fingers drummed a rapid staccato against the desktop. He stared out his study window, his mind in as much turmoil as his body.

Maria had left him. Although she was gone when he awoke and therefore said nothing of her intent to him, he knew she meant for their affair to be over.

He'd nearly gone after her immediately, but in the end he held back, knowing that he required a plan to proceed. He could not charge ahead and risk damaging their relations further.

Now, hours after waking, he was relieved when a knock came to his study door, grateful for a brief respite. Calling out for the person to enter, he watched as the portal swung open and Philip stepped into the room.

"Good afternoon," the young man greeted.

Christopher smiled wryly. "Is it?"

"I think so. You might agree, after you hear what I have to relay."

"Oh?"

Philip took a seat across from him. "Lady Winter was not intimate with Lord Eddington in Brighton, or at any other time."

Curious, Christopher asked, "Why tell me this?"

"Because I thought you would wish to know." Philip frowned. "If you had known before she sought you out, the evening might have progressed differently."

"Would I have wanted it to progress in another way?"

Philip began to squirm slightly as he became more confused. "I thought you might. You have been rather brooding since she left, and while I was asleep at the time, I have heard from others that Lady Winter did not look well when she departed."

"What purpose does it serve for me to know that she was not intimate with Eddington in Brighton?" Christopher leaned back in his chair.

"I've no notion," Philip muttered. "If you see no use for the information, there is nothing further to discuss."

"Very well," Christopher said dryly. "Allow me to rephrase. What would *you* do with the information, were you in my place?"

"But I am not in your place."

"Humor me."

Taking a shaky breath, Philip said, "I am not certain if Eddington's association with Lady Winter is the cause of your recent bout of melancholia, but—"

"I do *not* have melancholia," Christopher bit out.

"Um . . . Yes. Wrong word. 'Decline' might be better?" Philip risked a glance at Christopher's face and winced. "In any case, if Lady Winter and Lord Eddington were the cause, and I were to learn that they spent very little time together, I would conclude that perhaps they are not engaged in any lascivious activities."

"A reasonable conclusion."

"Yes, well . . ." Philip cleared his throat. "Therefore, since the events would make little sense to me, I would go to Lady Winter and ask her to clarify."

"She has never once told me a secret of hers," Christopher said. "That is our primary point of contention."

"Well . . . she did write to you. She came to you. I would consider that a positive sign."

Christopher snorted. "If only that were true. She came to say good-bye."

"But you do not have to say it in reply, do you?" Philip asked.

"No. However, it would be best if I did. For both of us."

Philip shrugged. *You know better than I.* That was his protégé's message. But it was tempered by an unspoken admonishment. His lieutenant did not believe he had exhausted all of his options, and Christopher supposed he was correct about that.

"Thank you, Philip," he dismissed. "I appreciate your concern and candor."

Philip made his egress with obvious relief.

Christopher rose and stretched, his body aching from muscles strained by Maria's passion. By God, the woman had ridden him to the best orgasm of his life, but the climax had been bittersweet. He had felt her withdrawal even as she opened herself as she never had before.

"Maria," he breathed, moving to the window where he could look out at the street below. She had come here to this cesspool in search of him. Christopher's forehead pressed against the glass, the heat of his skin misting the pane, the unanswered queries in his mind tormenting him.

There was no real need for the answers. Their relationship, such as it was, had nowhere to go. It was best that it end so miserably. Their estrangement should make it easier to do what he must—wrap her up in a pretty bow and deliver her to Sedgewick.

Why pursue the connection?

A knock sounded behind him, then, "Lord Sedgewick has come to call."

The irony almost made him laugh.

It took him a moment to collect himself, to lift his head from the glass and return to his desk. He nodded his readiness and waited for the viscount to enter.

"My lord," he greeted dryly, refusing to rise.

Sedgewick's lips whitened at the insult and then he sank into the seat Philip had recently vacated, crossing one ankle over to the opposite knee as if this were a social call.

"Do you have any information for me or not?" the viscount snapped. "You and Lady Winter were both gone a fortnight. Surely you learned something during that time."

"You assume we were together."

Sedgewick's gaze narrowed. "You were not?"

"No." Christopher smiled as the other man's face reddened. "Why such haste?" he asked, taking a pinch of snuff from the box on his desk with deliberate leisure. "It has been years since the deaths. What are a few weeks more?"

"My schedule is none of your concern."

Studying the peer with a trained eye, Christopher hummed softly. "You want something, a higher position within the agency, perhaps? And the length of time you have to acquire it grows short, yes?"

"What grows short is my patience. It is not one of my virtues."

"Do you have any virtues?"

"More so than you." Sedgewick rose. "A sennight, no more. Then back to Newgate you go, and I will find another to take up the task you seem not to be capable of."

Christopher knew he could end this now. He could promise to deliver a witness who would implicate Maria. But the words would not come. "Good day, my lord," he said instead, his nonchalance infuriating the foppish viscount, who then left the room in his profusion of lace and jewels.

A week. Christopher rolled his tense shoulders back and knew the time had come to make a decision. Shortly, the men he had assigned to investigate the girl named Amelia would return with their reports. Beth hopefully would have gleaned something interesting from her association with Welton. And the young man he had stationed in Maria's house could be called back to share what he had learned.

Christopher had pockets of information to tap. It was not like him to delay the reception of news. But then he had not been acting like himself since the night he first had sex with Maria.

What hold did she have on him?

He was still asking himself that question when he handed the reins of his mount to her groomsman in front of her house. He took the short steps to her door with the heavy stride of a man walking to the gallows, and he was not at all surprised to be told that she was not at home.

Telling himself to go, to leave, Christopher still found himself saying, "I *am* coming in. The manner in which I do so, however, is entirely up to you."

The grumbling butler stepped aside and Christopher took the stairs, anticipation warring with dread in a heady mix. He hoped for Quinn to appear and give him a fight. Though he was in poor physical condition, he didn't care. Fisticuffs would leave him no room to think about Maria, which was all he wanted—to be free of his pining for her.

He reached the second floor and found a familiar face there, although it was not Quinn's.

"How fare you?" he asked Tim, noting that his lackey was sporting a tidy queue and a Vandyke, the mass of his unruly beard gone.

"Well."

Nodding his approval, Christopher said, "See that we are not disturbed."

"Aye."

Moving to Maria's door, Christopher lifted his hand to knock, then thought better of it. Instead he turned the knob and entered her room without warning, pausing a step inside the threshold when he spied her standing before the window. Like all great sirens, she was *en déshabillé*, her lushly curved figure visible through the thin cotton chemise she wore. The sight of her tiny form framed by long, flowered and tasseled curtains made his throat nearly too tight to speak. Somehow, though, he was able to say, "Maria."

Her shoulders stiffened, and he watched as she took a deep breath.

"Lock both doors," she returned, without facing him, as if

she had been expecting him. "Simon will return eventually, and I want this resolved before there are any interruptions."

The air in the room was oppressive, filled with so many words left unsaid. Still, as Christopher turned the locks, he felt as if a great weight had been lifted from him, simply because he was in the same space as Maria.

He moved toward her but stopped a few feet away.

She finally turned to face him, revealing dark circles under her reddened eyes. A heavy mantle of weariness shrouded her slender shoulders. "I had hoped you would stay away."

"I want to."

"Then why are you here?"

"Because I want you more."

Maria's hand lifted to her heart. "We cannot have what we want. People who live as you and I do forfeit affairs of the heart."

"Is your heart engaged?"

"You know the answer," she said simply. There was nothing in her features or the depths of her eyes to give him any clue to her thoughts.

Christopher felt a drop of sweat glide down his temple. "That night I came to your room and we lay together . . ."

She turned back to the window. "A beautiful memory to treasure. Good-bye, Mr. St. John." Her voice was devoid of emotion.

He stood unmoving. His mind told him to go, yet he could not make his limbs cooperate. He knew she was right, he knew it was in both of their best interests to walk away and resume the separate lives they had led before meeting. Instead, he found himself walking toward her, coming up behind her, wrapping his arms around her.

The moment he touched her, she began to shake. He was reminded of that first evening in the theater, when he had held her similarly. She had been cool and collected then. The vulnerable woman in his arms now had been brought to existence by his effect on her.

"Christopher . . ." The sadness in her voice was the end of him.

"Release me," he said hoarsely, his nostrils buried in her fragrant hair. "Let me go."

Instead she turned in his arms with a pained cry and kissed him deeply.

Enslaving him further.

Chapter 16

Amelia slipped through the forest filled with anticipation. It was silly, perhaps, to be excited about a kiss that she planned rather than accepted in a moment of passion, but she enjoyed the idea anyway. She was also eager due to the missive in her pocket. She had stayed up far too late the night before, trying to find exactly the right words to write to her sister. In the end, she had chosen the short and direct route, telling Maria to contact Lord Ware to arrange a meeting.

The fence was directly ahead. After making certain that the guard was still far enough away to miss seeing her, she hurried toward it. She did not see the man hidden on the other side of a large tree. When a steely arm caught her and a large hand covered her mouth, she was terrified, her scream smothered by a warm palm.

"Hush," Colin whispered, his hard body pinning hers to the trunk.

Her heart racing in her chest, Amelia beat at him with her fists, furious that he had given her such a fright.

"Stop it," he ordered, pulling her away from the tree to shake her, his dark eyes boring into hers. "I'm sorry I scared you, but you left me no choice. You won't see me, won't talk to me—"

She ceased struggling when he pulled her into a tight embrace, the powerful length of his frame completely unfamiliar to her.

"I'm removing my hand. Hold your tongue or you'll bring the guards over here."

He released her, backing away from her quickly as if she were malodorous or something else similarly unpleasant. As for her, she immediately missed the scent of horses and hardworking male that clung to Colin.

Dappled sunlight kissed his black hair and handsome features. She hated that her stomach knotted at the sight and her heart hurt anew until it throbbed in her chest. Dressed in an oatmeal-colored sweater and brown breeches, he was all male. Dangerously so.

"I want to tell you I'm sorry." His voice was hoarse, gravelly.

She glared.

He exhaled harshly and ran both hands through his hair. "She doesn't mean anything."

Amelia realized then that he was not apologizing for scaring the wits from her. "How lovely," she said, unable to hide her bitterness. "I am so relieved to hear that what broke my heart meant nothing to you."

He winced and held out his work-roughened hands. "Amelia. You don't understand. You're too young, too sheltered."

"Yes, well, you found someone older and less sheltered to understand you." She walked past him. "I found someone older who understands me. We are all happy, so—"

"What?"

His low, ominous tone startled her and she cried out when he caught her roughly. "Who?" His face was so tight, she was frightened again. "That boy by the stream? *Benny?*"

"Why do you care?" she threw at him. "You have *her.*"

"Is that why you're dressed this way?" His heated gaze swept up and down her body. "Is that why you wear your hair up now? For *him?*"

Considering the occasion worthy of it, she had worn one of her prettiest dresses, a deep blue confection sprinkled with tiny embroidered red flowers. "Yes! He doesn't see me as a child."

"Because he is one! Have you kissed him? Has he touched you?"

"He is only a year younger than you." Her chin lifted. "And he is an earl. A gentleman. He would not be caught behind a store making love to a girl."

"It wasn't making love," Colin said furiously, holding her by the upper arms.

"It appeared that way to me."

"Because you don't know any better." His fingers kneaded into her skin restlessly, as if he couldn't bear to touch her, but couldn't bear not to either.

"And I suppose you do?"

His jaw clenched in answer to her scorn.

Oh, that hurt! To know there was someone out there whom he loved. Her Colin.

"Why are we discussing this?" She attempted to wrench free, but to no avail. He held fast. She needed distance from him. She could not breathe when he touched her, could barely think. Only pain and deep sorrow penetrated her overwhelmed senses. "I forgot about you, Colin. I stayed out of your way. Why must you bother me again?"

He thrust one hand into the hair at her nape, pulling her closer. His chest labored against hers, doing odd things to her breasts, making them swell and ache. She ceased struggling, worried about how her body would react if she continued.

"I saw your face," he said gruffly. "I hurt you. I never meant to hurt you."

Tears filled her eyes and she blinked rapidly, determined to prevent them from falling.

"Amelia." He pressed his cheek to hers, his voice carrying an aching note. "Don't cry. I can't bear it."

"Release me, then. And keep your distance." She swallowed

hard. "Better yet, perhaps you could find a more prestigious position elsewhere. You are a hard worker—"

His other arm banded her waist. "You would send me away?"

"Yes," she whispered, her hands fisted in his sweater. "Yes, I would." Anything to avoid seeing him with another girl.

He nuzzled hard against her. "An earl . . . It must be Lord Ware. Damn him."

"He is nice to me. He talks to me, smiles when he sees me. Today, he is going to give me my first kiss. And I'm—"

"No!" Colin pulled back, his irises swallowed by dilated pupils leaving deep black pools of torment. "He may have all the things that I never will, including you. But by God, he won't take that from me."

"What—?"

He took her mouth, stunning her so that she couldn't move. Amelia could not understand what was happening, why he was acting this way, why he would approach her now, on *this* day, and kiss her as if he were starved for the taste of her.

His head twisted, his lips fitting more fully over hers, his thumbs pressing gently into the hinges of her jaw and urging her mouth to open. She shivered violently, awash in heated longing, afraid she was dreaming or had otherwise lost her mind. Her mouth opened, and a whimper escaped as his tongue, soft like wet velvet, slipped inside.

Frightened, she stopped breathing, then he murmured to her, her darling Colin, his fingertips brushing across her cheekbones in a soothing caress.

"Let me," he whispered. "Trust me."

Amelia lifted to her toes, surging into him, her hands sliding into his silken locks. Unschooled, she could only follow his lead, allowing him to eat at her mouth gently, her tongue tentatively touching his.

He moaned, a sound filled with hunger and need, his hands cupping the back of her head and angling her better.

The connection became deeper, her response more fervent. Tingles swept across her skin in a wave of goose bumps. In the pit of her stomach a sense of urgency grew, of recklessness and flaring hope.

One of his hands slipped, caressing the length of her back before cupping her buttock and urging her up and into his body. As she felt the hard ridge of his arousal, a deep ache blossomed low inside her.

"Amelia . . . sweet." His lips drifted across her damp face, kissing away her tears. "We shouldn't be doing this."

But he kept kissing her and kissing her and rolling his hips into her.

"I love you," she gasped. "I've loved you so long—"

He cut her off with his lips over hers, his passion escalating, his hands roaming all over her back and arms. When she couldn't breathe, she tore her lips away.

"Tell me you love me," she begged, her chest heaving. "You must. Oh God, Colin . . ." She rubbed her tear-streaked face against his. "You've been so cruel, so mean."

"I can't have you. You shouldn't want me. We can't—"

Colin thrust away from her with a vicious curse. "You are too young for me to touch you like this. *No.* Don't say anything else, Amelia. I am a servant. I will always be a servant and you will always be a viscount's daughter."

Her arms wrapped around her middle, her entire body quaking as if she were cold instead of blistering hot. Her skin felt too tight, her lips swollen and throbbing. "But you do love me, don't you?" she asked, her small voice shaky despite her efforts to be strong.

"Don't ask me that."

"Can you not grant me at least that much? If I cannot have you anyway, if you will never be mine, can't you at least tell me that your heart belongs to me?"

He groaned. "I thought it was best if you hated me." His head tilted up to the sky with his eyes squeezed shut. "I had hoped that if you did I would stop dreaming."

"Dreaming of what?" She tossed aside caution and approached him, her fingers slipping beneath his sweater to caress the hard ridges of his abdomen.

He caught her wrist and glared down at her. "Don't touch me."

"Are they like my dreams?" she queried softly. "Where you kiss me as you did a moment ago and tell me you love me more than anything in the world?"

"No," he growled. "They are not sweet and romantic and girlish. They are a man's dreams, Amelia."

"Such as what you were doing to that girl?" Her lower lip quivered and she bit down on it to hide the betraying movement. Her mind flooded with the painful memories, adding to the turmoil wrought by the unfamiliar cravings of her body and the pleading demands of her heart. "Do you dream about her, too?"

Colin caught her to him again. "Never."

He kissed her, lighter in pressure and urgency than before, but no less passionate. Soft as a butterfly's wings, they brushed back and forth across hers, his tongue dipping inside, then retreating. It was a reverent kiss, and her lonely heart soaked it up like the desert floor soaked rain.

Cupping her face in his hands, he breathed, "*This* is making love, Amelia."

"Tell me you don't kiss her like this." She cried softly, her nails digging into his back through his sweater.

"I don't kiss anyone. I never have." His forehead pressed against hers. "Only you. It's only ever been you."

"Maria."

The sound of her name spoken in Christopher's raspy voice made Maria whimper with a mixture of need and fear. He heard the sound and pulled her closer, his lips moving urgently across hers.

She did not know how to handle the feelings he incited in her, the strange mixture of endless desire that went beyond the physical and wavering hope, as if something could come of this affair between them.

"I wanted you with me when I woke this morning," he said, his arms strong around her.

She stared up into his austerely handsome features, noting that his skin was pale beneath his tan and his countenance as weary in appearance as hers. "I wanted to stay, but *this*," she gestured between them, "cannot be between us."

"It was, perhaps, fortunate that you left. Otherwise, I might never have realized how it would feel to lose you completely."

Lifting her hand, she pressed her fingertips to his lips, stemming the intimate confession. She winced as he caught her wrist and pressed an ardent kiss into her palm. What happened to the pirate she first met in the theater? Physically, the man before her looked the same, perhaps even a little worse for wear, but the eyes that stared back at her were far different. Though familiar. For a long moment, she stared at him, trying to place why she felt such a mad fluttering in her stomach. And then it came to her in a flash of frightening comprehension.

"What is it?" he asked, frowning with concern.

She looked away, her gaze darting around the room, trying to find something, some object that would ground her in reality.

Christopher caught her shoulders, preventing her from escape. "Tell me. By God, we have too many secrets between us. Too much left unsaid. It's killing us."

"There is no 'us,'" she whispered, sucking in a fortifying breath only to find her senses inundated with the scents of bergamot soap and starch. The scent of Christopher.

"You know I wish that were true," he said softly, his head lowering, his lips parting an instant before they touched hers. His hand slipped into the neckline of her chemise and cupped her bare breast. She gasped at the lancing heat that burned through her, and he took advantage, his tongue gliding deep.

Expert fingers found her hardened nipple and pinched it, rolled it, plucked at it until her knees weakened.

He caught her up then, lifting her feet from the floor and carrying her to the bed.

"How will we end this," she asked, with her hot face pressed into his shoulder, "if we make love again?"

"That question requires reason to answer it," he murmured, laying her down carefully. Leaning over her, his hands on either side of her hips, he gave her that slow seductive smile that she was helpless to resist. "But there is no reason to what is between us. There never has been."

Maria was touched by his gentleness. Her heart began to race, and suddenly unable to look at the emotion in his eyes, she closed her own.

She felt the mattress dip as he sat beside her. His fingertip dipped into the hollow of her throat and then slid downward between her breasts. "Talk to me," he urged.

"I'd rather—"

His hand cupped the weight of her breast, then moist heat surrounded her nipple through her chemise. Her back bowed upward in startled pleasure and her eyes flew open.

Christopher sat up again and shrugged out of his heavy silk coat. "Tell me. Before I move on to more persuasive forms of coercion."

"I am a woman grown, but you make me feel like an adolescent," she confessed, experiencing a riot of emotions such as a girl of Amelia's age would—frightened but curious, anxious but eager. Her stomach fluttered in anticipation, although she knew well what was about to happen.

This time would be different, she knew. Beyond her experience.

A dark golden brow arched as his fingers moved to the ivory buttons of his waistcoat. "My first sexual encounter was against a wall in a filthy alley. She was a decade older than I, and an accomplished whore. I pretended to the others that I was highly knowledgeable in such matters, but she knew and took it upon herself to instruct me. She caught my hand, led me outside, and lifted her skirts. I was determined to hold to the lie, of course, so I rode her hard and well, and didn't stop until every one of the men I wished to impress had heard her coming."

Although his voice was light, she heard something beneath it that touched her deeply. Who was this man? How did he become the lover undressing in her bedroom? A man who would come to her, as she had gone to him, attempting to save a relationship that had nowhere to go?

Christopher stood and divested himself of the waistcoat, then quickly followed it with his shirtsleeves, breeches, stockings, and heels. Gloriously naked, he crawled onto the bed next to her. He rolled her into his side, arranging her into a similar position as the last time. Once she was properly situated, he sighed with deep pleasure.

Her hand over his heart, Maria looked out the window through her sheers and appreciated how, for the moment, she felt cocooned from the world at large.

"So tell me," he murmured, his lips in her hair, "what do you mean when you say you feel as an adolescent would?"

If we cannot discuss the present, that leaves us with only our pasts.

"Dayton was many years older than I," she said, her breath gusting through the light matting of golden brown hairs on his chest.

"I had heard that."

"He was very much in love with the first Lady Dayton. But even had he not been, I think he would have found my age off-putting regardless."

"Oh?"

Maria felt the expectation and curiosity within the tension of Christopher's frame. "But I was young and curious, and—"

"Hot blooded," he supplied with an affectionate kiss to the crown of her head, which she returned with one pressed to a hard brown nipple. "Do not attempt to distract me," he admonished. "You will finish your tale first."

"Dayton noted my growing preoccupation with ogling young men and took me aside. He asked if there was one of the servants in particular I found most appealing."

"You told him?" Christopher tilted her chin up to reveal his raised brows.

"Not immediately. I was too embarrassed." And she still was, if the heat she felt spreading across her cheeks was any indication.

"How lovely you are when you blush," he murmured.

"Don't tease, or I will not be able to finish."

"I'm not teasing."

"Christopher!"

He smiled, his eyes sparkling, making him look younger. Not adolescent, by any means. A man who had seen and done the things Christopher St. John had would never be able to recapture any hint of innocence, but the transformation of his features amazed her and affected her deeply. She had wrought this change in him.

She touched his cheek with reverent fingers and his smile faded, his gaze heated. "Hurry with your tale," he urged.

"One day, Dayton sent for me, telling me to meet him in the bachelor house. It was not an unusual request." It was where they had studied maps and cryptology, away from the prying eyes and ears of servants. "But when I arrived, it was not Dayton who awaited me, but the handsome young man who had caught my fancy."

"Fortunate bastard," Christopher said.

Maria returned her cheek to his chest, her hand cupping his lean hip. "He was kind and patient. Despite being young, randy, and obviously eager, he tended to my pleasure and comfort before he saw to his. It was an exceptional way to manage the task of losing one's virginity."

Christopher rolled and pinned her beneath him, gazing

down at her with liquid, heated eyes. "I feel rather dull-witted. I still cannot collect what it is about today's encounter that goads feelings of adolescence."

She pursed her lips, afraid to reveal any more.

"Must I resort to coercion, then?" Reaching between them, he tugged down her bodice and freed her breasts, his warm furred skin an intimate delight when pressed to her nakedness.

"Christ," he said, leaning his weight on one arm while rolling a nipple between the fingers of his opposite hand. "You are so beautiful."

"Silver-tongued devil," she teased, pressing a kiss to his chin before spreading her legs, allowing his hips to sink intimately between them.

"You like my tongue," he purred. "And I am prepared to use it on you to gain your confession. Now tell me how and why you feel like a schoolroom girl so we can move on."

"With a threat like that, why would I say anything?"

Christopher nipped her lower lip with his teeth. "Very well, I will guess, then, based on what you have told me so far. You feel apprehension, but also desire. Surprise, but also eagerness. Uncertain, but also decided. You don't want to have me, and yet you do." He smiled. "Am I close?"

Maria lifted her head and rubbed her nose against his. "I suppose the first time feels the same for everyone."

"I felt nothing of the sort the first time," he scoffed. "All I felt was a physical desire to spend my seed. Emotional feelings had nothing to do with it."

Her brows rose. "Then how do you know how I feel?"

"Because," he whispered, his lips lowering to hers, "I feel that way about you."

Chapter 17

Maria moaned softly as Christopher took her mouth in a luxurious kiss, showing no haste or urgency, enjoying her as if she were a delicious treat. His tongue slipped between her lips and then retreated, licking deep. All the while his large hand cupped her breast, kneaded it, his wickedly knowledgeable fingertips tugging at the taut point, making it harder and more tender.

She shivered beneath him, so aroused she could not bear to be still, her body writhing and aching.

"Maria."

God, how she loved the way he said her name, so fervently and filled with awe.

Her hands cupped either side of his spine and stroked the powerful length of his back. His muscles were so hard, his flesh gave not at all as she tried to pull him closer.

This was what she had wanted when she returned from Brighton, this deep passionate intimacy and wild conflagration of desire. Unlike Simon, Christopher did not retreat when she asked. The pirate forced her to acknowledge him, to take him . . . to take him *with pleasure.*

Suddenly, he pulled away, his breathing hard and erratic, his entire body shaking. He pressed his cheek to hers and groaned. "Do you have any notion of what you do to me?" he asked.

The yearning note in his voice brought tears to her eyes. "Is it anything similar to what you do to me?"

Christopher's hot, open mouth sucked erotically on her neck. "Bloody hell, I hope so. I do not think I could bear it were I in this alone."

Maria's hands moved to his shoulders and pushed. He grunted and continued his oral appreciation of her throat, his tongue rubbing back and forth across her fluttering vein.

"Allow me to perform a like service to your cock," she whispered.

Lifting his golden head, he looked down at her with dark, fathomless eyes. "Yes." He rolled to his back, taking her with him. His hand at her nape, he kissed her. A hard quick kiss that conveyed his gratitude.

It made her smile, that simple gesture. She slid down his big body with deliberately provoking movements, her mouth moving down his chest, her fingers teasing his nipple similarly to how he had teased hers. He tensed, his breaths shallow, waiting. Her tongue flicked rapidly across the tightened peak, wringing a cry from him.

"Do not dally," he urged hoarsely. "I need you."

She took further pity on him and wiggled down until she lay between his spread thighs. The muscles there were spasming, so great was his tension. She studied his balls, so heavy and full, drawn up tight in aching anticipation. His cock, so thick and hard, strained upward. She blew across it gently and it jerked, a spurt of semen escaping from the large, wide head.

"Delicious," she breathed, taking his phallus in hand and angling it to her mouth. As she drew it closer, more cum beaded the tip and slipped down along a fat, pulsing vein. Her tongue extended, pressing flat against the shaft and then licking slowly upward, cleaning him.

"Ah!" His fists clenched in her bed linens, his neck taut with strain. More of his seed leaked out, dribbling down the long length, pooling in the valley between her fingers and his rock-hard flesh. He watched her with dark, heated eyes. "Maria." His raspy voice was rough with urgency.

She lay on her side at eye-level with his cock. "Roll into me," she directed.

Side by side they faced each other, with her body much farther down the bed than his. She angled his erection into position for her waiting mouth and sucked him in, holding his hips as he cursed and jerked violently. Her tongue rubbed back and forth over the tender spot beneath the head of his cock. His groan was low and tormented, and for a moment, she felt like weeping. They were too close emotionally, each able to hurt the other. It made her want to give him all the pleasure she could, to give him some modicum of happiness in the midst of the mire that sucked them in.

Her eyes closed and she hollowed her cheeks, tugging on the swollen tip, her tongue swirling around the silky top, collecting the semen that now spilled profusely.

"Christ," he hissed, his large hands cupping the back of her head, holding her still as his hips pumped forward. She cupped his balls and rolled them with great care. Christopher's grip on her tightened painfully, making her nipples ache further and her sex slick with desire.

Maria sucked hard, her mouth tight as she could make it, and he shuddered hard.

"Yes . . . Maria . . ."

She opened herself to him as he had to her by coming here today. Aside from the hungry workings of her mouth, she remained completely motionless, allowing him to set the pace. He continued to groan, cry out, and shake, his words and pitch becoming more guttural as he fucked her mouth with increasing fervency.

Soon her lips were rimmed with his cum and her saliva, her mouth filled too full as his cock continued to swell. He cursed and writhed, the tension of his body betraying how frantically he drove toward release. He pumped deep, hitting the back of her throat, and then froze with a shout of mingled pleasure and mindless relief.

The hot salty wash of his semen flooded her mouth in a pulsating rush, and she serviced him, stroking his cock and gently squeezing his balls and sucking hard, so hard. He tried to push her away, to flee, but she held him captive, taking him, making him surrender, making him mutter incoherently.

"No . . . *Maria* . . . dear God . . . yes . . . no more . . . no more . . ." And finally a whispered plea, "*Don't stop . . .*"

She drained him, her hands and mouth still on him even as he lost that desperate hardness and softened against her tongue.

"Please," he begged, his hands falling away, his body slackening with tangible exhaustion. "I am undone."

Maria released him, licking her lips, her own body aching with unfulfilled desire, but she was pleasured nevertheless.

He watched her with dazed eyes, his face still flushed and glistening with perspiration. "Come here," he said hoarsely, his arms open and reaching for her.

She crawled to him, snuggled against him, rested her cheek over his violently beating heart. Her eyes closed as she breathed him in. His breathing slowed, became shallow and even, the sounds of deep sleep. She was close to following him when she felt the hem of her chemise rising, the skin of her legs exposed to the air.

Her head tilted back to find him looking at her, once again the controlled and intent man she knew.

"Christopher?" she queried softly, shivering as the heat of his palm covered the chilled skin of her thigh.

He pushed her to her back, rising to prop his head on his hand while the other slipped between her legs.

"Open," he rasped.

"You don't have—"

"Open." The upward press of his hand grew more insistent.

Aroused by the single-minded intent revealed in his actions, Maria spread her legs, a gasp slipping from her as his fingers tangled in her curls.

"How perfect you are," he murmured, parting the lips of her sex. "To become so creamy and hot from sucking my cock."

His long fingers rubbed lightly across her clitoris, making her sex clench tight with wanting.

"And your nipples." His head lowered, the heat of his mouth circling the aching tip, tugging on it with deep rhythmic suction. He released her and blew across the wet, erect point, making her whimper. "So delicious and sensitive that it makes this hungry little cunt"—two fingers slipped inside her—"suck me deep inside."

She started to pant as he worked in and out of her, his gaze rapt on her face, watching all the nuances of her pleasure.

"Yet despite how much I adore the outer shell of my beautiful, Spanish-blooded vixen"—his lips hovered above hers, taking in her gasping breaths while he fucked her with those wicked fingers—"it is my deeper affinity with her that binds me."

"Christopher." Her heart in her throat, she found it difficult to breathe. She felt herself falling and wanted to stop, but found she couldn't.

"Yes." His lips moved against hers, he was so close. "Shocking, is it not?"

Maria clenched the bedclothes and thrust her hips in time to the slow, drugging thrusts into her melting sex. She was so wet, so aroused, she heard her body suck him in and then release him with great reluctance.

"So tight and greedy," he murmured. "If I hadn't just come my last drop, I'd indulge."

"Later," she moaned, her eyes squeezing shut.

"Later," he agreed in that raspy bedroom voice. "Now look at me when you come. I want to see how much you like it when I make you climax this way."

Forcing her eyes to open, Maria was startled by the tenderness on his features. His hair was disheveled, softening his look further. She cupped her swollen, aching breasts, kneading them to relieve her torment.

He plunged deep, rubbed inside her, retreated. Thrust and withdrawal, in and out.

"Please," she whispered, writhing. Falling.

"Beggars we are when it comes to each other." He kissed her, a soft sweet kiss so at odds with the base pumping of his fingers. He lifted his head, pressed his thumb into her clitoris in a circular rubbing motion, and watched her orgasm with a cry of his name. Watched her shudder violently as her cunt convulsed around his fingers. Watched her fall all the way down.

Then he caught her. Held her. Tucked her against him.

And slept.

Amelia hurried over the fence and ran to the stream. Ware faced the river, his hands clasped at his back, waiting for her.

"I'm sorry," she said breathlessly, coming to a stop beside him.

He turned to her slowly, his gaze raking her from head to toe. "You failed to meet me yesterday," he said.

She blushed, memories of Colin's desperate kisses making her heart race. "I was detained. I feel terrible."

"You do not appear as though you feel terrible. Your eyes are bright and happy."

Unsure of what to say, she shrugged lamely.

Ware waited a moment and then offered her his arm. "Will you tell me about whatever it is that has made you glow?"

"Probably not."

He laughed, then winked at her, the friendly gesture relieving her immeasurably. She had worried about possible awkwardness between them. She was grateful to find that there wasn't any.

They strolled leisurely along the bank until they arrived at their previous picnic spot. Once again, a blanket waited in the midst of the lovely view. The shallow stream rushed over the smooth river rock in a delightful melody. The air was filled with the scent of meadow grass and wildflowers, and her skin warmed in the dappled sunlight.

"Are you angry with me?" she asked as she settled onto the blanket with a shy smile, her hands nervously smoothing the skirts of her white gown.

"Disappointed slightly," he drawled, shrugging out of his mustard-colored coat. "But not angry, no. I do believe it would be impossible to be cross with you."

"Others seem to find no trouble with it."

"More fool they. It's much preferable to be in charity with you." He sprawled across the blanket on his side, his head resting in his hand.

"If I begged a favor from you," she asked softly, "would you try to grant it?"

"Of course," he murmured, studying her.

He was always studying her. Sometimes she felt as if he was examining her even when he wasn't looking directly at her. She seemed to be a source of great interest to him, though she had yet to discern why.

Reaching into her reticule, she withdrew the letter she had drafted to Maria. "I would like you to post this for me. I'm afraid I lack her direction. But she is quite infamous, and it should not be too difficult to find her. Also, would you mind terribly if she were to reply to you?"

Ware reached out for the missive and gazed down at her handwriting. "The notorious Lady Winter." Glancing back up at her with an arched brow, he said, "I pray you will indulge me with the answers to some questions."

Amelia nodded. "Of course. Anyone would be curious."

"First, why ask me to post this instead of managing the task yourself?"

"I am not allowed to correspond with anyone," she explained. "Even discourse with Lord Welton must be done through my governess."

"I find that quite alarming," he said, his tone low and more serious than she had ever heard it. In truth, she had almost thought that Ware was never anything but mildly amused by circumstances around him. "I also dislike the look of the men who patrol the borders of the property. Tell me, Amelia. Are you a prisoner there?"

Taking a deep breath, she decided to tell her friend all that she knew. He listened attentively, as he always did, as if every word that left her mouth was of the utmost importance. She adored him for that.

By the time she finished her short tale, Ware was seated cross-legged before her, his blue eyes intense and the line of his mouth somber. "Have you never considered fleeing?"

Amelia blinked and then looked down at her intertwined hands. "Once or twice," she admitted. "But truly, I am not maltreated. The servants are kind to me, my governesses gentle and even tempered. I have lovely gowns and proper schooling. What would I do, if I were to leave? Where would I go? How foolish would I be to set out on my own with no destination and no means of support?"

She shrugged and looked up at him again. "If my father is correct about my sister, then he is only protecting me."

"You do not believe that," the earl said gently, setting his hand atop of hers, "or you would not ask me to post this for you."

"Wouldn't you be curious?" she asked, genuinely seeking his counsel.

"Of course, but then I am a curious fellow."

"Well, I am a curious female."

His blue eyes smiled. "Very well, my fair princess. I will humbly manage this task for you."

"Oh, thank you!" She tossed her arms around his neck

and kissed his cheek. Then, embarrassed at her exuberance, she recoiled, blushing.

Ware, however, had a soft smile on his aristocratic features. "Not the kiss I was hoping for," he murmured. "But it will do."

Chapter 18

Simon situated himself against the padded headboard and reached for the glass of wine that rested on the small table by the bed. His skin was heated by his exertions, so he ignored the linens and allowed the occasional breeze from the nearby open sash to cool him.

His throat worked with a large swallow, then he glanced down at the pretty blonde beside him with a lazy smile. "A drink, Amy?" he asked solicitously.

"Um." The girl sat up, revealing small but nicely curved breasts, and accepted the proffered glass.

"So tell me more," he murmured, studying her carefully beneath heavy-lidded eyes, "about this secret panel in Lord Sedgewick's house."

Amy swallowed the fine beverage with an unschooled gulp that made him wince inwardly. "'e uses it to 'ide 'is liquor."

"His contraband liquor."

"Aye."

"And access can be gained near the coal chute?"

She nodded, her curls swaying around her appealing features. "Makes the deliveries simpler. You won't steal it, will you?"

"Of course not," he soothed. "I simply find the idea quite clever and may implement something similar in my own home."

Simon dipped his finger into the glass, then painted the

maid's pretty mouth with it. She flushed, her gaze darting to where his semierect cock lay against his thigh. "We will return to that in a moment," he murmured, hiding a smile at how easy she was to distract.

Her lower lip thrust out in a pout.

"When does he receive callers?"

"Tuesdays and Thursdays from three to six."

He smiled. Once he finished here, he would visit the space and ascertain whether it was possible to hear clearly through the walls or not. If so, he would schedule a man to sit in that spot every Tuesday and Thursday in the hopes of learning more about the viscount. There was a reason Sedgewick had approached Maria at the masquerade, and Simon would learn of it.

But first he had to finish his business here.

He set aside his glass and glanced at Amy with a seductive smile. She shivered and lay back down quickly.

Ah, it is a strenuous job, he thought with an inner grin.

Then he set to work.

Amelia was so excited about the letter to Maria that she practically skipped through the trees toward the house. For the first time, she felt as if she was actively working toward something. She had a goal, and she had set in motion the steps required to achieve it. Lost in the heady excitement of that, she was once again caught off guard by grasping arms, but her startled cry was smothered by a warm, passionate mouth and her protest instantly turned into a plaintive moan.

"Colin," she breathed with her eyes closed and her lips curved in a smile.

"Tell me you didn't kiss him," he said gruffly, both of his powerful arms banded around her waist and lower back.

"Tell me I am not dreaming," she murmured, filled with pure pleasure at being near her love again.

"It would be better if you were," he said, releasing her with a sigh.

Opening her eyes, Amelia noted his frown and the harshly set line of his sensual lips. "Why are you so determined to feel so terrible about something so wonderful?"

His lips curved ruefully. "Sweet Amelia," he murmured, cupping her face. His overly long hair fell over his brow, framing those dark eyes she adored. "Because sometimes it's better to not know what you're missing. Then you can tell yourself that it wouldn't have been as wonderful as you thought. But once you know it, you can't help but pine for it."

"Will you pine for me?" she asked, her heart fluttering at the thought.

"Selfish girl."

"I have been wretched over you."

His eyes closed and he kissed her softly. "Tell me you didn't kiss him."

"Colin, have you no faith in me?" Rising to her tiptoes, she rubbed the tip of her nose against his. "I simply asked him for a favor."

"What favor?" he asked crossly.

"I asked him to post a letter to my sister for me."

He stilled. "What?" He waved his hand around them. "All of this is to keep her away from you."

"I need to know her." She pushed away from him and crossed her arms stubbornly.

"No, you don't. Jesus." Colin growled and set his hands on his hips. "You're always finding some mischief or another."

With his exotic handsomeness and tendency to brood, he looked divine to Amelia. She sighed with deep infatuation. That only made his scowl deepen. "Don't look at me like that," he muttered.

"Like what?"

He pointed a finger at her. "Like *that!*"

"I love you," she explained with all the girlish adoration

she held for him in her heart. "It's the only way I know how to look at you."

His jaw tightened.

"I so missed how protective you are," she said softly, her fingers linking together before her.

"That's exasperation," he corrected.

"Well, you would not become exasperated if you weren't protective."

Shaking his head, Colin moved away and took a seat on a stump. Around them, birds twittered softly and the discarded leaves on the ground rustled with the occasional breeze. Over the years they'd played in many forests and across many beaches, and run across countless miles of wild grasses. And wherever they were, she had felt safe because Colin was with her.

"Why didn't you ask me to post it for you, instead of Lord Ware?"

"I hope for a reply and it cannot come here. I needed his assistance both in the sending and receiving." She stopped dead in her tracks when she noted that he had dropped his head in his hands. "What is it?"

She dropped to her knees before him, uncaring of her white gown. "Tell me," she urged when he held his silence.

He looked at her. "There will always be things that I can't give you that men like Ware can."

"What things?" she asked. "Pretty dresses and hair ribbons?"

"Horses, manors, servants like me," he bit out.

"None of that has ever made me happy." Setting her small hands on his broad shoulders, she pressed an ardent kiss to his mouth. "Except for the servant like you, and you know I have never thought of you as inferior to me."

"Because you live a sheltered life, Amelia. If you were shown the world at large, you would see how things really are."

"I do not care what other people think, as long as you love me."

"I can't love you," he whispered, his hands lifting to circle her wrists and pull her arms down. "Don't ask me to."

"Colin." Suddenly she felt like the older one, the one whose task it was to comfort and protect. "You break my heart. But even in pieces, it has enough love for both of us."

Cursing softly, Colin seized her and said with his kisses what he would not say aloud.

Maria relaxed in the tub with her eyes closed, her neck resting against the rounded lip. Tonight she would go to Christopher and tell him about Amelia and Welton. She would tell him about Eddington, too, and together they would find a solution for their problems. Although it had taken her a few days to come to this decision, she knew in her heart it was the right one.

She sighed and slipped deeper into the warm water. Low male voices were heard in the gallery, then the door to the bedroom opened, followed by the door to her bathing chamber.

"You have been gone all day, Simon love," she murmured.

She heard him pull a chair closer and then he sat heavily. It was that and the deep breath he took, as if fortifying himself for some onerous task, that alerted her. Opening her eyes, she saw his grave features, so different from the merry charm he usually displayed.

"What is it?"

Simon leaned forward, resting his forearms on his thighs, his gaze intent. "You remember I told you about Lord Sedgewick's hidden liquor space? Today he had a visitor who imparted information that sheds light on his activities."

She sat up, her attention riveted. "Simon, you are a genius!"

But her praise did not earn her the lazy smile she loved.

"Maria . . ." he began, then he rose to his feet and came to her, lifting her hand from the edge of the tub.

Deep foreboding twisted her stomach into knots. "Tell me."

"Sedgewick is an agent of the Crown."

"Heavens, you frightened me with all your drama." She frowned, her thoughts rushing through all the possibilities. "They will never cease trying to solve the murders of Winter and Dayton. Of course, I am the primary suspect."

"Yes, the agency wants you." He exhaled harshly. "Enough that they have released a criminal to catch a criminal."

"Released a criminal—" She shook her head slowly, as understanding dawned. *"No . . ."*

Heedless of his expensive garments, Simon sank to his knees beside her, bringing them eye to eye. "Sedgewick is keeping the witness against St. John at an inn at St. George's Fields. The viscount has offered an exchange—St. John's freedom for information that would see you hang in his place. That is why he was not surprised to see St. John at the Campion masquerade and that is why he expected that you were there with the pirate.

Maria stared at Simon, searching his beloved features for any sign of mischief. It would be a dreadfully ill-conceived jest in such a way, but it would be preferable to the alternative; that her lover meant the ultimate betrayal—her death.

"No, Simon. No."

It was not possible to make love the way Christopher had with her and be lying.

Simon rose in a fluidly graceful movement, pulling her with him. He caught her up and sank to the floor, cradling her in a loving embrace. She clung to him, her wet body ruining his clothes, her tears silent but copious. He rocked her and hummed to her, held her and loved her.

"I think he cares for me," she said, her tear-stained face in his throat.

"He would be a fool not to, *mhuirnín*."

"I find it nearly impossible to believe otherwise." She drew in a shaky breath. "I had intended to ask for his assistance tonight."

If everything between them had been an elaborate subterfuge to win her trust, it was nearly a dazzling success. She had been prepared to bare her most precious secret, her one vulnerability, because she believed in him. She had even thought that Christopher *deserved* to know, because he had forgiven her for Eddington, even though she had given no explanations.

Eddington.

She pulled back, catching Simon's lapels with desperate urgency. "You know how St. John has been watching me, how he knew of Eddington's visit to Brighton and sent Tim to learn Amelia's identity. If he did those things with intent to harm . . . Dear God, I have been a fool to trust him with so much."

It was like being stabbed anew, this time in the heart. Would St. John attempt to use Amelia against her, too?

"I have already dispatched men to recover the witness," Simon soothed. "You will have your own leverage."

"Oh, Simon." Maria held him tightly. "What would I do without you?"

"You would rub along fine, *mhuirnín*. But I am in no hurry to be proven correct about that." He rested his chin on the top of her head. "What will you do?"

"I'm not certain. I suppose I will afford him the opportunity to redeem himself," she said, her throat tight and dry. "I intend to ask him outright how it was that he came to be released. If he refuses to tell me or evades the question, I will know his loyalty lies with his own interests and not with me."

"And then?"

She brushed the tears from her cheeks. "And then we do what we must. Amelia comes first, she always has."

* * *

Christopher stepped through the front door of his home with a whistle on his lips and a spring in his step. In all of his life, he could not remember the last time he had ever felt this . . . happy. He had not even known that he could *be* happy, for Christ's sake. He'd thought that feeling was beyond him.

Tossing his hat at his butler, he then yanked off his gloves and planned in his mind the best way to receive Maria when she arrived that evening. He would send men to escort her and ensure her safety, but what would he do with her once she was here? He'd stay buried inside her for hours, without question, but he would also like to continue wooing her. He relished the idea of exploring more of the unknown world of intimate relationships.

"Hmm . . ." He wracked his brain in his attempt to plan something neither of them would ever forget. He could ask his cook to prepare a variety of dishes known for their aphrodisiac qualities. And order flowers. Ones with a lush, exotic scent that would set the proper mood.

His lips twisted ruefully. Of course, all of that was directed toward the sexual part of the evening. He obviously knew nothing about romance or how to go about creating it. Rolling his shoulders back, Christopher considered a nap. He needed to think longer on the matter, but that required more energy than he had at the moment.

"St. John."

Turning his head, Christopher saw Philip filling the door to his study. "What is it?"

"The men you sent to research Amelia returned this afternoon."

His brows rose, then he nodded and moved into the room, taking a seat behind his desk. Lined up facing him were the four men he'd dispatched. All looked travel dusty and yet they were filled with a palpable excitement. Whatever they'd learned, they thought it was something he would appreciate.

"Go ahead," he said, his fatigue of a moment ago banished.

The four men looked at each other, and then Walter stepped forward. Two score in age with the gray hair and whiskers to show it, he had been with Christopher since the beginning of his less-than-illustrious career. In fact, Walter had been one of the men to watch him lose his virginity against the alley wall.

"I sent Tim ahead to tell you the news, but I hear he was waylaid."

Christopher smiled. "The tale is true."

"Well, I hope the delay isn't one you'll regret. Her name is Amelia Benbridge, the Viscount Welton's daughter."

Welton's *daughter*?

"Good God," Christopher breathed, leaning back heavily into his chair. "She is Lady Winter's half sister."

"Aye. Odd thing is, no one in the towns surrounding Welton's seat knew of her. When asked about the girl, everyone looked at us as if we were daft."

"How did you find her?"

"The vicar had the birth records."

"Well done," Christopher praised, even as he frowned in consternation and tapped his foot upon the Aubusson rug. Maria had been stabbed in an attempt to speak with her sister. They were obviously being kept forcibly apart. "I have to find her."

"Ah, well, we did."

Christopher's wide-eyed gaze shot to Walter's beaming face. "At one of the posting inns, Peter caught himself a pretty miss. He was talking to her, trying to wiggle under her skirts, and she says she's been hired as lady's maid to a viscount's daughter and the viscount she describes sounds like Welton. So we followed her to Lincolnshire and discovered the girl she tends is named Amelia Benbridge."

"Bloody hell."

"A dumb stroke of luck," Walter said. "But we'll take it, eh?"

"Yes, we will. Peter is absent," Christopher noted. "I assume he stayed behind to watch the girl? Excellent." He glanced at Philip, who waited by the door. "Fetch Sam."

His fingers drummed against the surface of his desk. "Welton hired this girl?"

"That's what she said."

Blowing out his breath, Christopher considered what he knew. Welton had Amelia. Maria wanted Amelia. Welton supported Maria's household and introduced her to men like Eddington. Christopher still had no notion of what Eddington was paying her for, but he now had no doubt that it was not for sexual favors. A picture was forming, but the image remained too murky to understand.

Sam stepped into the room.

"Tomorrow you are to go with Walter and the others to Lincolnshire," Christopher said. "There is a girl there. I need to know if she is the same girl Lady Winter sought. If it is, send word to me but remain with her. Follow her if she leaves. I want to know where she is at all times."

"Of course." The determined set of Sam's jaw told Christopher the man would do his best to redeem himself, just as Tim was doing.

"Clean up," Christopher said to the others. "Relax the rest of the night. Tup a willing maid. You will receive boons for your hard work."

"Thank you," they said in near unison, smiling.

He waved them out, then took a moment to collect his thoughts before rising and ascending the stairs to his bedroom.

Maria knew he had the resources to help her. Now that they had breached each other's outer defenses, would she share this with him? He hoped that she would.

With that goal in mind, he began to make plans for a seduction of a deeper kind. He wanted her heart, every dark corner and crevice of it.

Would she trust him enough to give it to him?

* * *

"The Earl of Eddington wishes to know if you are at home."

Maria looked at her butler through her mirror's reflection. His face was studiously impassive, as was hers, but inside she was a jumble of hurt and confusion. She nodded.

Bowing, the servant retreated.

Sarah continued to work on Maria's hair, weaving pearls and flowers into the elaborate arrangement, but when the knock came and Eddington entered, the abigail curtsied quickly and retreated.

"My Lady Winter," the earl drawled, striding into her boudoir. "You are, as always, an incomparable vision."

He had never once bothered to mince his steps around her, a comfort in bearing she wasn't certain she liked. The earl was dressed without fault in a striking burgundy ensemble, his dark hair restrained with the ends curled and hanging midway down his back. Lifting her proffered hand to his lips, Eddington then took a seat on the small stool beside her.

"Tell me something," he said, his heavy-lidded eyes studying her intently.

"I wish I had something to offer you," she murmured, unwilling to share news of Sedgewick until she knew for certain whether Christopher cared for her or not.

The earl sighed, as if quite put upon, then he opened his snuff box. He caught her hand, set the pinch atop the fluttering vein in her wrist, and sniffed.

"You are distressed over something," he noted, staring at the betraying pulsing of that thin blue line.

"My abigail cannot seem to manage the style I desired."

"Hmm . . ." He rubbed his thumb back and forth across her wrist. "What are your plans for the evening? Are you still on holiday?"

Maria tugged her hand back. "No. I have an assignation with a certain criminal of renown."

"Lovely." Eddington smiled with pleasure. Even though she was fairly immune to his lauded charms, she could not fail to note how attractive the man was. And a spy, too. Quite delicious, if one liked a rakish hero.

"Do you plan to ask St. John outright how he secured his release?" he asked conversationally. "Or do you plan to glean the information I need to recapture him in some other fashion?"

"If I tell you my secrets, what value would I have?"

"True." He stood and lifted the lid to her patch box. Selecting a diamond shape, he prepared it and secured it next to the corner of her eye. "The agency could use a woman of your talents. You should consider it."

"And you should go, so I can complete the task you set for me."

The earl stood behind her, setting his hands on her shoulders. "Do not dismiss my offer out of hand. I am sincere."

Maria met his gaze in the mirror. "I never dismiss anything out of hand, my lord. Most especially attractive offers made by men who stand to gain a great deal from my downfall."

Eddington grinned. "You don't trust anyone, do you?"

"Sadly"—she looked at herself in the mirror—"I have learned not to."

Tim pinned Sarah's delightfully robust figure to the master sitting-room wall, his hand cupping her fleshy buttock and urging her against his erect cock. The lewd embrace had been the sole focus of his interest until he had heard Lady Winter's discussion with Lord Eddington in the next room.

His eyes closed and his forehead rested against the wall some inches above Sarah's, who was so much shorter. It pained him greatly to learn of the betrayal. He had come to like and respect Lady Winter and had hoped her association with St. John would continue indefinitely. They both had a certain gleam in their eyes when referencing the other, and St. John had never looked happier than when he was in her ladyship's company.

"The earl has departed," Tim rumbled, stepping back. "Lady Winter will be needing you now."

"Will you come to my room later?" she asked breathlessly.

"I'll try. Go on now." He spun her about and urged her toward the nearby door with a pinch of her ass.

He waited until the latch had secured behind her, then he left the room.

Time was of the essence.

If he made haste, he could tell St. John about Lady Winter's true nature and return before he was missed.

Chapter 19

Colin whistled softly as he brushed the satiny-smooth coat of one of the carriage bays. His heart was both lighter and heavier, a strange mixture that he did not know how to manage.

It was beyond foolhardy, he knew, to seek Amelia out. She was far too young, and many stations above him. They could never be together. Not in any way. Their few stolen kisses were a danger to both, and he felt the cad for even stealing those.

She would be set free one day, exposed to the world at large and men like Lord Ware. She would look back on these days and her fervent girlish infatuation and wonder what she had been thinking to imagine herself in love with a groomsman. He was simply the only dish on the table, so she imagined herself hungry for him. But once she was set before a banquet, his common contribution would be like porridge amongst a multicourse meal.

"Colin."

He turned at the sound of his uncle's voice, watching as the rotund man entered the stable. "Yes, uncle?"

Yanking off his hat, Pietro ran a hand through his graying dark hair in a gesture rife with frustration. Aside from the differing widths of their middles, they looked very much alike, their Gypsy heritage unquestionable even though Colin's was diluted by a non-Gypsy mother.

"I know you've been seeing the lass in the woods."

Colin tensed.

"The guards tell me she's been meeting the lord from the neighboring property, and now you've interfered."

"I haven't." Colin resumed his exertions. "She saw him yesterday."

"I told you to stay away from her!" Pietro approached, anger evident in the set of his shoulders. "Take your needs to the village wenches and dairymaids."

"I have. I do." Breathing deep, Colin fought to control his temper. "You know I do."

And it ached when he did; every woman he took beneath him was a temporary relief from his raging desires, but nothing more. His heart had belonged to Amelia since he was a boy. His love for her had grown and changed, matured, even as his body did. She was guileless and innocent, her love for him pure and sweet.

He rested his head against the horse's neck. Amelia was everything to him, had been from the day Viscount Welton had hired his uncle. Pietro had agreed to work for far lower wages than other coachmen. It was the reason he had kept his job all these years rather than being replaced often, as the governesses were.

Colin would never forget the way Amelia had run up to him with that bright, open-hearted smile and placed a dirty hand in his.

"Play with me," she'd said.

Having come from a large band with many children, he had been afraid of loneliness. But Amelia had been a dozen playmates in one. Blessed with an adventurous spirit, she had been willing to learn all of the games he knew and then she'd set her mind to besting him at every one.

Over the years he'd come to appreciate her with a man's awareness enhanced by a joyous history of friendship and true companionship. He had grown into love with her, not fallen, his affection rooted deeply in the past. Perhaps Amelia's was, too, but how could he know for certain? He had experience with other females. Amelia had only him. Her feelings could change as she gained understanding of her choices. His never would. He would love her always.

Colin exhaled wearily. Regardless, even if she felt the same, he could never have her.

"Ah, boy," his uncle said, placing a large hand on his shoulder. "If you love her, leave her be. She has the world at her feet. Don't take that from her."

"I'm trying not to," he said hoarsely. "I'm trying."

Christopher sat in a wingback in his sitting room and stared into the glass in his hand. He was not quite certain what it was that he was feeling. It was rather the way he had felt when he'd overheard Eddington and Maria in Brighton, only now the tightening in his chest was nearly unbearable. Inhaling and exhaling was a conscious task.

"You should return," he said to Tim, his voice so low and raw, it startled him a moment. He scarcely recognized himself. He was not thinking, acting, or speaking like the man he had been before meeting Maria. "We do not want you to be missed."

He thought wryly about Tim's position in the Wintry Widow's household. She was so confident of her inevitable success that she freely allowed a serpent in her midst.

"Aye." Tim turned to go.

"If Eddington returns, I want to know the details of the exchange."

"Of course. I won't disappoint you again."

Christopher nodded, his gaze still deep in his glass. "Thank you."

He was vaguely aware of his bedroom door closing, but other than that, he was lost in thought. He prided himself on his ability to judge character and read people. He would not be alive today if he lacked that skill. Why then did he find it nearly impossible to convince himself that Maria felt no tenderness for him? The facts were there, clear and indisputable, yet in his heart he still believed in her.

Snorting, he lifted his glass to his lips and drained it. Therein lay his problem. His heart was directing him, and not his brain. Sadly, he loved her. That traitorous woman. His Jezebel, a seductress whose livelihood was dependent upon how many men she could lead to their rewards.

A knock came to the door, pulling him from his maudlin thoughts. "Come in," he called out.

Next he knew, he was rising to his feet by sheer habit, his pulse leaping into a passionate, riotous pace at the sight of his lover returning.

How much time had passed? A glance at the mantel clock told him nearly two hours.

Turning his head, he caught her gaze, saw the glimmer of pure pleasure that said she felt similarly, then it was quickly masked by a seductive smile. She was hooded, the black cowl framing her delicately seductive beauty, with those big, dark eyes and pouty red lips.

Christopher took a deep breath, then walked toward her before circling behind her. He set his hands on her cloaked shoulders and breathed her in. Warm, luscious woman. "I missed you," he murmured, reaching around her to the frogs at her throat.

"Will you always greet me dressed only in breeches?"

Always, as if there were a possibility of a future between them.

"Would you like me to?" He unclasped the cloak, gently lifted the hood from her head, and then allowed the entire weighty mass to puddle on the floor at their feet.

"I would prefer you naked," she said.

"As I would you, a preference I will see to directly." He began the task of undressing her, appreciating how much easier it was to accomplish when sober. His fingers moved nimbly, quickly freeing buttons and tapes.

"How was your day after I departed?" he asked.

"Lonely. I missed you, too."

Christopher's hands paused. He closed his eyes and inhaled deeply, trying to calm the part of him that flared white hot at her words. In his mind, he relived the afternoon—the way she had loved him, the way she had opened to him. That startled, almost frightened look she'd had when she came for him. The way she shivered when he touched her and melted when he kissed her.

When they were in bed, they were stripped and bared to each other beyond mere clothing.

"I have delicacies to feed you," he murmured, kissing the angry scar on her shoulder, "and flowers to woo you. I did not intend to start the evening in bed, but I find I cannot wait."

His hands slipped into the gaping back of her gown and reached around to cup her breasts through her chemise. He found her nipples hard, and he tugged on them with his fingertips in exactly the way she liked.

Maria's head fell back against his shoulder with a low moan.

"I love your breasts," he growled, his lips to her ear. "Tonight I intend to suck on them until you come with my cock deep inside you. Remember how that felt? How tight you gripped me?" He rolled his hips. "My cock is hard with the mere remembrance of it."

"Christopher." There was something sad and plaintive in the way she said his name, and all around them hung a heavy air of melancholy.

Impatient to reach the heart of the matter, he released her to tear open the back of her gown, which sent tiny, cloth-covered buttons flying out to either side.

"You will leave me with nothing to wear," she said, her

breathlessness betraying her secret desire to be taken. He knew this, of course, and suspected that Quinn's relatively easy acquiescence to her ending of their sexual relationship was the other man's downfall. Perhaps if the Irishman had pursued Maria more doggedly, she would not be here in Christopher's house now.

His impatience grew at the thought and he tore at her tapes and ties with even more ferocity. Her chemise rent with a loud ripping sound, and then Maria turned and was in his arms, her bare breasts pressed to his bare chest. He caught her up, taking the mouth she offered, lifting her feet from the floor.

Her tiny hands cupped his face; her soft, sweet lips worked frantically beneath his. Desperation, he could taste it and felt it in his own blood.

He nearly ran to the bed, so quick was his stride. He tossed her down and tore at his breeches.

"Spread your legs."

Wariness passed over her features, and Christopher knew why. He was not affording her the chance to hide.

Stepping free of his lone garment, he joined her on the bed, his hands catching her knees and opening her wide. She struggled, but he gave her no quarter, pinning her hips so he could take her cunt with his mouth.

"No," she cried out, her hands gripping his hair. "Not that way . . ."

Framing the ebony curls with his hands, Christopher parted her, exposing the soft pink skin and the hood that shielded her clitoris. With the pointed tip of his tongue, he rubbed it, teased it, coaxed it to come out and play. The moment it emerged, he wrapped his lips around the surrounding area and sucked gently. Maria moaned and arched upward, all the while begging him to cease, to fuck her with his cock, to give her time to regroup and be less vulnerable. She did not say the last, of course, but he knew it.

He also knew the moment she opened her eyes and saw the mirror above his bed, because she gasped and stiffened.

"Appreciate the view?" he purred before returning to his ministrations.

Maria stared up at the lewd reflection of Christopher's golden head between her legs and was devastated by what she saw. Glassy eyed and flushed from head to hipbone, she looked nothing like the grim, determined woman she had seen in the mirror at home. The woman she saw now was lost to the pleasures bestowed by a man she craved with a deep-seated, almost innate hunger. A man who had sought her out with the express purpose of leading her to the gallows in his place.

She could forgive that, knowing she had come to him with a nefarious purpose. She understood how many individuals relied on his support for their livelihood and that they were likely his motivation for saving himself. He would not bother for his own sake.

She knew this because she understood *him*, the man she thought he was, the man who once had a brother he loved as much as she loved Amelia. But the fact remained that his motives might not have changed from their original purpose and the man between her legs might be a man who wanted her dead.

"Maria."

She squeezed her eyes shut and felt him move. He pressed a kiss to her clitoris, then moved up to lie beside her.

"You are far from shy," he murmured, "yet the sight of my making love to you has chilled your desire." Cupping her hip, he rolled her into him so that the heat and hardness of his erection pressed into her belly. "Is it too intimate?"

Maria opened her eyes and studied him, noting both the soft affection in his deep blue eyes and the intensity of his perusal.

"Is it 'making love'?" she queried in a small voice. "Or is this sex between two people who fit well together?"

"You tell me."

They stared at one another, and she felt the questions between them like another body in the bed. "I wish I knew."

"Let us find out together, then." Lifting her thigh, he moved
into place, the wide, smooth head of his cock slipping through
the folds of her sex. "Take me inside you," he rasped. "Let
me in."

Was it possible to learn a man's character through sex?

"Tell me what happened to the witness who would have
testified against you," she whispered.

"Who wishes to know?" he rejoined.

Her breath caught, then grew more labored. "Christopher."

Could he know? Was it possible? Surely, if he knew what
she was about, he would not be touching her the way he was
now.

"Let me inside you, Maria." He nudged against her, pressing against the small slitted entrance to her body. "Make love
to me, and I will give you the answers you seek."

As she settled her leg over his hip and reached behind her
to position him properly, her hand shook and her indrawn
breath shuddered in her tight lungs. She circled his thickness
with her fingers and altered the angle of his penetration. He
slipped in a fraction, spreading her wide, making her neck
arch in pleasure.

"More," he murmured. "All the way inside you. As deep
as I can go."

She pressed down, filling herself with his heat and hardness, whimpering at how big he was and how much she enjoyed him.

Christopher caught her chin and turned her head to look
upward. "Watch."

Afraid to look, but helpless against the desire she had to see
them together, Maria focused her lust-dazed vision and stared
up at their reflection. His large, muscular body dwarfed hers,
the top of her head was below his chin, the foot of her
straightened leg ended at his midcalf. The skin of his torso

and arms was tanned by the sun and seemed impossibly dark next to hers, which had rarely felt the direct kiss of sunlight. His golden hair was even paler when compared to her raven tresses. They were opposites on the exterior, yet inside they were the same.

They were perfect together.

"See?" he whispered, bringing her gaze up to meet his in their reflection. Together they watched as his cock disappeared inside her. Her lids grew heavy with the drugging pleasure of the slow glide, but she refused to close her eyes again. Christopher withdrew, his cock now slick and shiny with her cream, then his buttocks clenched and he sank into her again.

Her gaze lifted as he moved, her attention riveted by his gloriously perfect features, now flushed with lust. As he pumped into her again, unadulterated pleasure swept across his face, and when she looked at herself, she saw the same intensity.

"Now, tell me," he whispered, in that deliciously raspy voice she adored. "Are we making love?"

She moaned as his hips buffeted hers in a perfect thrust.

"Tell me, Maria." His gaze locked with hers in the mirror. "I am making love to you. Are you making love to me?" He pulled out and thrust again. Harder. Deeper. "Or is this nothing but sex?"

Could he fool her so well? Was he that expert at deception that he could fake this level of intimacy?

No matter how she tried to reconcile the information she had with the man in her arms, she couldn't.

Maria wrapped her arms around his neck and pressed her cheek to his. It was then she felt the wetness of tears on her skin. Whether they were hers or his, she could not tell.

"It's more than sex," she whispered, watching the flare of something sweet and possessive cross his beloved features.

He crushed her against him and began to fuck her in earnest, his lean hips working his cock into her with expert precision. She took him in return, with similar fervor, her gaze locked on the deeply erotic sight of their straining, inter-twined bodies and the rigid, swollen shaft that pumped into her so quickly it was scarcely more than a blur.

Her mouth opened on a silent cry, her body tensing in the grip of a powerful, devastating orgasm. He growled and stroked through her spasms, murmured sex words and rever-ent praise that prolonged her climax until she thought she would die of it. Only when she settled weakly in his embrace did he ride her to his own completion, his cock jerking hard, then spurting harder, filling her, flooding her with his seed.

Breathing erratically, he took her mouth, sharing the air in their lungs.

Making them one.

Chapter 20

Amelia woke to a hand held over her mouth. Scared beyond measure, she struggled against her assailant, her nails clawing at his wrist.

"Stop it!"

She stilled at the command, her eyes opening wide, her heart racing madly as her sleep-fuzzy brain came to awareness of Colin looming over her in the darkness.

"Listen to me," he hissed, his gaze darting to the windows. "There are men outside. A dozen at least. I don't know who they are, but they are not your father's men."

She yanked her head to the side to free her mouth. *"What?"*

"The horses woke me as the men walked by the stable." Colin stepped back and yanked off her counterpane. "I snuck out the back and came round to fetch you."

Embarrassed to be seen in only her night rail, Amelia yanked the covers back over her.

He yanked them off again. "Come on!" he said urgently.

"What are you talking about?" she asked in a furious whisper.

"Do you trust me?" Colin's dark eyes glittered in the darkness.

"Of course."

"Then do as I say, and ask questions later."

She had no notion of what was happening, but she knew

he wasn't jesting. Sucking in a deep breath, she nodded and slipped from the bed. The room was lit only by the moonlight that entered though the window glass. The heavy length of her hair hung down her back in a thick, swinging braid and Colin caught it, rubbing it between his fingers.

"Put something on," he said. "Quickly."

Amelia hurried behind the screen in the corner and disrobed, then slipped the chemise and gown she had worn earlier over her head.

"Hurry!"

"I cannot close the back. I need my abigail."

Colin's hand thrust behind the screen and caught her elbow, tugging her from behind it so that he could drag her to the door.

"My feet are bare!"

"No time," he muttered. Opening her bedroom door, he peered out into the hallway.

It was so dark, Amelia could barely see anything. But she heard male voices. "What is going—"

Moving with lightning speed, Colin spun and covered her mouth again, his head shaking violently.

Startled, she took a moment to understand. Then she nodded her agreement to say nothing.

He stepped out into the hallway with silent steps, her hand in his. Somehow, despite her shoeless state, the floorboard beneath her squeaked, when it hadn't under Colin's boots. He froze, as did she. Below them, the voices she had heard were also silent. It felt as if the house were holding its breath. Waiting.

Colin placed his finger to his lips, then he picked her up and hefted her over his shoulder. What followed was a blur. Suspended upside down, she was disoriented and unable to discern how he managed to carry her from her second floor bedroom to the lower floor. Then a shout was heard upstairs as she was discovered missing, and pounding feet thundered above them. Colin cursed and ran, jostling her so that her teeth ached and her braid whipped his legs so hard, she feared hurting him. Her arms wrapped around his lean hips and his pace picked up. They burst out the front door and down the steps.

More shouting. More running. Swords clashed and Miss Pool's screams pierced the night.

"There she is!" someone shouted.

The ground rushed by beneath her.

"Over here!"

Benny's voice was music to her ears. Colin altered direction. Lifting her head, she caught a glimpse of pursuers, and then more men intercepted them; some she recognized, others she didn't. The new additions to the fray bought them precious time and soon she could not see anyone on their heels.

A moment later she was set on her feet. Wild-eyed, she glanced around to catch her bearings and found Benny on horseback and Colin mounting the back of another beast.

"Amelia!" He held out one hand to her, the other expertly holding the reins. She set her hand in his, and he dragged her up and over, belly down across his lap. His powerful thighs bunched beneath her as he spurred the horse and then they were off, galloping through the night.

She hung on for dear life, her stomach heaving with the jolting impacts. But it did not last long. Just as they reached the open road, a shot rang out, echoing through the darkness. Colin jerked and cried out. She screamed as her entire world shifted.

Sliding, falling.

Until she crashed to the ground.

Then there was nothing.

Christopher woke to warmth and softness. The scents of sex and Maria permeated both the air and the linens beneath him. She lay draped over him, her leg over his, her arm across his torso, her ripe, luscious breasts pressed to his side. He reached down and adjusted the sheet tented over his morning cockstand.

The only words they had exchanged over the long night were love words, sex words. Nothing of pain, betrayal, and lies. It was entirely against his nature to avoid the unpleasant, and because Maria was so like him, he knew it was against her nature as well. But they had an unspoken agreement to say with their bodies what they would not say aloud.

Turning his head, he pressed a kiss to her forehead. She murmured sleepily and cuddled closer. A snuggling kitten could not have been more adorable.

He ran his free hand through his hair and formulated his plan. There was only one way to ascertain her loyalty. He had to test her, provide her with an obvious way to betray him and then see if she took the opportunity.

Her mouth touched his chest in a soft kiss.

His gaze caught hers.

"What are you thinking about?" she asked softly.

"You."

Sadly, it appeared the bright light of morning was too great an intrusion. There was a heavy weight of wariness between them.

"Christopher . . ."

He waited for her to speak and then it seemed that she changed her mind.

"What is it?" he asked.

"I wish there were no secrets between us." Her hand stroked over his chest. "You said you would tell me whatever I wished to know."

"And I shall." He looked up at the reflection of them together and knew he wanted to wake up in this manner every day. "I beg your company this evening. Primitive man that I am, I have ruined two of your gowns, and I cannot live with myself without making amends."

"Oh?" She rose up beside him, her hair a delightfully ruined tumble of dark tresses and strings of pearls. He smiled, remembering his thoughts in the theater about her being too concerned with her appearance to enjoy a good, hard fucking. How wrong he had been.

He hoped he wasn't wrong about the depth of her affection for him. Tonight he would know the truth.

"There is a place here in Town where I store goods," he said. "I should like to take you there. There are some lovely Parisian silks and linens that I would like to show you. Once you have selected your favorites, I can make restitution for your maltreated garments."

Her lovely face impassive, she asked, "When will you answer my questions?"

He gave an exaggerated sigh. "You are supposed to be overjoyed at this display of my largesse. Instead you wish to pick at my brain."

"Perhaps I find your brain more intriguing than gowns," she purred. "That would be a compliment, you know."

"Very well. If we manage the evening without mishap, I will sit at your service and bare my every secret to you."

And he would. If she did not betray him tonight, he would bare his heart to her, and perhaps, if he was fortunate, the vision he saw above him would indeed be the one that greeted him every morning for the rest of his life.

Maria knew it was not a coincidence that Lord Eddington arrived within an hour of her return. He was watching her, following her. Driving her mad.

"I will receive him," she said when advised of the earl's call. A moment later, Eddington entered her private sitting room with a smug curve to his smile that she found more than slightly alarming. Maria feigned nonchalance and affected a lazy smile. "Good afternoon, my lord."

"My dearest," he murmured, lifting her hand to his lips.

She studied him carefully but found nothing amiss in his customary flawless exterior.

"Tell me something worthwhile," he said.

"I do wish there were something to tell." She shrugged. "Unfortunately, St. John was less forthcoming than I had hoped."

"Hmm." He adjusted his tails, then relaxed into the settee. "You did not tell me you had a sibling."

Maria froze, her heart stilling before racing madly. "Beg your pardon?"

"I said, I was not aware that you had a sister."

Unable to remain seated, she stood. "What do you know?"

"Very little, sadly. I do not even know her name." His gaze hardened. "But I know where she is, and I have men there to fetch her, if necessary."

Something inside Maria turned hard and brittle. "You tread on dangerous ground, my lord."

The earl pushed to his feet and closed the small distance between them. "Give me *something*," he bit out. "*Anything* that I can use, and your sister will be safe."

"That is not sufficient to relieve my concerns." Her chin lifted with no more strength behind it than pure bravado. In truth, her breathing was so shallow that she felt as if she could faint. "I want to see her with my own eyes."

"She will be untouched and unaware, if you follow through with your end of our bargain."

"I want her *here*!" Her fists clenched at her own helplessness. *Amelia* . . . "Bring her to me. Then I will give you whatever your heart desires, I swear it."

"You have already promised to give me—" Eddington paused. His gaze narrowed. "There is more behind your demand than mistrust."

Maria's stomach knotted, but outwardly she arched her brow in an icy show of disdain.

The earl caught her chin and tilted it from side to side, examining her. "I suspect you don't know," he murmured pensively. "How many secrets do you have?"

She yanked free of his grip. "Do you know her location or not?"

"By God . . ." Eddington whistled and sank heavily onto

the settee. "I've no notion of what is transpiring in your life, but let us dispense with the lies for a moment." He gestured to the opposite sofa. "Sit."

Maria complied only because her legs were shaking too much to support her safely.

"Does Welton know where his daughter is?"

She nodded. "He keeps her."

"But her location is unknown to you?" His eyes widened as understanding dawned. "Is that the hold he has on you?"

She said nothing.

"I can assist you in return for the service you provide to me." Eddington bent low, resting his forearms on his thighs. "I know where your sister is. You must know something about St. John that will help me catch him. This can be a mutually beneficial association."

"You wish to use her against me, as Welton does." Her hands fisted in her lap. "If anything untoward happens to her, you will pay dearly. I promise you that."

"Maria." It was the first occasion the earl had ever used her first name and the familiarity shook her, as he most likely intended. "Your position is untenable. You know this. I can achieve my aims without helping you. Accept my terms. They are more than fair."

"Nothing about this is fair, my lord. Nothing."

"Your trust is safer with me than it is with St. John."

"You do not know him."

"Neither do you," he argued. "I am not the only one who knows where Lady Amelia is. St. John knows as well."

Her smile was mocking. "Ply your wiles on someone more gullible than I."

"By what means do you think I found her? I sent agents to investigate Welton because of his connection to you. St. John's men were ahead of us, making inquiries of their own. *They* discovered your sister. The pursuing agents simply followed."

She frowned, considering, looking back on the last few days with examining eyes.

"Damn you." The earl's hands fisted at his knees. "I believed you would be a match for St. John, but he has deceived you as well."

"I am not so easily goaded that you can toss out such an accusation and I will accept it on its face. My doubt in your claim does not mean that St. John has my sympathies or loyalty, only that between the two of you, I see a great deal of similarity. In this case, is there a lesser of two evils?"

"Be reasonable," he cajoled. "I strive for the good of England. St. John strives for his own selfish welfare. Surely that gives me some advantage?"

Her mouth curved disdainfully.

"Maria. Surely there is some tidbit you can pass on to me that will implicate St. John in illegal activities or will provide some clue about that witness. Is there anyone you might have seen visiting St. John, someone he has talked about? Think carefully. Your sister's fate lies in the balance."

Weary of it all and heartsick, she knew she had to bring this triangle to its conclusion. She could not go on like this. It was too draining, and she needed what little energy she had remaining to bring Amelia safely home. "He has asked me to accompany him this evening," she whispered. "He has smuggled goods stored nearby."

"He will take you there?"

She nodded. "I pity you if you arrest him for smuggling. The people will riot."

"Leave that concern to me," he said, with obvious excitement. "You just lead the way."

Christopher cursed under his breath. "You are certain that was what he said? That he ordered the capture of Amelia?"

"Yes." Tim nodded. "They were speaking low, but I heard it clear. They are awaiting word now. Eddington didn't say as much to Lady Winter. He said he was watching her sister, not nabbing 'er."

"We can only hope that Walter, Sam, and the others were able to fend them off," Philip said.

"Hope is too fickle to base assumption on," Christopher argued. "To be safe, we must assume that Eddington was successful."

"So how will you proceed?" Philip's gaze was sympathetic behind his spectacles.

Rubbing the back of his neck, Christopher settled his hip more securely against the front of his desk. "I will offer myself to Eddington in trade."

"By God, no!" Tim roared. "She means to betray you."

"What choice does she have?" Christopher countered.

"Eddington is an agent," Philip said. "I doubt he would hurt the girl."

"I have my doubts, as well. But by law, he should return the girl to Welton and I think he will, if Maria does not provide the assistance he has demanded of her." Christopher looked at Tim. "Return to Lady Winter, but escort her to me this evening."

"You would sacrifice yourself for her benefit, when she will not do the same for you?" Tim asked in obvious outrage.

Christopher offered a slight smile. How could he explain? How could he put into words the greater weight he gave to Maria's happiness than to his own? Yes, he could confront her with his knowledge of Eddington, but where would that leave them? He could not proceed with his life knowing he had thrown her to the wolves, leaving her at the mercy of Welton and Eddington and men like Sedgewick who wished to harm her.

"Philip and my solicitor are aware of the steps I have set in place to see to the welfare of all of you, should something untoward happen to me."

"I care naught about that!" Tim argued. "'Tis *your* welfare that concerns me."

"Thank you, my friend." Christopher smiled. "I am grateful."

"No." Tim shook his head. "Yer daft. Lost yer mind o'er a woman. Never thought to see the day."

"You have said that Lady Winter refused him information until he baited her with her sister. I hold no blame on her for this. She truly has no other choice if she has any hope of reclaiming her sibling."

"She could choose you," Tim muttered.

Hiding his pain, Christopher gestured for them to leave him. "Go now. I have some matters to arrange."

The men departed reluctantly, and Christopher sank into his seat behind the desk and released his breath. Who would have thought his relationship with Maria would end like this?

Regardless, he could not find the will to regret their affair. He had been happy for a time.

For that, he would gladly pay whatever cost was required.

Chapter 21

The ride to the St. John residence felt as Maria imagined a ride to Tyburn would feel.

Somewhere behind her, Eddington and other agents followed.

The knowledge ate at her with a viciousness that caused her physical pain. She wanted Amelia back more than anything in the world, but her heart told her the price she would pay was too great.

There was no escaping how deeply attached she was to St. John. Despite all of the things she had discovered about him over the length of their liaison, she could only seem to dwell on his kindnesses—his handling of Templeton, his concern over her injury, the way he made love to her.

As she exited the carriage and stared up at Christopher's house with its empty planters and burly guards, the minute details of their association filled her mind. Heated moments and tender ones. Moments of comfortable silences and moments of verbal sparring. They shared a startling affinity and similar pasts.

Lifting her skirts, Maria ascended the short steps without haste and swept through the waiting open door. Many of those who lived under his protection lined the downstairs, watching her gravely, their eyes dipping to the foil in her hand. Her gaze met each and every one of theirs, challenging them to interfere.

None did.

She climbed the main staircase to reach Christopher's bedroom and knocked on the door. When she heard his voice call out to her, she entered.

Christopher stood before the mirror, shrugging into a beautifully embroidered waistcoat that was held out by his valet. The colorful floral pattern was a lovely accent to his butter yellow breeches and the matching jacket that hung on the nearby rack. The entire ensemble reminded her of their first meeting in the theater, and her chin lifted.

"I have something to tell you."

Christopher's gaze met hers in the reflection, then he caught sight of her weapon. With a low murmur, he dismissed the servant and faced her. "Why, Lady Winter, had I known my lover would send you in her stead, I would have dressed warmer."

"Your garments are perfect." Her mouth curved. "Less material between the tip of my blade and your skin."

"Do you mean to run me through?"

"I might."

He raked her with a skeptical glance.

"I urge you not to think of my skirts as an advantage in your favor. I have trained as much in gowns as I have breeches."

His hands came up in a signal of surrender. "Pray tell, fair lady, what service can I provide that would spare me from certain death?"

Maria set the tip in the Aubusson rug and rested her hand casually atop the hilt. "Do you love me?"

Christopher's brow arched. "Gads. How unsporting of you to solicit a declaration of love under duress."

Her foot tapped impatiently.

He smiled and stopped her heart. "I adore you, my love. I worship you. I would kiss your feet and supplicate myself for your favors. I offer you all that I have—my vast riches, my many ships, my cock, which weeps for your attentions—"

"Enough." She shook her head. "That was odious."

"Oh? I should like to see you do better."

"Very well. I love you."

"That's it?" His arms crossed, but his eyes were soft and warm. "That is all you have to say?"

"Stay home tonight."

He tensed. "Maria?"

She inhaled deeply, then released her breath in a rush. "You asked me many times what association I have with Eddington. He is an agent of the Crown, Christopher. He is out there now, waiting to follow us and catch you in the thick of things."

He stared at her pensively. "I see."

"I know about Sedgewick."

When he opened his mouth, she held up her hand. "No explanations. I mention it only because Simon found the witness. Sedgewick demanded the man's cooperation as ransom for the safety of his family—a wife, two sons, and a daughter. Tim and several men freed them. The viscount has nothing against you now."

His brows dipped together in a deep frown. "You render me speechless."

"Good. I prefer not to be interrupted. I was told that you know about Amelia." Her voice was shakier than she would have liked. "That you found her and are watching her. Is that true?"

"That is my hope, yes." He stared at her with fathomless eyes. "I have asked for a firm identification before bringing the news to you. I did not want to raise your hopes needlessly."

"Where is she?"

"If the girl I know of is indeed your sibling, she is in Lincolnshire."

"Thank you." Maria tugged up her blade and paused before turning away. "Be careful," she said softly, her hand over her heart. "I wish you well, Christopher. Godspeed." She moved toward the door.

"Maria."

That low, raspy voice curled around her spine. Tears fell, and she brushed them away as her pace quickened. Her hand curled around the doorknob, but before she could turn it she found herself trapped. Christopher's arms caged her, his body pressed tightly to hers.

"You forfeit your dream to reunite with your sister in favor of sparing my life." He pressed his cheek ardently to her temple. "You tell me of your love for me. Yet you cannot ask me for assistance?"

"Our lives diverge here," she whispered, her throat too tight to speak any louder, "as they should. You are free and safe, my path goes on. I will have Amelia, never doubt it. But I cannot do it this way—at your expense. I will find something of equal value to Eddington."

"You show me no mercy by sparing me for a life without you in it," he said roughly.

Maria began to shake, and he wrapped his arms around her.

"I *know*, Maria. I know he has offered Amelia in return for me. I know how much she means to you. You risked your life attempting to save her." He hunched over her, burying his hot face in her neck. "What I did not know was that you would confess all to me and attempt to save my life, despite knowing of Sedgewick and the rest. *My God...*" His voice broke. "How deeply you must love me to take this action. I am not worthy."

"You know?" Her hands clutched at his.

"Tim came to me today. He related Eddington's visit and your agreement. He also overheard Eddington speaking to a man waiting in his coach for him. He said he ordered the retrieval of your sister some days ago and was awaiting news. I pray my men were successful in preventing her abduction, but we cannot be certain."

She struggled against him until he freed her, then she spun to face him directly. "We must assume he has her, then."

He looked at her with such tenderness. "So despite your attempt to spare me, I must still go tonight. I have no goods here in Town—that was simply a ruse to see if you would betray me—but I have my confession and I will exchange that for Amelia."

Maria swiped furiously at her tears, hating that she was unable to see his face as he said this to her. "You knew of my agreement with Eddington . . . and you were still prepared to go?"

"Of course," he said simply.

"Why?"

"For the same reason you knew of Sedgewick and attempted your sacrifice regardless. I love you, Maria. More than my life." His smile was bittersweet. "Today I believed I loved you as much as I was able. Now, however, I love you many times more than that."

Maria reached back for the doorknob to support her weakening knees, but it was not enough. She sank to the floor in a puddle of lavender skirts and white underskirts, her foil across her lap.

"That's it?" she whispered. "That is all you have to say?"

"Teasing wench." He crouched before her and cupped her face in his large hands. He pressed his smiling lips to hers with heartbreaking reverence. She clutched his wrists and kissed him back with near desperation.

"I love you." The raw emotion in his voice made her push up to her knees and surge into his arms. His returning embrace was so tight, it crushed the breath from her.

"They have set us against each other," she said. "Must we allow them to break us apart?"

"No." He pulled back to look at her. "Do you have a suggestion? Until we have Amelia, we are weakened."

"We need to limit the number of players in this game. We have too many annoyances, and they are distracting us from our goals."

Christopher nodded, his mind lost in thought. "Together we should be clever enough to find a way . . . Welton, Sedgewick, and Eddington. Eddington may have Amelia, so we tolerate him . . . but Welton and Sedgewick . . ."

A possibility entered Maria's head and she quickly tried to discredit it. When the odds remained in their favor, she smiled.

"I love it when you look wicked," Christopher said.

"Shall we change the rules, my love? Shall we reverse our positions and set *them* against one another?"

"Devious and audacious." He grinned. "Whatever it is, I like it."

"We need parchment and ink, and three of your fastest and most obstinate riders. These notes must be delivered, regardless of where the recipients are."

"Done." Christopher stood and pulled her to her feet. "Who would have thought that setting the two most wanted individuals in England against each other would lead to a collaboration on so many levels?"

"*We* might have thought of it"—she winked—"had we been orchestrating the matter."

He laughed and hugged her close. "I pity the world now that we act as one."

"Save your pity for yourself," Maria said. "You have me for the rest of your life."

"Never a dull moment, love." He kissed the tip of her nose. "I would not have it any other way."

Chapter 22

To the unsuspecting eye, the occupants of a single un-marked carriage and multiple outriders were the only persons at the darkened wharf.

Maria stepped down from the coach and walked in plain view, the footman at her side holding a lamp aloft to draw all attention to her. Behind her, in the darkness, Christopher was slipping down through a hidden trapdoor in his carriage. He would see to his part of their plan while she saw to hers.

"Damn it, Maria!"

Welton's harsh voice made her jump, but then a slow inner smile warmed her. As she turned around, she kept her face mildly disdainful.

"What the devil is this?" he muttered, striding toward her with his greatcoat flaring around his long legs. "Why so dramatic a location? And with damnable short notice? I was busy."

"'Busy' to you means gaming or whoring," she said scornfully. "Forgive me if I feel little regret for the inconvenience."

He stepped into the circle of light, and as always, Maria was taken aback by the masculine beauty of his features. She supposed she would never cease expecting to see some outer evidence of his inner rot, yet he appeared to neither age nor suffer the ill effects of remorse.

"It is not safe to meet with you anywhere else," she said,

stepping back when he came too close so that he would be forced to speak loudly. "Eddington did not wish to bed me, as you assumed. He suspects me of the deaths of Winter and Dayton. He means to see me hang for your crimes."

The viscount cursed viciously. "He can prove nothing."

"He says he has found the person who concocted the poisons you used."

"Impossible. I killed that crone myself when she became greedy. A blade in the heart permanently silenced her."

"Regardless, he has found someone who will testify against me and he means to see me hang."

Welton's green eyes narrowed dangerously. "Then why are you here? Why are you not in custody?"

She gave a bitter laugh. "He noted my association with St. John. You can imagine how it pleases him to have the leverage to extort my cooperation."

"He will have to go the way of Winter and Dayton, then." His finely etched lips pursed with thought.

Maria marveled at the ease with which the viscount talked about murder. By what design would such evil hide within a perfect physical shell?

"You would poison another agent of the Crown?" she asked, her voice pitched louder in mock horror.

He laughed. "I am amazed I can continue to surprise you. Don't you know me well enough by now?"

"Apparently I can still be appalled at the depths to which you aspire. You killed Dayton and Winter for their money. While I detested your avarice, I understood your motivation. Greed is a universal vice. But murdering Eddington simply because he annoys you is . . . Well, I would have thought that beyond even you."

Welton shook his head. "I will never understand you. Here I have provided you with titles and wealth, and now I seek to ensure your freedom and you are, as ever, completely ungrateful."

"By God!" boomed a voice that startled them both. "This is excellent!"

The tapping of heels drew their gazes to the approaching shadows that appeared to be two men. Lord Sedgewick and Christopher entered the small circle of light.

"What is the meaning of this?" Welton asked, moving toward Maria.

Christopher swiftly sidestepped into his path, protecting her from possible harm. "This is the end of the road for you, my lord."

Sedgewick rocked back on his heels, his smile wide. "You've no notion what this will do for my career. To have caught the man responsible for the deaths of Dayton and Winter. Brilliant, St. John, absolutely brilliant."

"You have nothing," Welton said as he looked at Maria. "She will testify that I am innocent of any wrongdoing."

"Not so," she said with a wide smile. "I look forward to affirming Lord Eddington's relation of tonight's events."

"Eddington?" Sedgewick asked, scowling. "How does he signify?"

"I am the man who will see you stripped of your duties," Eddington said, joining the growing crowd. "And of course there is Lord Welton here, whose confession of his crimes was heard by too many people to be discounted."

More lanterns flared to life around them, revealing an astonishing number of individuals—Runners, soldiers, and lackeys.

It was altogether too perfect. The three men toppled each other. Eddington mitigated Sedgewick's hold over St. John, and Sedgewick mitigated Welton's hold over Maria.

"Dear God," Welton breathed. His head whipped toward Maria, his features contorted with pure rage. Finally, he looked like the monster he was. "You will correct this, Maria, or you will never see her again. *Never.*"

"I know where she is," she said simply. "You have no hold

on me, or her. With your imprisonment, I will care for her. As
I should have all of these years."

"I have associates," he hissed. "You will never be safe."

Christopher's gaze narrowed. "She will always be safe,"
he said in a low, fervent tone. "Always."

Maria smiled. "May God have no mercy on your soul, my
lord."

Eddington watched as Welton was clapped in irons by a
Runner and Sedgewick was led away by two agents. As the
wharf cleared, leaving only his carriage and St. John's, he set
his hands at the small of his back and heaved out a deep sigh
of satisfaction. After this night, he would assuredly be granted
the recently opened position of commander that Sedgewick
had sought with such reckless determination.

Lost in plans for his use of his new power, he failed to reg-
ister the patter of footsteps behind him until the sharp tip of
a blade pierced through his clothing and poked at his flesh.

He stilled. "What is the meaning of this?"

"You will be my guest, my lord," Lady Winter murmured,
"until my sister is returned to me."

"You must be jesting."

"I caution you against underestimating her," St. John said.
"I have felt her blade more times than I care to admit."

"I could call out for help," Eddington said.

"How unsporting of you," Lady Winter said.

A grunt of pain was heard, quickly followed by several
more. Eddington turned his head and found his coachman,
footmen, and outriders engaging in fisticuffs with what appeared to be a lone man of Irish descent. That the Irishman
was winning was in no doubt.

"Good God!" Eddington cried, watching with pure awe.
"I have never seen such a show of pugilistic expertise in my
life."

He was so engaged by the spectacle that he offered no
protest when his hands were bound behind him.

"Come along now," Lady Winter said when he was secured. She poked him with her knife again for good measure. "Who is that man?" he inquired as St. John's lackeys restrained those who groaned in surrender on the ground. But no one replied.

Later, he was pleased to see the Irishman again when the man entered Eddington's guarded room with a decanter of brandy and two glasses. Truly, as far as prisons went, Lady Winter's opulent home was the finest of them. His "cell" was decorated in shades of ivory and gold, with brown leather wingbacks before a marble-framed grate and a canopied bed covered in a golden floral embroidered silk counterpane.

"It is almost morning, my lord," the Irishman said, "but I hoped you would share a nightcap with me." His mouth curved wryly. "Lady Winter and St. John have already retired."

"Of course." Eddington studied the other man as he accepted the proffered glass from him. "You are the kept paramour I have heard whispered about."

"Simon Quinn, at your service."

Quinn settled into a wingback before the grate and held his glass in two hands, seeming not at all injured by his earlier activities. He glanced aside with a look that would chill boiling water. "Lest you think this is merely a social visit, my lord, I feel I should tell you bluntly that if Lady Winter's sibling arrives with any injury at all, I will beat you to a bloody pulp."

"Christ." Eddington blinked. "You've put the fear of God into me."

"Excellent."

Eddington tossed back his drink. "Listen, Quinn. It appears your present occupation will be . . . eliminated."

"Yes, it does appear so."

"I have a proposition for you."

Quinn's brow raised.

"Hear me out," Eddington said. "Once this matter with

the sister is resolved, I will assume a position of some power. I could use a man of your talents, and working on this side of the law does have decided benefits." He studied the Irishman to see how his proposal was being accepted.

"How are the wages?"

"Name your price."

"Hmm . . . I'm listening."

"Excellent. Now here are my thoughts . . ."

Chapter 23

"Once again, I find myself amazed with you," Christopher murmured, his lips to Maria's forehead as they reclined in her bed.

She snuggled closer, her nose pressed to his bare chest so she could breathe in the delicious scent of him. "I *am* amazing."

He laughed. "How you managed after the deaths of your parents . . . All those years under Welton's thumb . . ." His arms tightened. "We will go away after the wedding. Anywhere you like. *Everywhere* you like. We shall leave those memories behind and make new ones. Happy ones. All three of us, my love."

"After the wedding?" She tilted her head back to look up at him. "A bit presumptuous, I would say."

"Presumptuous?" Both of his brows rose up to his hairline. "You love me. I love you. We marry. That is not presumptive, it's expected."

"Oh? And when did you begin to do the expected?"

"When I unexpectedly fell in love with you."

"Hmm."

"What does that signify? That noise you made." Christopher scowled. "That was not an affirmation."

"And what is it that I am supposed to be affirming?" Maria hid her smile by looking away. The next she knew, she was flat on her back with an ardently piqued pirate and smuggler of renown looming over her.

"My marriage proposal."

"I was not aware you made one. It was more of a declaration."

"Maria." He heaved an exasperated sigh. "Don't you wish to wed me?"

Her hands came up to cup his face. To his credit, he was only distracted a moment by her bare breasts. "I adore you, as you well know. But I have been married twice. I think that is plenty enough for any woman."

"How can you compare a union with me to what you experienced with them? A man who cared for you like a dear friend, and a man who used you merely for his own gratification?"

"Would you be happy in the wedded state, Christopher?" she asked, discarding pretense.

He stilled, his gaze intent. "You doubt it?"

"Did you not say that the only way out of your livelihood is death? Either yours or of those you love?"

"When did I—" His eyes widened. "By God, have you a spy in my midst?"

Maria smiled.

"Vixen," he muttered, kneeing her legs open and settling his hips between them. "Yes, I said that. Perhaps it is selfish of me to ask you under those very real circumstances, but I have no choice. I cannot live without you."

He reached between them, cupping her sex in his hand and stroking her. "Neither of us has made any effort to prevent conception," he said softly, "and I am glad of that. The thought of you increasing with my child fills me with awe. Imagine how clever and industrious our issue will be."

"Christopher . . ." Her eyes stung and her vision grew blurry, even as her body awakened to his touch, growing liquid with desire. "How would we ever manage such a mischievous lot?"

"Just the way we managed the lot last night." Gripping his cock, he teased her creamy opening with the wide tip and then began to slip inside her. "Together."

Her eyes slid closed as he filled her, her head falling to the side to expose her throat to his mouth. "And if something were to happen to me or our children," she asked, "would you promise to hold yourself blameless? Or would you damn yourself forever?"

Christopher stilled, his cock a thick, throbbing presence within her. Something dark passed over his features, remembered pain and thoughts of more, perhaps.

"You could have left your life of crime long ago," she murmured, her arms clasped around his back. "The life you embraced to save your brother, and in the end it was the death of him, yes?"

The shudder that moved through him shook her, too.

"And yet you stay," she whispered, "caring for those who are loyal to you, seeing to their families when they pass on, providing a home and food on the table for many."

"I am not a saint, Maria."

"No. You are a fallen angel." The comparison seemed even more apropos now, with his handsomeness offset by the blue satin lining of her canopy.

He growled. "There is nothing angelic about me."

"My darling." She lifted her head to press a kiss to his shoulder. "If we stay unwed, you will know that I stay with you because I wish to. Because I make that same wish every day, and you are not responsible for binding me to you."

"Could you not make the wish to wed me and be done with it?"

She laughed and tugged him closer. He held back a moment, an immovable object unless he wished to be moved. Then he sighed and rolled over, taking her with him, keeping them joined. He reclined his golden head into the mass of pillows and gazed up at her.

"I am the bastard son of a nobleman," he said with the uninflected tone she had come to realize meant that he was discussing something that disturbed him. "My mother was the unfortunate recipient of her employer's lust until she had the temerity to start increasing. Then she was discharged from her position as scullery maid and sent back to the village in shame."

"Your brother . . . ?"

"Was legitimate. But I had the better circumstances. I was happy in the village. He was miserable in the manse. Our pater was half mad and viciously tempered. I think he raped my mother for the power of the act, not so much the physical release. Still, she loved me. The only affection Nigel ever knew was mine and his wife's."

"I am sorry." Maria brushed the hair back from his forehead and then kissed him in the space between his brows.

"So you see, my love"—he caught up her hand and set it over his heart—"I wish to have children within wedlock. I wish to share a home and a life with you. I wish to share a façade of normalcy with you."

"A façade?" She smiled.

"Will we ever be normal?"

"God forbid," she said with mock graveness.

"You wound me," he retorted. "Jesting at a time like this. I am laying my heart at your feet and you tease me."

Maria lifted their joined hands and set them over her own heart. "Your heart is not at my feet, it is here, beating within my breast."

Christopher kissed her fingertips, his dark blue eyes alight with love. "We can manage, I promise you that. My steward and Philip are capable of seeing to my affairs while we are away. Philip is the most recent addition to my lieutenants. There are several, and together they can effectively rub along without me."

"Good heavens," she breathed, blinking down at him. "Whatever will you do with yourself surrounded by an increasing wife and her soon-to-be-marriageable sister?"

"An increasing wife . . ." His voice was even raspier than usual. His hand cupped her nape and pulled her down, his lips pressing hard to hers. "I want that, damn it. I want it now. With you. I never thought I would. But I do, and I need you to give it to me. No other woman would be able to tame me. After all, how many notorious suspected murderesses are there?"

"I am not certain. I could investigate—"

He rolled again, pinning her beneath him and thrusting deep. She gasped in surprise, and he reared back and thrust harder.

"Have I mentioned lately," she said with laughter in her voice and heart, "that aggressive behavior only makes me more obstinate?"

"Maddening, contrary wench!" he growled, punctuating each word with a lunge of his hips. Reaching down, he anchored her leg on his hip and fucked her with passionate, fervent abandon.

He moved with the precision of a man who not only knew how to give a woman pleasure, but who wanted to especially. Who made it the goal of the entire sexual encounter to please his partner. To please *her*. He watched her closely, picking up on all the ways she responded to him, and adjusted his exertions accordingly.

"You like that?" he murmured when she whimpered in pleasure. He repeated the movement exactly. "You know as well as I that you crave me. Crave the feel of me inside you, stretching that tight, delicious cunt. Imagine days and nights spent like this, your ripe little body fucked so well it is nearly too much to bear."

"Ha! I can wear you into exhaustion." She meant to scoff, but her voice sounded slurred by lust instead.

"Prove it," he whispered darkly, pumping deep and true, filling the room with the liquid sounds of their sexual congress. "Marry me."

Lost to the feel of him inside her, Maria writhed and whispered hot sex words in his ear, her nails digging into his clenching buttocks. He was wild, untamed despite his claims to the contrary, his desperation for her evident in the way he made love to her, as if he would never have enough. Would never get deep enough.

"Are you certain you wish to experience this level of agitation every day of your life?" she whispered before she bit his earlobe.

In retaliation, he plunged balls-deep into her and circled his hips, rubbing her clitoris with his pelvic bone, throwing her headlong into a pulsating climax.

"Christopher!" She shivered violently, her cunt milking his cock until he groaned and came, spurting inside her.

"I love you," he gasped, clutching her so tightly she found it hard to breathe. "I love you."

Maria wrapped him with her body, her heart pounding with her returning depth of affection for him. "I suppose I should marry you," she breathed. "Who else would drive you insane?"

"No one else would dare. You are the only one."

"And certainly no one could love you as much as I do."

"Certainly not." He nuzzled his damp head into her cheek, imprinting her with his scent. "I used to wonder why my pater had to be who he was, why my brother had to inherit destitution, why the only recourse I knew of led me to this life."

"My love . . ." She knew well how he felt. Had she not asked herself similar questions every day?

"I knew the moment I held you in the theater, that you were the reason for everything. Every single turn my life has made led me to you. Were I not the man I am, the agency would never have approached me and I would not have found you, my soul mate. In fact, you are so like me, it is nearly frightening, yet you continue to surprise and astound me."

"As you continue to surprise and astound me." She walked her fingers up his spine and laughed when he squirmed. "I never thought you would wish to be married. I cannot picture it."

"Then we will commission a portrait," he said dryly. "Say yes, my darling Maria. Say yes."

"Yes."

He lifted his head and arched a brow. "Why do I feel as if that was too easily won?"

"Oh?" Maria batted her eyelashes at him. "I recant, then, and will proceed to resist you further."

Christopher rumbled a warning and twitched inside her.

She grinned. "Do you collect that the more I frustrate you, the more sexually focused you become? It is quite delicious."

"You will be the death of me."

"I warned you."

"You will pay."

"Ooh . . . When do you intend to collect?"

"As soon as we can procure a wedding license and a priest."

"I await your pleasure," she purred.

As he deliberately flexed inside her, his smile was pure wickedness. "Well, then. You shan't be waiting long."

"Simon love." Maria rose to her feet from her perch on the parlor settee and held out her hands.

Simon approached her with his slow, sultry stride, his smile deeply affectionate. Dressed in soft gray, he was understated, as usual, but dramatically attractive all the same. He caught up her hands and bent to kiss her cheek. "How are you faring?"

"Not so well," she admitted, resuming her seat with him beside her. Christopher had returned to his home to change his garments and make arrangements for the advent of any news of Amelia. Maria waited at her residence, unwilling to leave in case she missed word sent to her here. She'd wanted to gather a team and venture out in search, but Christopher had begged her to allow him to manage that part of the affair and offered several excellent reasons why. In the end, she had relented, albeit reluctantly. "I cannot help but worry."

"I know," he soothed, stroking the back of her hand. "I wish I could be of more help."

"Your presence alone is of great comfort to me."

"Ah, but I am slightly *de trop*, yes?"

"Never. You will always have a place of prominence in my life." Maria took a deep breath. "St. John has asked me to wed him."

"Wise man." Simon smiled. "I wish you great happiness. I know of no one who deserves it more than you."

"You, too, deserve to be happy."

"I am content, *mhuirnín*. Truly. At the present moment, my life is perfect." Simon grinned and settled more comfortably in the brocade-covered seat. "So, tell me, how much time do I have before I must leave you?"

"You are not going anywhere. I want you to keep this house. You have happy memories here, yes?"

"The happiest of my life."

Maria's eyes stung, and she swallowed past the lump in her throat. "Once I have Amelia, we plan to go away. Travel. See all the places that were kept from me while I was in service to Welton. I hope the adventure will help rebuild the bond Amelia and I once shared."

"I think that is a fine idea."

"I will miss you terribly," she lamented, her lower lip quivering.

Simon lifted her hand to his lips and kissed the back. "I will be here for you always, for whatever you may need. This is not the end. For you and me, there will never be an end."

"And I will always be here for you," she whispered.

"I know."

She blew out her breath. "So you will take the house?"

"No. I will maintain it for you. Fortuitously," he continued, smiling, "this is the perfect location for my new appointment under Lord Eddington."

Maria's mouth fell open. "He lured you into the agency?"

"Not quite. He anticipates some matters of delicacy that would best be handled by someone with less scruples than most."

"Dear God." Her hand lifted to brush along his cheek. "Be careful, please. You are a member of my family. I could not bear it if something untoward were to befall you."

"I request the same level of care from you. Take no risks." She held out her hand. "We have an agreement, then."

He tilted his head in a slight bow, captured her proffered hand, and held it to his heart. "A lifetime pact."

"So tell me," her lips curved, "what does Eddington have in mind for you?"

"Well, here are his thoughts . . ."

Maria paced the length of her lower parlor and cursed under her breath. Unable to resist, she stared at the weary and travel-dusty man in the corner and felt almost as if she would faint.

"Excellent work," Christopher was telling him, once again praising the man for saving Amelia from those who sought to take her.

The next Maria knew, her lover's hands were on her shoulders. "Maria? Are you ready?"

Her gaze lifted to his.

Christopher smiled down at her, his eyes soft and adoring. "Sam rode ahead once they reached the outskirts of London. The party with Amelia will be arriving shortly."

She managed a jerky nod.

"You are so pale."

Her hand went to her throat. "I am afraid."

"Of what?" He pulled her closer to him.

"Of believing that she is coming, of believing this is the end." Tears welled, then flowed freely.

"I understand." Christopher stroked the length of her spine soothingly. Simon approached from his position at the window and offered both a handkerchief and a comforting smile.

"What if she does not like me? What if she resents me?"

"Maria, she will love you," Christopher soothed. "There is no help for it."

Simon nodded. "No help for it at all. She will adore you, *mhuirnín.*"

They all heard the rap of the door knocker. Maria tensed. Christopher released her and moved to a position at her side, his hand offering support at the small of her back. Simon moved to the door.

It took forever, it seemed, before another travel-stained lackey entered. Maria held her breath. A moment later a smaller body appeared. Dressed in a gown far too large for her young frame, Amelia paused hesitantly inside the threshold. Her green eyes, so like Welton's but filled with innocence, took in everything around her with rapt attention. Her gaze locked on Maria and roamed the length of her, so curious and wary. Maria did the same, noting all of the differences time had wrought in the many years they had been apart.

How tall Amelia had grown! Her piquant face was surrounded by a curtain of long, black hair so like their mother's. But Amelia's eyes retained the child's innocence Maria remembered from their past, and the gratitude she felt for that was nearly overwhelming.

A sob broke the silence. Maria realized it was hers and covered her mouth with the kerchief. Her free hand lifted of its own accord, reaching out. It shook violently, as did her entire frame.

"Maria," Amelia said, taking a tentative step forward, a lone tear slipping free and sliding down her cheek.

Maria, too, took one tiny step, but it was enough of a welcome. Amelia ran the short distance between them. She threw herself into Maria's arms with enough force that Christopher caught Maria's back and saved them both from a tumble.

"I love you," Maria whispered, her face buried in Amelia's hair, dampening the raven locks with her tears.

Together, they sank to the blue and green Aubusson rug in a puddle of floral skirts and lacy underskirts.

"Maria! It was so awful!"

Her sister wailed loudly, making it difficult to understand everything she said, the words pouring out of her mouth in a jumbled deluge. Horses and fighting and someone named Colin . . . Something about Colin being killed . . . and Lord Ware and a letter . . .

"Hush," Maria soothed, rocking Amelia. "Hush."

"I have so much to tell you," Amelia cried.

"I know, my darling. I know." Maria glanced up at Christopher and saw his tears. Simon, too, stood with reddened eyes and a hand over his heart.

Maria rested her cheek on the top of Amelia's head and hugged her tightly. "But you will have the rest of our lives to tell me everything. The rest of our lives . . ."

Epilogue

The slight scratching on the open door drew Simon's attention from the maps spread out across his desk. He looked up at the butler with both brows raised. "Yes?"

"There is a young man at the door asking for Lady Winter, sir. I did tell him that neither she nor you were at home, but he refuses to leave."

Simon straightened. "Oh? Who is it?"

The servant cleared his throat. "He appears to be a Gypsy."

Surprise held his tongue for the length of a heartbeat, then Simon said, "Show him in."

He took a moment to clear the sensitive documents on his desk, then he sat and waited for the dark-haired youth who entered his study a moment later.

"Where is Lady Winter?" the boy asked, the set of his shoulders and jaw betraying his mulish determination to get whatever it was he came for.

Simon leaned back in his chair. "She is traveling the Continent, last I heard."

The boy frowned. "Is Miss Benbridge with her? How can I find them? Do you have their direction?"

"Tell me your name."

"Colin Mitchell."

"Well, Mr. Mitchell, would you care for a drink?" Simon stood and moved to the row of decanters that lined the table in front of the window.

"No."

Hiding a smile, Simon poured two fingers of brandy into a glass and then turned around, leaning his hip against the console with one heel crossed over the other. Mitchell stood in the same spot, his gaze searching the room, pausing occasionally on various objects with narrowed eyes. Hunting for clues to the answers he sought. He was a finely built young man, and attractive in an exotic way that Simon imagined the ladies found most appealing.

"What will you do if you find the fair Amelia?" Simon asked. "Work in the stables? Care for her horses?"

Mitchell's eyes widened.

"Yes, I know who you are, though I was told you were dead." Simon lifted his glass and tossed back the contents. His belly warmed, making him smile. "So do you intend to work as her underling, pining for her from afar? Or perhaps you hope to tumble her in the hay as often as possible until she either marries or grows fat with your child."

Simon straightened and set down his glass, bracing himself for the expected—yet surprisingly impressive—tackle that knocked him to the floor. He and the boy rolled, locked in combat, knocking over a small table and shattering the porcelain figurines that had graced its top.

It took only a few moments for Simon to claim the upper hand. The time would have been shorter had he not been so concerned about hurting the lad.

"Cease," he ordered, "and listen to me." He no longer drawled; his tone was now deadly earnest.

Mitchell stilled, but his features remained stamped with fury. "Don't ever speak of Amelia in that way!"

Pushing to his feet, Simon extended his hand to assist the young man up. "I am only pointing out the obvious. You have nothing. Nothing to offer, nothing with which to support her, no title to give her prestige."

The clenching of the young man's jaw and fists betrayed his hatred for the truth. "I know all of that."

"Good. Now"—Simon righted his clothing and resumed his seat behind the desk—"What if I offered to help you acquire what you need to make you worthy—coin, a fitting home, perhaps even a title from some distant land that would suit the physical features provided by your heritage?"

Mitchell stilled, his gaze narrowing with avid interest. "How?"

"I am engaged in certain . . . *activities* that could be facilitated by a youth with your potential. I heard of your dashing near rescue of Miss Benbridge. With the right molding, you could be quite an asset to me." Simon smiled. "I would not make this offer to anyone else. So consider yourself fortunate."

"Why me?" Mitchell asked suspiciously, and not without a little scorn. He was slightly cynical, which Simon thought was excellent. A purely green boy would be of no use at all. "You don't know me, or what I'm capable of."

Simon held his gaze steadily. "I understand well the lengths a man will go for a woman he cares for."

"I love her."

"Yes. To the point where you would seek her out at great cost to yourself. I need dedication such as that. In return, I will ensure that you become a man of some means."

"That would take years." Mitchell ran a hand through his hair. "I don't know that I can bear it."

"Give yourselves time to mature. Allow her to see what she has missed all of these years. Then, if she will have you anyway, you will know that she is making the decision with a woman's heart, and not a child's."

For a long moment, the young man remained motionless, the weight of his indecision a tangible thing.

"Try it," Simon urged. "What harm can come from the effort?"

Finally, Mitchell heaved out his breath and sank into the seat opposite the desk. "I'm listening."

"Excellent!" Simon leaned back in his chair. "Now here are my thoughts . . ."

Don't miss *Ask for It*, the first book in Sylvia Day's Georgian series.

London, April 1770

" A re you worried I'll ravish the woman, Eldridge? I admit to a preference for widows in my bed. They are much more agreeable and decidedly less complicated than virgins or other men's wives."

Sharp gray eyes lifted from the mass of papers on the enormous mahogany desk. "*Ravish*, Westfield?" The deep voice was rife with exasperation. "Be serious, man. This assignment is very important to me."

Marcus Ashford, seventh Earl of Westfield, lost the wicked smile that hid the soberness of his thoughts and released a deep breath. "And you must be aware that it is equally important to me."

Nicholas, Lord Eldridge, sat back in his chair, placed his elbows on the armrests, and steepled his long, thin fingers. He was a tall and sinewy man with a weathered face that had seen too many hours on the deck of a ship. Everything about him was practical, nothing superfluous, from his manner of speaking to his physical build. He presented an intimidating presence with a bustling London thoroughfare as a backdrop. The result was deliberate and highly effective.

"As a matter of fact, until this moment, I was not aware. I wanted to exploit your cryptography skills. I never considered you would volunteer to manage the case."

Marcus met the piercing gray stare with grim determination. Eldridge was head of the elite band of agents whose sole purpose was to investigate and hunt down known pirates and smugglers. Working under the auspices of His Majesty's Royal Navy, Eldridge wielded an inordinate amount of power. If Eldridge refused him the assignment, Marcus would have little say.

But he would not be refused. Not in this.

He tightened his jaw. "I will not allow you to assign someone else. If Lady Hawthorne is in danger, I will be the one to ensure her safety."

Eldridge raked him with an all-too-perceptive gaze. "Why such passionate interest? After what transpired between you, I'm surprised you would wish to be in close contact with her. Your motive eludes me."

"I have no ulterior motive." At least not one he would share. "Despite our past, I've no desire to see her harmed."

"Her actions dragged you into a scandal that lasted for months and is still discussed today. You put on a good show, my friend, but you bear scars. And some festering wounds, perhaps?"

Remaining still as a statue, Marcus kept his face impassive and struggled against his gnawing resentment. His pain was his own and deeply personal. He disliked being asked about it. "Do you think me incapable of separating my personal life from my professional one?"

Eldridge sighed and shook his head. "Very well. I won't pry."

"And you won't refuse me?"

"You are the best man I have. It was only your history that gave me pause, but if you are comfortable with it, I have no objections. However, I will grant her request for reassignment, if it comes to that."

Nodding, Marcus hid his relief. Elizabeth would never ask for another agent; her pride wouldn't permit it.

Eldridge began to tap his fingertips together. "The journal Lady Hawthorne received was addressed to her late husband and is written in code. If the book was involved in his death . . ." He paused. "Viscount Hawthorne was investigating Christopher St. John when he met his reward."

Marcus stilled at the name of the popular pirate. There was no criminal he longed to apprehend more than St. John, and his enmity was personal. St. John's attacks against Ashford Shipping were the impetus to his joining the agency. "If Lord Hawthorne kept a journal of his assignments and St. John were to acquire the information—bloody hell!" His gut tightened at the thought of the pirate anywhere near Elizabeth.

"Exactly," Eldridge agreed. "In fact, Lady Hawthorne has already been contacted about the book since it was brought to my attention just a sennight ago. For her safety and ours, it should be removed from her care immediately, but that's impossible at the moment. She was instructed to personally deliver the journal, hence the need for our protection."

"Of course."

Eldridge slid a folder across the desk. "Here is the information I've gathered so far. Lady Hawthorne will apprise you of the rest during the Moreland ball."

Collecting the particulars of the assignment, Marcus stood and took his leave. Once in the hallway, he allowed a grim smile of satisfaction to curve his lips.

He'd been only days away from seeking Elizabeth out. The end of her mourning meant his interminable waiting was over. Although the matter of the journal was disturbing, it worked to his advantage, making it impossible for her to avoid him. After the scandalous way she'd jilted him four years ago she would not be pleased with his new appearance in her life. But she wouldn't turn to Eldridge either, of that he was certain.

Soon, very soon, all that she had once promised and then denied him would finally be his.

Read on for an excerpt from the third of Sylvia Day's Georgian books, *A Passion for Him*.

London, 1780

The man in the white mask was following her.

Amelia Benbridge was uncertain of how long he had been moving surreptitiously behind her, but he most definitely was.

She strolled carefully around the perimeter of the Langston ballroom, her senses attuned to his movements, her head turning with feigned interest in her surroundings so that she might study him further.

Every covert glance took her breath away.

In such a crush of people, another woman most likely would not have noted the avid interest. It was far too easy to be overwhelmed by the sights, sounds, and smells of a masquerade. The dazzling array of vibrant fabrics and frothy lace . . . the multitude of voices attempting to be heard over an industrious orchestra . . . the mingling scents of various perfumes and burnt wax from the massive chandeliers . . .

But Amelia was not like other women. She had lived the first sixteen years of her life under guard, her every movement watched with precision. It was a unique sensation to be examined so closely. She could not mistake the feeling for anything else.

However, she could say with some certainty that she had never been so closely scrutinized by a man quite so . . . compelling.

For he *was* compelling, despite the distance between them and the concealment of the upper half of his face. His form alone arrested her attention. He stood tall and well proportioned, his garments beautifully tailored to cling to muscular thighs and broad shoulders.

She reached a corner and turned, setting their respective positions at an angle. Amelia paused there, taking the opportunity to raise her mask to surround her eyes, the gaily colored ribbons that adorned the stick falling down her gloved arm. Pretending to watch the dancers, she was in truth watching him and cataloguing his person. It was only fair, in her opinion. If he could enjoy an unhindered view, so could she.

He was drenched in black, the only relief being his snowy white stockings, cravat, and shirt. And the mask. So plain. Unadorned by paint or feathers. Secured to his head with black satin ribbon. While the other gentlemen in attendance were dressed in an endless range of colors to attract attention, this man's stark severity seemed designed to blend into the shadows. To make him unremarkable, which he could never be. Beneath the light of hundreds of candles, his dark hair gleamed with vitality and begged a woman to run her fingers through it.

And then there was his mouth . . .

Amelia inhaled sharply at the sight of it. His mouth was sin incarnate. Sculpted by a master hand, the lips neither full nor thin, but firm. Shamelessly sensual. Framed by a strong chin, chiseled jaw, and swarthy skin. A foreigner, perhaps. She could only imagine how the face would look as a whole. Devastating to a woman's equanimity, she suspected.

But it was more than his physical attributes that intrigued

her. It was the way he moved, like a predator, his gait purposeful and yet seductive, his attention sharply focused. He did not mince his steps or affect the veneer of boredom so esteemed by Society. This man knew what he wanted and lacked the patience to pretend otherwise.

At present it appeared that what he wanted was to follow her. He watched Amelia with a gaze so intensely hot, she felt it move across her body, felt it run through the unpowdered strands of her hair and dance across her bared nape. Felt it glide across her bared shoulders and down the length of her spine. *Coveting.*

Enjoy more of Sylvia Day's Georgian series with *Don't Tempt Me.*

Paris, France—1757

With her fingers curled desperately around the edge of the table before her, Marguerite Piccard writhed in the grip of unalloyed arousal. Gooseflesh spread up her arms and she bit her lower lip to stem the moan of pleasure that longed to escape.

"Do not restrain your cries," her lover urged hoarsely. "It makes me wild to hear them."

Her blue eyes, heavy-lidded with passion, lifted within the mirrored reflection before her and met the gaze of the man who moved at her back. The vanity in her boudoir rocked with the thrusts of his hips, his breathing rough as he made love to her where they stood.

The Marquis de Saint-Martin's infamously sensual lips curved with masculine satisfaction at the sight of her flushed dishevelment. His hands cupped her swaying breasts, urging her body to move in tandem with his.

They strained together, their skin coated with sweat, their chests heaving from their exertions. Her blood thrummed in her veins, the experience of her lover's passion such that she had forsaken everything—family, friends, and esteemed future—to be with him. She knew he loved her similarly. He proved it with every touch, every glance.

"How beautiful you are," he gasped, watching her through the mirror.

When she had suggested the location of their tryst with timid eagerness, he'd laughed with delight.

"I am at your service," he purred, shrugging out of his garments as he stalked her into the boudoir. There was a sultriness to his stride and a predatory gleam in his dark eyes that caused her to shiver in heated awareness. Sex was innate to him. He exuded it from every pore, enunciated it with every syllable, displayed it with every movement. And he excelled at it.

From the moment she first saw him at the Fontinescu ball nearly a year ago, she had been smitten with his golden handsomeness. His attire of ruby red silk had attracted every eye without effort, but Marguerite had attended the event with the express aim of seeing him in the flesh. Her older sisters had whispered scandalous tales of his liaisons, occasions when he had been caught in flagrant displays of seduction. He was wed; yet discarded lovers pined for him openly, weeping outside his home for a brief moment of his attention. Her curiosity about what sort of shell would encase such wickedness was too powerful to be denied.

Saint-Martin did not disappoint her. In the simplest of terms, she did not expect him to be so . . . *male*. Those who were given to the pursuit of vice and excess were rarely virile, as he most definitely was.

Never had she met a man more devastating to a woman's equanimity. The marquis was magnificent, his physical form impressive and his aloofness an irresistible lure. Golden-haired and skinned, as she was, he was desired by every woman in France for good reason. There was an air about him that promised pleasure unparalleled. The decadence and forbidden delights intimated within his slumberous gaze lured one to forget themselves. The marquis had lived twice Marguerite's eight and ten years, and he possessed a wife as lovely as he was comely. Neither fact mitigated Marguerite's immediate, intense attraction to him. Or his returning attraction to her.

"Your beauty has enslaved me," he whispered that first night. He stood near to where she waited on the edge of the dance floor, his lanky frame propped against the opposite side of a large column. "I must follow you or ache from the distance between us."

Marguerite kept her gaze straight ahead, but every nerve ending tingled from his boldness. Her breath was short, her skin hot. Although she could not see him, she felt the weight of his regard and it affected her to an alarming degree. "You know of women more beautiful than I," she retorted.

"No." His husky, lowered voice stilled her heartbeat. Then, made it race. "I do not."